# Road
## to
# ROSEWOOD

# Road
## to
# ROSEWOOD

# ASHTYN NEWBOLD

SWEETWATER
BOOKS
An imprint of Cedar Fort, Inc.
Springville, Utah

ISBN 13: 978-1-4621-2182-3

Published by Sweetwater Books, an imprint of Cedar Fort, Inc.
2373 W. 700 S., Springville, UT 84663
Distributed by Cedar Fort, Inc., www.cedarfort.com

LIBRARY OF CONGRESS CATALOGING-IN-PUBLICATION DATA

Names: Newbold, Ashtyn, 1998- author.
Title: Road to Rosewood / Ashtyn Newbold.
Description: Springville, Utah : Sweetwater Books, An imprint of Cedar Fort, Inc., [2017]
Identifiers: LCCN 2017058116 | ISBN 9781462121823 (perfect bound : alk. paper)
Subjects: LCSH: Man-woman relationships--Fiction. | Nineteenth century, setting. | England, setting. | LCGFT: Novels. | Romance fiction. | Domestic fiction.
Classification: LCC PS3614.E568 R63 2017 | DDC 813/.6--dc23
LC record available at https://lccn.loc.gov/2017058116

Cover design by Shawnda T. Craig
Cover design © 2018 Cedar Fort, Inc.
Edited by Jessica Romrell
Typeset by Kaitlin Barwick

Printed in the United States of America

10  9  8  7  6  5  4  3  2  1

Printed on acid-free paper

For every adventurous spirit
No matter how small

# ONE

*I* thought you would be better at piquet," I said, raising my eyes above a perfectly fanned hand of cards. My curls bounced as I shifted in my chair to face Nicholas. My feet dangled above the ground.

Nicholas leaned his elbow across the small table in the middle of the library at Rosewood. He lived in the smaller house next to Rosewood where I spent a great deal of time during my summer visits with my family. I enjoyed staying at Aunt Edith's house and playing with Kitty, but usually only if Nicholas was there too. Today Mama had taken a trip to town with the adults, so Nicholas had been enlisted to watch over Kitty and me—although I despised the idea of requiring supervision at my age. I was eleven after all.

"I thought you would have grown taller since last summer," Nicholas said.

I threw my cards face down onto the table. "I have grown taller."

"Your curly little head only reaches the second to the bottom button of my waistcoat. Last year it reached the third. Either you have grown shorter or I have grown taller." A grin marked his face as he studied his cards.

I shook my head, but couldn't help but smile. He always teased me about being short. I was the shortest girl of my age that I knew, and much shorter than Kitty. She watched silently, her eyes darting between the two of us. I raised my eyebrows at her. "I haven't grown shorter, have I?"

She stifled a giggle. "Perhaps you might consider wearing your hair atop your head to add an inch or two."

"I have not grown shorter!"

Nicholas laughed. "Very well. Then can you see that I have grown taller?" He pushed away from the table and stood, stretching his neck.

I moved over to him and stood on the tips of my toes, looking straight ahead at the second button of his waistcoat. "Perhaps we have both grown, but you have just grown a slight bit more than I have," I conceded.

Kitty chewed her fingernail, observing us critically from her chair. "I do believe you have grown a bit, Lucy."

Nicholas chuckled, patting the top of my head like an older brother might do. I did not appreciate it. I watched his face, wondering how much closer I would be to his height when I was sixteen just like him. But there was no way to know. My eyes flashed to the chair I had been using at the card table. Giggling, I pulled it around to where it stood right in front of him. I stepped on top of it, using Nicholas's shoulder as a balance. "I am taller!" I said, nearly toppling over with my laughter. Kitty's eyes widened. She had always been the proper sort of girl. She did not climb atop chairs and make a cake of herself like I had made a habit of doing.

Nicholas raised one eyebrow, forming a deep, curving crease in the right side of his forehead. "You are a silly little girl, Lucy."

That made me frown. "You are a strange little boy."

"I am not a little boy."

"But you are not old enough to be married," I countered.

He reached around me, tipping the chair I was standing on. I shrieked as I fell, but he caught me by my arm as if he had planned it all along. My laughter rang through the room, but I tried to frown at him.

"How old should I be when I get married, then, Lucy?"

I caught my breath, sitting on the floor with my dress tucked under my feet. "Thirty."

"Thirty?" he scoffed. "I will be an old man by then."

"Fine. Twenty-five," I declared, staring up at him from the ground, fluttering my lashes.

The maid dusting the bookshelves in the corner chuckled. I didn't know what I had said that had been so humorous. Kitty leaned across the table, propping her face on her hands, watching the exchange with a sly grin pulling on her lips. As my dearest friend and cousin she knew all my secrets. And one of those secrets was that I wished to marry Nicholas when I was all grown up. But something about Nicholas's amused smile made me wonder if he knew my secrets as well.

He leaned over with a sigh to sit beside me on the ground. He flinched as if the movement had hurt him. His family was not among the wealthiest in town and his father had died in recent years. His mother was strange—she hardly spoke and seemed to require more care than most grown women I knew. Because of these things, Nicholas worked hard at his house during the early hours of the day. I smiled at the lean muscles in his adolescent arms. It was the first summer I had noticed or cared.

It was then that I began to wonder how many girls fancied Nicholas. Just how easy would it be for him to find a wife? My eyes flicked up to his face. He was smiling in amusement, with brown eyes like mine, dramatic eyebrows and a dented chin, freckled cheeks, and messy golden-brown hair.

"How old will I be when you are twenty-five?" I blurted.

Kitty chewed her nails faster, blinking quickly.

He chuckled, rubbing his jaw with his thumb and forefinger. "You'll be . . . twenty."

I stood up, twirling my skirt as I moved across the room. "I will attend balls and be pretty and we can dance together!" I immediately clamped my mouth shut, feeling my round cheeks heat up.

"You wish to dance with me?" Nicholas asked, leaning back on his hands. "You needn't wait until you are twenty. I'll teach you now. Surely your mama wouldn't have you at your first ball without learning to properly dance."

I jumped toward him, feeling the ribbons in my curls slide a little with the motion. "Are you being serious?"

He nodded. "I'll teach Kitty as well." He motioned for her to join us in front of the table. As she approached, we exchanged a grin that felt wide enough to cross all of England. Twice.

"Very well . . . which of my students would like to be first?"

I was not usually shy, but the thought of dancing with Nicholas was daunting. Kitty and I stood in silence before Nicholas threw his head back in exasperation. "Come now, Lucy. Stand on my feet," he said, nodding toward his boots. He had a little smile on his lips.

I pressed my lips together in concentration, grabbing his outstretched hands and standing on his boots. "Does this hurt your toes?"

He grinned. "No, you're just a little thing."

"I am not!" I said through a giggle.

Nicholas took a step, then another, an awkward sideways shuffle that made me laugh harder. "This is not the proper way to dance!"

"No, but it is much more fun, is it not?"

I tipped my head back, holding his hands at arm's length, and squeezed my eyes shut, letting the stomps of his boots echo through the empty room and off the domed ceiling. When I looked up, far, far up at his face again, I remembered thinking for the first time how wonderful it would be to dance with him when I was old enough to dance the proper way.

"You are a horrendous dancer," I said. "I don't believe any girl will marry a boy that dances in such a way."

And Nicholas laughed. I quite enjoyed the sound.


## NINE YEARS LATER

### 1820

*Dearest Lucy,*

*I cannot believe it has been so many months since we have spoken in writing, but much longer in presence, I might add. Six years is far too long. I miss my dearest cousin. Please forgive my neglect of your letters; I expect you will, once you are informed of my reason. It was with recent events that I found myself rather bereft of a proper companion* to share a most thrilling piece of news with. I am writing to tell you that I am engaged to marry! His name is Mr. John Turner, and I love him very much. We met at the start of the season in a small London ballroom and have been courting through the spring. I received his proposal last week, and cannot comprehend the dullness of my life without him. Is that not strange? You must still imagine me as I was six years ago when we both thought ourselves to be so grown up, chasing after Nicholas Bancroft.

I would be so delighted to hear from you. If it puts you at ease, I promise that I will return a response promptly. You must think me to be a most careless friend. If you demand it, I will repay you with a jaunt to town and one of your favorite scones, should you ever visit us here at Rosewood again.

Yours,

Kitty

Dear Kitty,

It is not fair of you to claim that you have missed me so dearly, when truly you have been finding such joy in your cherished courtship. My sincerest congratulations on your engagement! Upon my word you shall deliver that promised scone by post, because surely I will not be permitted to visit you there in Dover. What should make this summer different than the last? You are right, I do still imagine you at the age of fourteen, singing in the drawing room, and of course, chasing Nicholas Bancroft. Where has life taken him?

I do wish I could find passage to Rosewood to see you before your wedding. It isn't likely my parents will allow it. I cannot tell you how much I long to travel to the South. My heart aches with every passing day I remain in Craster. I fear I do not belong here any longer. It seems I never have.

Please send my love to your family.

Lucy

*Dear Lucy,*

*My poor cousin! Are you certain that you cannot travel here to Rosewood? Surely my family will welcome you without a moment of hesitation. If there is a thing I know about you, Lucy, it is that you are quite skilled in the art of persuasion. Do you remember the day you persuaded me to swim in that pond full of toads?*

*Perhaps your parents will allow you this trip. Surely if they knew the depth of your melancholy they would provide you with anything necessary to remedy it. Let us strike a bargain. I will inquire after the date you may be welcome to arrive, if you will consider the possibility of traveling here, even if it means you must do it alone.*

*Is not your happiness worth it?*

*Kitty*

*Dear Kitty,*

*You must remember my sister, Rachel? She has recently been engaged to marry a man from Yorkshire. She will be leaving soon and I fear I will feel even more lonely than ever without her. There are days I find little reason to leave my bedchamber. Perhaps a trip to Dover is precisely what I need to lift my spirits. The problem of the matter lies not only with my parents' misgivings, but also with their intentions for me. With Rachel soon to be married, they feel the need to offer me equal opportunity to spread my wings in society. They wish to offer me a season in London. However, I am older than many debutantes, and I have no desire for anything at all of late. I do not want new dresses, new hats (quite unlike me, I know), nor do I want a husband. All I can dream of is green, trimmed grasses, and the sort of sunshine that requires a parasol, although it would suit my spirits well to let the sunlight grant me a freckle or two.*

*When I am asked to be a proper lady I feel that the boot is quite on the other leg. I don't wish for stuffy London ballrooms like I did as a child, but for open hills and horses.*

*Did you make mention of how Nicholas is faring?*

*Yours,*

*Lucy*

Dear Lucy,

Have your persuasions met success? My family would love to receive you at Rosewood and I will be living with my husband just two miles from the estate.

Unfortunately I have little good to say with regard to Nicholas Bancroft. He has not been living in his family residence for well over a year since his marriage. Did you not know of this? It was a bit of a scandal actually, the way he ran off to marry an unknown woman in London. Nicholas has always been spirited I suppose, but it seems love has made him reckless.

I hope you will receive this news lightly. I trust your childhood adoration of him has been put to rights? I should hate for him to hurt you again.

Yours sincerely,

Kitty

# Two

*D*roplets of water hit the window like tears. Not silent, contained tears, but the kind that fall uncontrolled, shaking the world with sobs. I watched the gray, late summer sky as it fell to a dark line at the horizon of the unsettled sea. Wind blew rain at the window again, blurring the familiar castle ruins on the distant headland, and I wondered if the wind was strong enough today to carry me away from this town.

My fingers touched the window before I sunk deeper in my chair, wrapping my arms around myself. Chill bumps inched over my skin.

Kitty's latest letter had arrived this morning. I had read it so many times that I imagined the words would never leave my memory. Opening the book on my lap, I pulled the folded parchment out from between the pages.

*Dearest Lucy,*

> *It is settled. You are always welcome here at Rosewood. At what time may we expect your arrival? I cannot contain my excitement. Six years is far too long. My husband will be very pleased to meet the woman I spent so many adventurous summers with as a child. I do hope you will be coming soon, for we have always had nothing but open arms for you. Mr. Turner's home is beautiful as well, and quite*

*comfortable, but we will certainly stay at Rosewood during your visit. Please do write back soon.*

*With love,*

*Kitty*

The drawing room door opened and I jostled from my spot at the window, nearly dropping my letter.

"What is that you are reading?" It was my sister, Rachel, in the doorway, her smile wide as she walked into the room and gazed ahead out the window. She had always enjoyed storms and the color gray.

My eyes were dry, stinging with hours of missed sleep. I stared at her as she crossed the room to me, pressing the letter to my chest.

Speaking had been very difficult lately.

Rachel knelt down on the floor beside my chair, her brown eyes wide and filled with concern. She had always been the first person to know when I was troubled. She had always known the best way to make me feel stronger. She understood me too well, in a way that made me even more vulnerable. I hardly ate. I hardly slept. I stared out of windows and occasionally at the flames in our fireplace. While the conditions of this town filled Rachel with joy and comfort, they did nothing but plague me with sorrow. It was as though I were a fish on land, gasping for breath because there was somewhere else I belonged. There was a place I could breathe, live, find happiness. Rachel knew as well as I did that it wasn't here in Craster.

"A letter from Kitty," I breathed, "inviting me to come to Rosewood."

Rachel lifted her brow in a look of surprise. "Mama and Papa will take quite a lot of convincing."

"I do not care what they say. If they love me, and I am sure they do, they will allow me to do this. It is necessary for my happiness."

Over Rachel's shoulder, I saw the outline of a top hat stooping under the doorway. I nodded at the man who had just stepped into the room. Rachel turned, and I watched the way her eyes sparked with joy at the sight of her husband. They had been married just a fortnight before. I almost smiled, but a pinching started in my stomach and rose to my heart.

Certainly it was the same manner in which Nicholas looked at his wife.

Mr. Harding doffed his hat at me and turned his smile on Rachel. "I am sorry to interrupt, my dear, but the coach has arrived."

Rachel stood, brushing one of my dark curls from my forehead. "I will visit again in two months." Dropping her voice to a whisper, she added, "And when I do, I expect you to be at Rosewood. You must write me of all your adventures there." Her lips twisted into a sad smile. She didn't like to see me like this.

"I will." I squeezed her hand.

"When do you plan to leave?"

My fingers twitched over the letter in my lap. "As soon as I am able."

She threw me a look of suspicion. "Surely you plan to involve Mama and Papa in the travel arrangements? Papa will insist on everything being good and proper."

I bit my lip.

"Lucy." Rachel's eyebrow arched.

It felt as if I were being forced to confess to a stern nanny, much less my caring sister. "I did not plan to inform them. I need to do this on my own."

"Lucy, I must insist that you make the proper arrangements."

I almost snapped at her, but saw that she was genuinely concerned. "I plan to travel by mail coach. It is the most affordable option."

Rachel was quiet for a long moment.

"You won't tell them, will you?" My heart pounded with dread. This was my grand opportunity. I could not afford to have anyone stop me. My heart would break all over again, this time at the hand of shattered dreams. I couldn't carry on day to day with the same coastline, the same storms, the same bleak shops. The only thing that Craster shared with the countryside was the sky, but it was a different color there. I felt choked in confinement, seeing what I longed for but unable to touch it. Rachel had found love, joy, and contentment. I wanted the same.

"You should not be angry with them, Lucy." Rachel's voice was soft. "Mama and Papa had their reasons for keeping away these years."

My jaw tightened and I looked out the window again. Yes, reasons that they would never speak of. Secret things.

When I didn't reply, Rachel stood, smoothing her skirts. "I will not stop you from leaving. But please write to me often. Be safe." When she met her husband at the door, she gave me a final glance over her shoulder before disappearing from sight.

What Rachel did not know is that I had already replied to that letter from Kitty. It had come weeks before, and I was leaving within the week.

I had been wrong, Rachel didn't always understand completely. Mama and Papa may have had their reasons for keeping away from Rosewood, but I also had my reasons for being angry. By keeping me away from the countryside, they had deprived me of five summers— five summers I could have changed Nicholas's mind. What if he had seen me grown up? I was no longer a little child. Year after year, I begged to be allowed to go visit again. I told my parents it was because of my cousins, and the sunshine, and the beautiful village, and it was, but they knew that I missed Nicholas the most.

The handsome men are always the ones to be chased. It didn't matter whether they were intelligent, or humorous, or kind. I swallowed hard, clearing the lump in my throat. No girl had known Nicholas like I did. They hadn't seen what was in his heart. I had always considered myself fortunate to have seen it, but now that it was certain that I could not have him, I regretted every moment. I had seen what was in his heart, and I had seen that *I* was not there. But a day had yet to pass that I didn't wonder what might have happened if he had seen me turn sixteen, seventeen, eighteen—what might have changed? Now I was twenty. It had been too long.

I could never know what might have happened because Mama and Papa had taken that from me. The blame and the hurt welled up inside me until I couldn't breathe. It was too late. Nicholas was married. I was not surprised at the news, but only at the pain that followed. I had thought my heart to have been stronger than that.

But I was still traveling to Dover. I would stay at Rosewood with my cousins and have a liberating and beautiful few months. I would put my past behind me and start anew. Before my mind could be reversed, I bolted to the stairs and found a place at the writing desk in my bedchamber. My heart raced, bringing tremors to each finger as I dipped the quill.

*Dear Kitty,*

    *I am pleased to hear that I will be welcome. You may expect my arrival on the twenty-fifth day of September, should all go as planned. I hope this note receives you well.*
    *With love,*

    *Lucy*

After ringing for my maid to post the letter, I turned in my chair, chewing my lip with concern at the prospect of packing my trunk. It was tucked behind the gowns that hung in my wardrobe. Moving across the room, I faced the gowns in my wardrobe, wringing my hands together. These gowns would need to be packed eventually, and it so happened that my 'eventually' expired tomorrow. I would be leaving Craster. My heart quaked with excitement and fear at the thought.

Kneeling down, I pulled the trunk out from behind the skirts of those dresses, hands shaking as I unclasped the latch. Staring down into the contents of my trunk, I frowned. The trunk was almost full already with my hats and other necessities.

Laying the gowns out on the floor, I first tried rolling them, but the densely packed fabric crushed the fine feathers of the hats. I breathed a sigh of frustration, settling on bringing only half of the dresses to Rosewood. Surely I could have more dresses made upon my arrival. Or perhaps I could learn to make them myself.

Or I could learn to make hats.

The idea sent a tingle of joy rolling over my skin. There were plenty of much larger shops in Dover, and I could only imagine how much the local milliner's had grown since I had last visited six years before.

After I was satisfied with the arrangement of my belongings, I sat back on my bed, breathing deeply and trying to formulate a plan. Mama and Papa would need to be informed of my planned departure.

It was something I had been putting off for weeks. I had no idea of how they would react, but I knew that I couldn't let them change my mind. *Nothing* could change my mind.

"Lucy?"

My head snapped toward my door. It was Mama's voice.

"Are you there?"

In panic, I leapt from my bed, landing in front of my trunk and sliding it forcefully underneath my bed. I cringed at the deep, grating sound of the leather as it scratched across the floor. Pushing my dark hair from my eyes, I found my place on my bed again and clasped my hands in my lap.

"Yes." My voice cracked and I cleared my throat. "What is it?"

The door eased open and Mama walked in. She was smiling, as she always did when she knew I wouldn't be. She thought it would make me smile more willingly if she never stopped. I wanted to smile, but I had found it very difficult lately.

"Lucy, dear, what are you always doing up here in your bedchamber?" She crossed the room to sit beside me on the edge of my bed. "I have missed my cheerful girl." She rubbed my arm. I loved her, but there were times she cared too much. She tried too hard to make me cheerful rather than understand why I could not be. She didn't know the pain she had caused me by not letting me leave Craster. How could she have known? I had kept it hidden for years. I had never shed a tear in front of her; I had never complained. I had never confided my attachment to Nicholas to her or anyone else. Yet something buried deep inside of me found her and Papa to blame for these feelings of confinement and sorrow.

"Would you like to take a walk with me to visit Charlotte and James? Their piano duets always seem to remedy your spirits. Perhaps Clara and Thomas?" Mama was trying to pull my eyes to hers, but I could not look at her for fear I would cry. She hadn't seen my tears since I learned of Nicholas's marriage. She couldn't know how much the news had affected me.

When I didn't answer, Mama squeezed me closer. "Where is my cheerful girl? Shall we run you up a new hat?"

"I am not a girl, Mama," I croaked. "I am twenty."

She fell quiet, pulling away so she could see my face more clearly. I glanced at her, feeling the sting of tears as emotion tore through my skull. I could not contain them now. Ducking my head, I scooted to the other side of the bed to hide my face from her as my tears slid down my cheeks. What had come over me?

"Oh, Lucy," Mama whispered. "If I knew what was troubling you I would do everything in my power to help you. Please—please tell me what I can do. Please tell me what is wrong. It seems you haven't smiled in weeks."

I wouldn't mention Nicholas's marriage. There were some secrets that felt too precious to reveal to anyone. I kept those tucked deep in my heart where no one could find them. I took a deep, quaking breath and smeared the moisture off my face. "I wish to leave."

She stared across the bed at me. I expected to see disbelief in her expression, but instead I saw understanding. "I know."

Sniffing, I turned so I faced her.

"I know you wish to leave, but we cannot allow you to travel alone. As you know, Rachel was just married, and your Papa and I cannot hire a coach at this time. We simply do not have the remaining funds, and—"

"That is not why," I said, my voice sharp.

Mama's eyes widened and she crossed her arms. Her face quickly softened and she tried to move closer again, but I stood.

"You have known how much I longed to return to Rosewood all these years, yet you have refused because *you* didn't wish to go. I know that Aunt Edith has passed away, but that was years ago. You still have your niece, your brother-in-law . . ."

Mama's gaze fell down and her shoulders tightened.

"Will your grief keep you from seeing them? It will not keep me. I have stayed away for you long enough." Emotion tore through me and brought new tears to my cheeks. "I do not belong here. I want fresh country air and horses and flowers. I am tired, so very tired, of the ocean and the color gray." I breathed, feeling stronger than I had in weeks, finally bearing my soul to my mother. "I miss Kitty."

She stood, gripping my hand, and gave a sad smile. "I understand that you wish to leave. Perhaps one day, but we are approaching winter now. Perhaps next summer we may go."

I shook my head.

"You have been happy here too," Mama whispered. "Have you not?"

"I have tried. But I do not belong here." The truth of the words filled me with determination. I was leaving whether Mama condoned it or not. There were two options. Mama allowed me the trip and I would travel there by mail coach in two days, or Mama refused, and I would still travel there by mail coach in two days, however, I would be forced to sneak away. I had been saving my pin money for months, and had even sold back some of my lightly used hats to the milliner and gowns to the mantua maker. Mama did not know this, nor did she know that I had been assisting the town seamstress in her mending for a shilling a week for months now. Since Kitty's first note I had been preparing, allowing hope to take root inside me. It had flourished far more than I had intended.

"Please allow me to travel to Rosewood." My voice was desperate. "If only for a few months to revive my spirits."

Mama watched me. She appeared more tired and frail than I remembered. She was always working to lighten the burdens of others. She had been a mother to Rachel and me, but she had also been like a mother to many others in town, always spreading her love and kindness. I had tried to be like her, to distract myself with goodwill, but I found it to be exhausting, while Mama thrived off of it. I needed to take this opportunity for myself. I needed to return to Rosewood at last.

"I'm sorry, dear. I'm afraid I cannot allow you to take this trip. Your papa will agree. We cannot afford a private coach for that great a distance at this time, and I will not have you traveling alone, even if we could afford you such an excursion. I'm sorry, Lucy. Perhaps next year. Or perhaps the funds might be put to better use. Perhaps a season in London?"

I shook my head, my mind racing. So it seemed I would be *sneaking* after all.

Mama hurried around me, wrapping me up in her arms. "I will speak with your papa about getting you a little extra pin money for some new dresses. I know how much you love visiting the milliner. It may not be enough, but I will try my best to help you." She stepped back to look in my eyes. "Now. Shall we take a trip to visit the Worthams?"

I thanked her and nodded. The Worthams were my dearest friends here in Craster. I would miss them very much. A visit to them would be perfect, for soon I would be away for months. Mama swiped away a tear that still balanced on my lower lashes. Her face split into a smile. "Off we go."

Hooking my arm through hers, I felt a flutter of excitement and a bit of rebellion over the prospect of traveling to Rosewood anyway . . . against the wishes of my parents. I swallowed hard.

"Off we go."

The walk to the Worthams' was fairly short. Mama and I were silent as we walked, and I took the opportunity to make a list in my mind of all the things I would be glad to escape about this place. It was not a difficult list to compile; it only took a quick glance in any direction.

First, the air smelled of fish and salt, and was always chilly and wet with mist. Spring and summer had their virtues, but we were quickly approaching fall and winter, when the sand would freeze and the water would appear a dismal gray. Rain would fall when snow did not, and the village was always full of more freezing, poor people than could be helped. Today the sky was light, edged in blue and covered in a thick layer of clouds. The sun was not to be found.

We followed a rough stone pathway to the front door to the small house of the Worthams, winding around rich green plants that would soon fade to brown. The rooftop rose up in two peaks, brought together by a row of red tile shingles. As we approached the door, I exhaled all my concern and fear and imagined invisible threads at the corners of my mouth, pulling it up into a smile.

"Lucy! Mrs. Abbot!" Charlotte stood in the open doorway seconds later, one petite hand on her growing belly. Her other hand, marked by scars and missing fingers, held the door open. She had come to be happy here despite the most tremendous of hardships. She had suffered injury and loss, but somehow she had grown stronger and altogether kinder because of it. I admired her for it.

A deep voice rumbled behind her and a head of dark hair and striking eyes appeared above her. "So the Abbots have come to be graced with our company again," Mr. Wortham said, stepping up beside his wife. "You are quite fortunate that Charlotte did not devour what remains of our lemon cake. She saved a slice for each of you."

Charlotte gasped before falling into laughter. "Please ignore the incorrigible man beside me. In truth I have saved *half* a slice for each of you."

I smiled as I watched the two of them. How perfectly matched they were. Perhaps observation of love would be my only means of feeling the joy that accompanied it. I knew I was destined for spinsterhood. I had once fancied Mr. Wortham, actually, at a time I had dared to think of men and courting. But it had been nothing more than a superficial adoration, and Nicholas had always been deep below the surface, striking my heart with every thought of him. Sadness threatened my composure again, so I focused on my dear friend and tried to be happy because she was.

We were welcomed into the house and ushered to the small sitting room that adjoined the entryway. The Worthams employed no servants, but relied on their own skill and work to run the tiny household. While most of society would scorn them for it, most people in the small town of Craster found it admirable. This was not a place of easy living and comfort. Was it wrong that I wished for precisely the opposite?

Mama and I were seated on two wooden chairs, while Charlotte and James sat on the low sofa across from us near the pianoforte that used to be ours. Mama and Papa had given it to them for their wedding a year before. I had been surprised by their generosity. Something bitter inside of me wondered if the money that had been used to pro-cure a new pianoforte for our home could have been used in allow-ing me to travel. I shushed my mind and scolded myself for being so selfish.

"I trust you are feeling well, Charlotte?" I asked.

She shifted, laughing lightly. "The babe has grown a mite larger since we had our last visit."

"That is why I'm betting we have a robust little man on the way," James said, throwing a smile at Charlotte.

"Not so. Why can it not be a robust and strong-willed little girl?" Charlotte wrinkled her nose at him, to which he sat back in defeat.

"I suppose it may be. God has three more months to decide." He wrapped his arm around her and she lay her head on his shoulder before straightening again as if remembering something important. "I must fetch the cake." She moved to stand but James stopped her.

"I'll prepare the tray for our guests," he said, exiting the doorway with long strides. "Will it be another slice for you as well, my dear?" he called over his shoulder.

"I will leave that up to you," Charlotte said before turning to me. My thoughts had been wandering again, and I had forgotten to keep up my smile. Charlotte noticed, and her pale blue eyes twinged with curiosity. She seemed to sense the tension between my mother and me, but decided to leave the subject untouched. I thanked her with a little smile.

The conversation was simple, the usual talk of the people in town and the success of the village. I marveled at the excitement that the two other women in the room could bolster at a topic that was so unstimulating that I felt choked by it. I was sinking into the floor, fighting the invisible chains at my ankles. Oh, how opinions differed among friends.

Shortly after James returned with a humorously large slice of cake for Charlotte and ordinary slices for Mama and me, we decided to take our leave. My heart stung a little as I hugged Charlotte in fare-well. I could not tell her of my plans to leave, not with Mama so near.

So when she asked, "May I call upon you the first part of next week?" I nodded my head yes. Surely she wished to inquire after the dullness in my eyes, but I would have no explanation, for I would be halfway across the county by then.

# THREE

$\mathcal{I}$ had never been a devious person. I had always honored the rules of my family and of society, living a righteous and honest life. However, there was a phrase that I had often been told by my father that I had never forgotten: A folly is never so grievous if it is done for a just and worthy cause.

It was time I grow up and claim my independence, whether Mama and Papa approved or not. Summer was nearing its end, and I wasn't going to miss the chance at a few sunny days at Rosewood. I had a plan.

The village smelled of fish today, as usual, but there was the over-riding smell of freedom that brought me a squeal of delight. The cob-blestone streets opened into a fork, and I knew the left was the way to the milliner. People passed me in all directions, most with a friendly nod to offer. They had not forgotten the generosity my mother and father offered them each year at the Christmastide parties. I felt out of place each time I took the short walk to the village in my clean and colorful dresses, neat basket, and straw hats and bonnets. I was among the few families in Craster that did not struggle daily in need of money. But still all the people offered me respect, which was some-thing you could not buy or sell.

Excitement pulsed within me with every beat of my heart, every breath I took. I had few qualms about my lies to Mama and Papa.

They would understand that this was necessary for my happiness and my independence. They could not keep me here forever. I missed my aunt and cousin, and my uncle's sister and son that often stayed at Rosewood in the summer as well. I missed those old hills and woods that I played in so often as a child.

There had only been two things I ever looked forward to living and growing up in this town: the annual Christmastide parties and the day I could climb in a carriage and travel to a much warmer and brighter place where I had friends and a handsome older boy to pine after.

I secured the ribbon of my bonnet under my chin in one quick motion. My hat had been in operations for weeks, and it was finally ready. With quick and determined steps, I made my way to the millinery shop and pushed open the heavy door. A bell rang above me and I experienced a moment of melancholy at the sound. Would I ever hear it again? I didn't know if I could ever bear to come back here once I made my escape.

Fresh fabric and dye filled my nostrils, along with the enthralling smell of the rose perfume Mr. Connor used as a fragrance for the papers on the walls. The shop was dimly lit today, bogged down by the drab clouds and rolling thunder that betrayed rain. I tugged on my gloves and surveyed the store for Mr. Connor.

The sound of creaking floorboards and the rustle of fabric reached my ears from the adjoining workspace that Mr. Connor spent much of his time in. The narrow door opened near the back of the shop and he stepped halfway through the doorway before throwing his hands in the air.

"Oh, Miss Abbot!" He stepped away from the door and around the wooden counter, stumbling over a box as he went. "I was beginning to wonder if you had taken offense to my opinion of your color choice in your latest hat, to which I would be most contrite."

I couldn't help but smile at the man and his eccentric choice of attire. He wore a bright yellow waistcoat with an assortment of fobs dangling over his round belly, conservative knee breeches, and robin's-egg-blue stockings. His waistcoat was embroidered with what appeared to be small birds, complete with a long tailcoat. His head was glistening with a sheen of perspiration from his work.

"Not to worry, Mr. Connor. Your opinions will never cause me offense, unless of course you claim that I look anything less than fetching in my most unconventional hats, much like the one we have been planning." I smiled at his deep chuckle.

Mr. Connor held a cushion of pins in one hand and used the other to steady himself on the edge of the counter. I followed his gaze to the highest shelf on the right side of the shop.

"There you have it, Miss Abbot. The *pièce de résistance*. I hope you are pleased with the final product. I must admit, I have never been more entertained by a project before."

"Perhaps you have not known me long enough."

Mr. Connor's graying hair was styled in what appeared to be an attempt at the Caesar style, and it was heavily waxed, for it didn't move an inch when he threw his head back in laughter.

I walked to the assortment of shelves. My hat was there, at the very top. I stood on the tips of my toes in an attempt to see it closer but could only glimpse the feathers that I had chosen myself. I sighed in frustration. Why must I be so short?

Mr. Connor walked to the shelf and reached above me to lower the hat to my hands. "You will be the talk of the town donning this beauty, to be sure."

I examined the hat in my hands. It was perfect. Turning to the mirror that leaned against the wall, I placed the hat over my dark curls. The brim was wide and heavy, where it fell low, shielding half my eyes and bathing the rest of my face in shadow. The hat was covered in a blue sheen of silk, with a basket-weaved edging and dramatic green ribbons that tied under my chin. The crown was rounded and tall, accented with an array of exotic feathers, strings of pearl, and three distinct red bows. It was large enough that I could tuck my hair inside and have my entire head covered.

This hat was to be more than a fashion accessory. If I intended to make my escape from this town without the spread of gossip, I needed to be as well disguised as I could manage. Gossip spread in this town faster than the shells washed over the shore. If the town did happen to recognize me, then at least I would be gossiped about while looking so staggering. I bit my lip against a smile.

"Oh, I love it, Mr. Connor! Thank you."

He was beaming. "It has been a delight to have a customer that shares my taste in unwonted fashion. I must own, I was tempted to run up such a hat for myself."

I turned away from the mirror and lifted the hat from my head. I smiled as I looked at the interior. A small tag had been pasted inside, my name written in the elegant hand of Mr. Connor.

"And why not?"

He chuckled, taking the hat and moving to the counter for a box. "There are far too many children in this town and I should hate to frighten them."

Here was another person I would miss. My smile spread to my ears as I swept my gaze over the shop again. I would miss this shop as well.

"Thank you for being such a dear friend, Mr. Connor." To my surprise, my eyes filled with tears.

"Have I upset you?" Mr. Connor looked down at me with round crystal blue eyes, deep wrinkles settling between his eyebrows.

I conjured up a smile. "Of course not."

"It seems I have." He rubbed his jaw. "Let us put that to rights, straight away." With a look that almost appeared devious, he handed me the box that contained the hat. His eyes twinkled. "For you, Miss Abbot, free of charge."

My jaw dropped and I looked at him with wide eyes. "I cannot accept such a service. You are much too kind!"

He shook his head. "There is no such thing as too much kindness, my dear."

I didn't know what to say. The old man looked down at me with mirth gleaming in his eyes at my complete bafflement. Mr. Connor had always treated my family and me with kindness, but never had he done something such as this. How could he afford to give away such a fine hat, surely one that took hours to make? In light of his kindness I now felt entirely like a selfish child.

"Mr. Connor, I—"

He held up a finger. "No more argument. You know very well that I will win any battle of the sort."

I wrapped my arms around the box and wished I could show my gratitude in something more than mere words. I squared my shoulders to show my sincerity. "I thank you. How very generous of you. I will wear it at every opportunity."

He laughed, a rasped sound behind it. "That is payment worth far more than pounds, shillings, and pence."

I cracked one more grateful smile before turning to the door. "Farewell, Mr. Connor! Your generosity will not be forgotten by me, I assure you."

"I do hope you shall visit again soon," he said, shaking his head as I scurried out the door. I was bursting to tell someone of my plans to leave, and Mr. Connor was far too trustworthy a friend. Soon I would be spilling all of my secrets and fears to him. Hurrying down the road toward home, I mulled over my plan again in my mind.

The closest thing to a coaching inn nearby was called The Rook's Nest, a small establishment that boasted three rooms and stabled one strong team of horses at a time. It was a two-mile uphill walk from the heart of the village, which meant I would need to be leaving soon in order to arrive before nightfall and claim a place on the mail coach that would pass through once, then move on, heading south toward London. I would take the most inexpensive seat if possible, likely on top of the coach itself. It would be an uncomfortable journey but worth every second.

I had a letter prepared for Mama and Papa, hoping it would ease their worry to some degree. My maid would deliver it to them tomorrow, although she had no idea of its contents. It was brief and concise, with enough explanation, I hoped, to prevent Mama from fainting. It read:

*Dear Mama and Papa,*

*I have secured passage to Dover by mail coach and plan to arrive at the end of the month. Please trust that I am safe and happy. Do not worry over me, for I will write you often and promptly upon my arrival at Rosewood. I am sorry you did not understand my desire to leave, but it is my sincerest hope that you will not punish me, or call me home for pursuing the thing upon which my chief hopes of happiness depend.*

*Sending my love,*

*Lucy*

The sun was just a crescent at the horizon when I trudged along the final cobblestones that led to The Rook's Nest. My feet ached from the walk, and my cheeks were flushed with exertion, thin strands of hair clinging to my neck and forehead. Fortunately, I had my hat to cover the mess that had become of my hair.

Stopping just outside the doors, I nearly burst into laughter again at the idea that I would be wearing my hat as I marched into the inn. Who could take me seriously with such an accessory? I choked back a giggle that would certainly dub me as a child. I didn't care what other people thought of it. I loved it.

With one firm motion, I set the hat on my head with one hand and pulled open the door to the inn with the other. The entry was dimly lit and smelled of dirty travelers and cinnamon. The candles that lit the walls were melted to stubs, and cinnamon sticks and sage hung beneath them in an attempt to freshen the air and serve as decoration, I gathered. A faint step caught my ears and I turned toward the sound. A thin woman with her hair pulled back tight seemed to materialize behind the front counter. She walked around to greet me.

"Good evening, miss." Her eyes caught on my hat and she dragged her gaze away with apparent effort. "How may we be of assistance?"

"I am waiting for the next available mailing coach to arrive," I said, squaring my shoulders in attempt to appear as if I were an independent lady rather than a mischievous young woman who was hiding from her parents.

One pale eyebrow lifted as she puffed out a breath. "May we interest you in a meal before your intended travel?"

My gaze crossed the room to where a stoutly man sat on a wooden stool, sipping from a jug and eating toast from a tray. He caught me staring and gave a nod, cheeks full of his unknown drink.

I tore my eyes away. "No, thank you."

The woman sucked in her cheeks and turned away without another word, bustling around the corner where she had appeared from.

The coach arrived not twenty minutes later, to my relief, and I rushed outside with my traveling trunk. The sky was almost black now, dotted with faint stars. It seemed the clouds insisted on blocking light even from the night sky.

This was a quick stop—there were not many parcels coming in and out of Craster. Feet racing over the cobblestones, I paid the driver his first sum for a top seat. I swallowed hard. Was I really doing this? My fingers fidgeted with my skirts as I looked up at the legs dangling down from the top of the coach. There were two men and three women, one with a young child on her lap. There was no room on the back of the coach for my trunk to be strapped down, so I would have to keep it with me, at least for the first length of travel. Inside the coach I could see the outline of faces. The horses that were being led away from us heaved in exhaustion, anxious for water and rest.

"Up you go, miss."

I turned at the voice behind me. The coachman was bent over, ready to hoist me up onto the coach, making a step with his hands. I glanced over my shoulder at the fading coastline as the sky darkened. I wondered what Mama and Papa were thinking right now. Had Suzanne delivered the note yet?

There was a space directly between the woman with the child and an elderly man. The man extended his hand to help pull me up. I resisted the urge to turn around and run back to the safety of my house. I pressed my lips together and forced myself to nod. Taking the man's hand I stepped into the hands of the coachman, shifting awkwardly and sliding myself into place on top of the coach. My legs shook and I drew a deep breath to calm my nerves. I hadn't known it would be this terrifying. This terrifying and exhilarating. Tightening the ribbons of my hat, a laugh of disbelief escaped my lips.

None of my traveling companions were exiting the coach at this stop, so before long the coachman returned to the box and set the new team of horses moving. With an extensive creak, the wheels started rolling and I clutched my small trunk by the handle and used the other hand to keep my balance. Shifting my eyes to the side, I realized the old man beside me had been watching me, a wide and rather toothless grin on his face. He doffed his hat and looked at my own hat with curiosity. I touched it, pushing the brim lower on my face and giving him a shaky smile in return. When I looked away, I could feel the gaze of the old man still on my head. I cleared my throat, sneaking one more look. He was still grinning.

Perhaps the hat had not been my finest idea.

Turning my attention to the darkening sky, I tried to clear my mind. It would be a long, long several days, but I would not regret a moment. I closed my eyes as I left Craster, reminding myself that dreams are worth chasing, even if it means leaving behind comfort and ease for a time. It was long past time for me to move forward and take a risk. I had been living in boredom for too many years, sinking in monotony. Unmoving, cold, and always feigning contentment. It seemed that my dreams had been given to me so my heart had something to chase. After all, sitting still for too long without exertion has been known to make for a weak heart.

As the night breezes picked up and whipped my skirts and pulled at my ribbons, I felt the start of a smile—the kind that reached my eyes. And I turned my face up to the sky and breathed.

# FOUR

*W*ould ye like a hot meal, miss?" The voice repeated words I had heard from countless faces over the course of almost a week of travel. My stomach grew tight with a rumble and I looked up at the new face.

"Yes, thank you." I breathed out a long sigh as I set my hat on the counter. It would not fit in my trunk, and my neck had begun to ache from the weight of it. The feathers had bent with the wind and the entire hat was caked in dust. No matter how unpractical it was, I couldn't deny that it made me feel sophisticated and steered my mind from my undisciplined behavior for a time.

This woman was dressed neat and prim, and I noticed that her breath did not smell. Perhaps this inn would be more comfortable than the last five. The woman's eyes surveyed my appearance with a look of concern. "And a washing? It seems ye've gathered a hearty helping of dirt." She studied my face.

I ran my hand over my cheek, pulling back a pale brown smudge. My seat atop the coach had provided me with direct sunlight, which led to freckles and sweat. The sweat allowed the dust that billowed up from the road to stick to my face in a uniform layer.

Today had been particularly hot and dusty. I was certain I had never looked so homely in my life.

For the last several days we had traveled half the night, stopping every fifteen miles for a new team of horses and to deliver and load new packages. My arms were numb at each stop, and the muscles had been sore and aching from holding my small trunk and gripping the side of the carriage as to not fall off on the bumpy roads. To distract myself, I had thought of all the activities I would find to entertain myself during my stay at Rosewood. I imagined the color of the sky. We were nearing London, which meant that Dover was only a few days from my reach.

Deciding between washing or eating first, I decided to wash, reminding myself that I was not so uncultured. Yet.

I opened my mouth to give the innkeeper's wife my decision, but stopped at the sound of hearty laughter from across the room to my right. The fire was burning bright in the corner where a group of men talked and laughed nearby. My eyes swept over the room.

That was when my heart stopped.

The walls spun, and I choked on a breath.

Blood rushed from my head and I nearly lost my balance.

"Are ye well, miss? You are quite pale—"

Her words didn't seem to reach my ears. My eyes were set across the room, where another man was sitting on a four-legged stool with his arms crossed, deep-set eyes surveying the sparse crowd. I made a sound—half gasp, half screech—and turned away from him so quickly the innkeeper's wife jumped back a step.

I put my hand on my head, scrambling for my hat on the counter. Pushing it low over my eyes, I ducked down, tucking the last of my curls under the brim of the hat.

"'Ave ye seen a ghost?" The woman looked over my shoulder in confusion, eyes wide.

My face and heart were on fire. I closed my eyes and opened them again, darting my gaze between the woman in front of me and the door. How quickly could I leave? Five seconds, perhaps three? It was just in my imagination, I tried to tell myself. But then I sneaked another look over my shoulder.

Sitting by the fire, rubbing his hands together, was a man that looked precisely like Nicholas Bancroft. I stared, heart racing. How could it be him? Kitty had said that he married a woman in London. We were near London, so I supposed it was possible.

Peering out from beneath the brim of my hat, I studied his appearance in brief glances. He was turned slightly away from me, face illuminated by the dying flames. *No. No, no.* I begged fate to allow it to be an entirely different man, not Nicholas. It wouldn't be fair. He had broken my heart but now I wouldn't have a chance to break his. He was married. My hands shook as I studied the side of the man's face.

"Come now, lady. We'll have a nice cup a' tea prepared for ye. Does't sound like a welcome diversion?"

I tore my eyes from the man at the fire, allowing the woman to lead me to a chair by the arm. She pulled out a chair and practically pushed me down into it. What seemed like just seconds later there was a tea tray in front of me. My hands shook as I tried to lift my cup.

"Perhaps a washing'll ease your spirits?" The woman's voice pierced the air. "If you will follow me we'll get ye washed." She gestured at the hallway that stemmed directly from the wall that mysterious man sat against. I shook my head fast. Washing would be a welcome escape, but not if it required passing him in such close proximity. I stole another glance at the man and gasped, looking away. He was facing me now. And it was *certainly* Nicholas.

"Do ye care to answer my question?"

My cup clattered to the tray, but I caught it before more than a drop of tea escaped. "No, no, I . . . quite enjoy being dirty." My voice was distant and barely a squeak. I thanked the heavens that my face had been caked in filth on the drive. Perhaps Nicholas would not recognize me through it.

The woman watched me as if I had come from another century or planet. She blinked twice. "I've ne'er heard a lady say such things."

I couldn't focus on her words. It was impossible to believe that Nicholas was sitting across the parlor. But I slid my eyes across the tea tray and lifted them slowly to the fireplace again. My stomach twisted. He was still there.

And he was watching me.

My hand flitted to the ribbons at my neck and I pulled hard, ensuring that the hat was shielding as much of my face as I could manage. My hands shook. Every breath struggled to come as I met his eyes and tore mine away, all within the same second. Disbelief and shock wrapped around my stomach in an embrace that left me on the brink of collapse.

He could not know I was here. He would speak to me, pretending that he hadn't hurt me. My heart thudded hard and fast, stealing all my strength and leaving my mind in shambles. Where was this wife of his? I didn't know if I could bear to see them together.

I turned my attention back to my tea, sipping it too quickly, burning my tongue. I swallowed hard, trying not to choke as the searing liquid tore down my throat. Loud voices were absorbed in the walls, leaving behind hushed tones of quiet and tired travelers. I could feel the heat of eyes watching me, burning through the back of my head and all the feathers of my hat. Glancing around the room, I found mostly conservative people, wearing their most comfortable clothing for travel. I had not chosen my attire in an attempt to conceal myself in a crowd. I hadn't known it would be necessary.

When I looked behind me again, Nicholas was gone. Scowling, I sneaked a glance around the room, pausing with a leap of my heart when I spotted him moving toward the counter where I sat.

I gasped a silent breath, pulling down on my hat and pushing away from the counter.

"Miss?" The woman that had helped me before had to catch my tea tray from clattering off the edge. Before I could escape, Nicholas sat down in a chair two places away from mine, resting his elbows on the counter.

I turned my head away, my breath streaming out in panic. My legs were shaking. What was wrong with me? It had been six years. I was not a child any longer.

The warmth that filled the room did not help the heat on my face and the heat racing through my veins. How absurd, how utterly unexpected that I had crossed paths with Nicholas here. Tingles climbed over my skin again. Memories scratched the surface of my heart but I didn't let them through.

"Would you object to me joining you here?" A voice hit my ears from my left, setting my pulse racing again. I would recognize that voice anywhere. My throat was so dry I couldn't choke out a single word. Instead I chose to ignore him. It didn't have the result I intended. Nicholas cleared his throat and I heard a faint rustle that told me he moved one chair closer.

How could I hide from him now? Though familiar, his voice was different than I remembered, deeper somehow, as if in all those years that had passed he had gathered burdens to weigh it down.

In my panic, I turned sharply in my chair. I could feel his presence beside me, warm and steady, reaching out with hands ready to crush my heart all over again. I did not want to introduce myself to him. I did not want him to know who I was. It wasn't fair for me to be forced to relive the memories he had given me. I needed a doctor. No, I needed Nicholas to take fifty steps backward and face the corner so I did not have to see his face and worry that he would recognize mine.

And what the devil was he doing asking for my company?

Gathering my wits to some degree, I tried to imitate the sound of elegant refinement I had heard from my mother in social gatherings, but took it further, elongating my vowels and lifting my chin. I adopted a lower pitch than my normal voice, hoping he wouldn't hear the girl he once knew. Keeping my face turned away and my hat low, I said, "I'm afraid I must make known my objection. I am one to delight in solitude, though I thank you for your offer of companionship."

I kept my eyes averted, but I thought I heard a sound of disbelief come from Nicholas. "I only asked as a courtesy." I heard his chair scrape across the floor and settle closer to mine. "The bar is the privilege of all lodgers, but I understand from your objection that you would rather enjoy that privilege without conversation. Am I correct in assuming this?"

I nodded, jerking my hand to my hat when I felt it slipping. I picked up a chunk of bread from my tray and took several large bites, hoping he wouldn't attempt to continue the conversation if my mouth was full. I didn't dare look at his face, keeping mine turned away from his view. Luckily he didn't seem to recognize me at all.

"Where have your traveling companions gone?" he asked.

I took another bite. "Did we not agree to put an end to the prattle?" My voice was muffled by the bread.

"I only wish to know how they tolerate your warmth and kindness."

I didn't dare sneak a glance at his face, despite how much I wanted to. I was desperate to know what all these years had done to his appearance.

I swallowed, nearly choking. "Unfortunately, their tolerance is running thin," I rasped. "They have formed a union against me, plotting to throw me off the top of the coach." I bit my lip. Why did I not keep my mouth shut?

"Is it your warmth and kindness that deters them, or your choice of headwear?"

I could hear a smile in his voice.

How dare he insult my hat? He had crossed a definite line. If Nicholas Bancroft was just going to saunter into my life in such an unexpected way, he could not go about insulting my choice of head-wear. No matter how extreme it was.

When I didn't answer immediately, he leaned closer, prompting me to turn another several degrees away from him. He sat back. "I must say, when I saw your hat I was simply too curious to remain by the fire. I have never seen such an accessory in my life." He chuckled.

I sucked in my cheeks, rolling my eyes where he couldn't see them. "In my defense, this hat has been the cause of much enter-tainment and conversation. I expect it should become the new rage in London."

I had half a mind to reach up and tear the hat off my head and smudge the dirt off my cheeks so he would know it was me. Then I would demand a long overdue apology. Hearing his voice, thinking his name but not speaking it . . . it was torture. He had wronged me, and I wanted him to know it. I knew I could never hate him, but I *could* wish to give him a firm slap across the face.

"Ah. And is it London to which you are traveling?" he asked.

I couldn't give him the true answer, so I said, "Yes, London. I find it to be most diverting."

"Even with the season at its end?"

"I do not need parties and crowded society to entertain me."

"Oh, yes. You need only your hat."

I almost smiled. For a moment I forgot that I was not sitting under a tree at Rosewood begging Nicholas to stop teasing me, when really I enjoyed every second. Instead I was here in a crowded inn, crossing paths for one evening before I would move along and never see him again. My heart pinched. I wanted so badly to see his wife, to understand what she had given him that I could not.

My defenses were weakening. I straightened my posture. "It is not only this one hat, sir. I have at least twenty just the same at home to entertain me."

He chuckled, and I sensed him turn his attention away from me. I stole one look at his face and felt my cheeks tingle. Why must he be so handsome? Nicholas was smiling, a wide grin of astonishment at my manners I assumed, staring ahead. My heart skittered. There was something new and strange about him, something I couldn't quite place. Perhaps it was that he was now a married man, no longer the boy I had known. But there were also the obvious things—the wider shoulders, the more solid jaw, the deeper set eyes and denser stubble on his cheeks. I cursed fate for not granting him with bald patches and moles.

But his smile was the same as I remembered, and when he started turning his head to me again, with one eyebrow raised, I noticed that the crease above his eyebrow still appeared, deep as ever.

I looked away fast.

"I shall presume that you are quite wealthy if you claim to have the funds to support such . . . fine millinery," he said. It wasn't just a part of a light conversation. He sounded genuinely curious.

His boldness shocked me. There was definitely something different about Nicholas. It wasn't just the depth of his voice, but the way he spoke. He had changed.

"Inquiring after my wealth will not act in your favor for a pro-longed conversation." My voice sounded remarkably like a child impersonating an elderly woman. "But if you must know, it is in my favor to assume that I am more wealthy than any person of your acquaintance by half."

"Ah. And surely you keep a portion of your wealth with you in your travels, do you not?" His voice was charming, sly, smooth enough that I nearly answered his question before wondering why he had posed it. I scowled to myself.

Why was he still here? Why was he speaking to me? Dread pounded in my chest as I began to question his motives. How much *had* Nicholas really changed? I was not wealthy. It was a lie. The reticule of coins at my side contained just enough for my travels.

When I didn't reply, Nicholas cleared his throat. "Why do you conceal your face from me?"

My eyes flew open and my heart skipped a beat. I was not tal-ented in the area of quick wit. "I am unsightly," I choked. "Ugly as the back end of a horse, mind you." My face blazed with heat. *Lucy Abbot, stop speaking!* My eyes squeezed shut. Could I possibly humiliate myself further? "Please, if you will, leave me be. If I may be as bold as you, I must state that I am not fond of speaking with strange men. I will be leaving again very soon."

"Why do you travel through the night?"

"Mail coach."

"Could you not afford a private coach?"

I stiffened. "I enjoy the adventure of a rooftop seat, sir. Now, if you will excuse me, I must be off."

I flashed my eye away from him and ducked my head again. My heart was racing. I needed to get away from him. The coach would be leaving again soon. I glanced out the small window near the door. The coach was still being prepared, the horses still resting. But we would be on the road again within the hour, so I decided to wait outside the inn until then. After paying the innkeeper for the meal, I stood and brushed my hands over my skirts. "Good evening."

I glanced at Nicholas one more time, making sure to shield my face. My forehead ached, so I rubbed between my eyes with two fingers. Pain of a very different sort tingled in my heart and out to the tips of my fingers. I wished I could speak to him as Lucy, not as this strange traveler without a face. But I knew it would only hurt me more to look at Nicholas again and know that he could never be mine.

Outside, I positioned myself behind the coach where I wouldn't be seen from inside the inn. I saw Nicholas stand up and exit the doors, circling around the back of the inn and out of sight. I scowled. Why had he been acting so strangely?

The parcels and letters were being loaded onto the coach in front of me. It was almost time to leave again. My eyelids weighed tons, but I had no trouble keeping them open. Dozens of questions about Nicholas Bancroft rankled my brain until I couldn't contain any more of it.

To my relief, it seemed that he had not recognized me. I had changed since those old summer days too. My face was longer, not the perfectly round circle of cheeks it had once been. I had nearly grown into my large brown eyes, and perhaps I had grown a little taller. I wondered which of Nicholas's waistcoat buttons I reached now. But when I reclaimed my seat on top of the coach and we started our trip away from the inn, I accepted that I would never know.

## SUMMER 1812

*Breezes ruffled my hair like bird feathers, and I savored the scent of flowers and rich grass that accompanied it. The gardener of Rosewood had kindly allowed me to borrow the shears for a spell, and I had plucked away at least fifteen different flowers, all of which I now wore pinned to my white muslin dress and tucked in the twists of my hair. The gardener had remarked with a grunt that I looked like the flower garden itself, but I had claimed that I looked like a beautiful grown-up lady. Nicholas would agree with me, I just knew it.*

*Skipping through the vast property of Rosewood, I found my way past the vegetable garden that the two homes shared and onto the property of the Bancrofts' small house. I pressed my hands flat against my chest to keep the flowers from falling as I ran, praying the wind would not claim the daisies from my hair. My stockings slid down my legs—they had always been too large, and I felt the trickle of perspiration on my back.*

*The stables were on the west corner of the back lawn, and I assumed that Nicholas would still be there, finishing his morning chores. Peeking through a crack in the door, I saw him standing at a stall, currycomb in hand.*

*With a deep, flourishing bow, I entered through the door, unable to stop my giggling. The flecks of hay I had unsettled at my entry floated in the air around me and I wrinkled my nose at the smell of horses and the pile of muck that Nicholas had shoveled out.*

*The light was dim as Nicholas glanced up. For a moment his eyes were heavy, as if I had interrupted a deep thought. But I was sure I had imagined it, because his face spread into an amused grin a moment later. "Lucy, you have frightened the poor animals to death."*

*I sputtered out a breath. "Is it because they do not recognize me?" My eyes jumped to the horse at the stall he stood at. Nicholas stepped aside as I approached the horse I knew to be named Ginger. His eyes were dull, his breathing labored. His whiskers twitched as I held my hand out to his muzzle. "Is he all right, Nicholas?"*

*He scuffed his boot across the floor, leaning an elbow on the wall. "He's aging, becoming tired, that's all. You might cheer him up with all your colorful flowers."*

*I turned my face up to Nicholas. He raised one eyebrow in surprise as he noticed the flowers that covered my dress and hair. One side of his mouth was smiling, and his chin quivered with suppressed laughter. I batted my eyelashes, just as I had once seen an older girl do to Nicholas in the village.*

*"Are you flirting with me?" he asked, chuckling and resuming his combing of the aging horse.*

"No," I said, my voice defensive. "I wish for you to tell me that I look all grown up."

"I am not a liar, Lucy."

I scowled at the ground, grumbling to myself.

"Please repeat yourself. I didn't quite comprehend that." There was a smirk in his voice.

Searching my mind for an idea, I hurried around Nicholas and picked up the shovel that rested against the neighboring stall. Grown up ladies surely knew how to clean the stables.

A sleek black horse looked up from its water as I dragged the tall shovel away. I grunted with the effort. "I wish to help you."

Nicholas breathed out, long and slow. "Your Mama would be fit to be tied if she learned that I had employed you as my assistant in the stables."

Ignoring him, I pushed the shovel into the stall of the black horse. It was much heavier than I had first determined.

"Lucy," Nicholas warned, exasperation entering his voice.

Deciding that dragging the shovel would be much more effective, I turned around and backed myself into the stall with the horse, pulling the shovel forward over a pile of unpleasantly scented mush. My slipper slid out from under me and I balanced on the handle of the shovel. The sharp metal tip crashed into the foot of the horse.

An agitated cry came from the horse as it threw its leg forward. My eyes widened and I saw Nicholas lunge forward to calm the animal. Dropping the shovel, I stumbled back against the wall and fell, rather dramatically, into the trough. My feet fell over my head and I gasped for air as the water submerged my head. Sputtering, I came to my knees as hay and water dribbled off my face and soaked through my dress. Flowers floated all around me.

Nicholas had calmed the horse, but he threw me a look of disapproval before offering his hand to pull me out. My cheeks burned with embarrassment and shame. Before I knew it, hot tears carved a path through the cold water on my face and I was trembling. If there was any person in the world that I hated to disappoint, it was Nicholas.

His features softened. "Come now, Lucy," he said, pulling his jacket off and handing it to me. I wrapped myself up, warm and safe in the soft *fabric and the smell of him. I dared to look at his face as tears wobbled on my lower lashes. His eyes were firm, but there was something that hinted at amusement there too, hiding so as to not encourage me. My chin quivered and he pressed his thumb against it. It always seemed to stop my tears.*

*"What am I to tell your mama now, hmm?"*

*I sniffed. "That I am a disobedient, buffle-headed niddicock."*

*He threw his head back in laughter, resting one hand on his thigh as he bent over to my height. His eyes had softened, and now they captured mine with a look of brotherly concern. That bothered me. I wanted him to look at me the way he had looked at that other girl in town, the much older one with the parasol.*

*"You are not a buffle-headed niddicock. You are much too adventurous for your own good. If you wish so much for a swim, there is a pond in the woods. Surely the toads will welcome you."*

*I scrunched my nose, feeling lighter and more at ease. "Why do you tease me so, Nicholas? You know how I despise toads."*

*He winked and stepped back, picking up the comb he had lost in his attempt to save me from the horse.*

*"Will you come play with me?" I asked.*

*He sighed. "I have work to finish, Lucy. Perhaps try Kitty or William today."*

*My hopes dropped. It was my turn to be disappointed. Glancing up one more time, I saw that I was no longer in his attention. His shirt was wet from the splash I had made, and had come untucked from the dirty trousers he wore. Nicholas had already set to work again, and he did not see me leave. The horses seemed to whinny in delight as I closed the door behind me, as if I had been a burden to them as well as Nicholas. My lips pressed together to hold in my tears as I plucked wet pieces of straw from my dress. I did not wish to play with Kitty or William. I wanted to play with Nicholas. I wanted to be important.*

*Mama was not angry with me when I arrived soaked to the bone with horse water, but only burst into laughter along with the rest of the party that was gathered in the drawing room at Rosewood. She instructed me to dry myself in the sun while playing with the other children. Nicholas was not a little child, but it seemed that I still was.*

*One day that would change, I assured myself. One day we would both be all grown up and he would take notice of me. Just a few more years.*

*And so I felt the beginnings of a smile on my lips as I raced little William to the woods.*

# FIVE

$\mathscr{I}$ rested my head on the soft leather of my trunk and tried to fall asleep, despite the encounter at the inn that had left my mind spinning. Even a person with a talent for sleeping would find such an act impossible. But with my arms wrapped around my trunk, I had given in to exhaustion. My eyes blinked open. We had not been traveling long. I stretched my back, sitting up straight and wiping away the puddle of drool that had collected on the top of my trunk with my sleeve. It seemed I was becoming less and less civilized with every mile of this never-ending journey.

My traveling companions didn't seem to be affected by my odd behavior. I was seated beside two women now, each much older than me, with stern brows and weary eyes. It was just the three of us with rooftop seats, with two passengers on the back and three inside. The road was at a slight downhill, and the horses seemed to trot faster.

I had just nestled into my traveling trunk again when the coach veered sharply to the left. My eyes flew open as I caught my balance. The disquieted horses panted and squealed, tossing their heads against the tightened ribbons. We rolled to a stop but I could still hear the trotting of horse hooves.

"We've nothing to give," the woman beside me whispered. Her gaze was fixated on something to the right, fear filling her expression in every line.

Dread poured over me, quickening my pulse as I followed her eyes. The air was split by a deafening sound. I didn't comprehend where it came from until I saw the coachman standing near the front wheel, one pistol in each hand.

A masked man on horseback raced toward us. Noise surrounded me, swimming in my ears and making me light-headed. Shouts came from behind, and two other men appeared on horseback, each also wearing Venetian masks. I muffled a scream as the three men came closer. The coachman fired another shot, missing the first approaching man by inches. My heart was in my throat.

Highwaymen had been rumored to roam the roads near London, but I had never seen them with my own eyes, or encountered them in my own scant travels. My muscles seized in panic. I had my trunk with me, containing a few pieces of jewelry and some moderately fine gowns. I had very few coins in my reticule but still enough to draw interest. I squinted. The first man to reach us jumped from his horse. He was short but thick, and his strength was proven as he pushed the coachman from behind, knocking him to his knees and pressing down on the back of his neck with one forearm. The coachman cried out, prompting the wicked man to press him down farther.

I couldn't speak. I could hardly breathe. My hands were slick with sweat as I gripped the edge of the coach. How had I been taught to deal with highwaymen? Be courteous, brief, and offer them any items of value on your person. Do not show defiance. Maintain a calm countenance.

A second highwayman had reached the coach now, dismounting and joining the one that held the coachman captive, helping secure ropes around him. Tall and thin, the second highwayman's hands moved quickly as he tied the ropes and turned to face the passengers. My heart was in my throat. The only man that remained on horseback circled around again, keeping a distance—silent, while his comrades were sneering at the helpless coachman they had overcome.

The tall man on foot stepped forward, only his mouth seen past his black mask. He too held a pistol in his hand. He laughed, flashing a set of narrow teeth. "Stand and deliver," he said, an edge of boredom in his voice, as if he had done this countless times. He flung the door to the coach open. I could see the top of his head from my vantage point, bald with dark strands of wishful hair. Screams resounded from inside the coach beneath me.

The passengers on the back of the coach had already begun untying packages and flinging them toward the highwaymen. A young man, likely of sixteen or seventeen years, struggled to keep hold of his small trunk as the thin man wrestled it from his grasp. Reaching into his pocket, the highwayman threw a handful of dust at the young man's face, forcing his eyes shut as he tore the trunk away. I tensed and could contain myself no longer.

"Sir!" I shouted. My mouth clamped shut. *What had I done?* My mind refused to clear itself. The frightening man brought his eyes up to me, a sneer forming a curved line at his mouth. "You may take what is mine, but please leave the poor boy alone." My voice shook.

"Come down from there." His eyes flashed dark under the bright moonlight.

I had never come down from the coach without assistance. The ground appeared to be several feet away and two terrifying men stood to greet me at the bottom. Never had my seat atop the coach felt more welcome.

"Perhaps it would be quicker if I were to throw my things down to you?" I suggested. Swallowing hard, I fiddled with the latch on my reticule before tossing a handful of coins down below. I kept three shillings inside—I needed it for the remainder of my travels.

Meeting the man's eyes again, I saw that he was not pleased with my plunder. With a glance over his shoulder, he brought the other man forward. My feet dangled over the edge of the coach, and the thin man lunged forward, gripping my ankle and attempting to drag me down. The horseman circled around again. I thought I heard him speak, but couldn't be sure. The deep tones sounded angry. My mind spun with sheer panic.

I screamed, holding helplessly onto the woman next to me with one hand and grabbing the edge of the carriage with the other. My trunk slid off my lap and fell to the dirt with a thud. In my struggle, my hat was knocked from my head, landing somewhere near the men that stood below. My dark curls fell over my eyes and my face burned with tears.

The woman had pulled herself from my grasp and the rooftop of the coach was too slick to keep hold much longer. The highwayman behind me had one arm wrapped around my waist, pressing me close as he attempted to pull me down to the ground. My screams were hoarse as I lost my grip and fell backward into the arms of the highwayman. He roughly set me on my feet but did not release my arms from his tight grasp.

The other man stooped over in front of me to pick up my hat that had fallen. Turning it over in his hands, he stopped, staring through his mask at the tag inside. "Miss Lucy Abbot." Chuckling, he tossed my hat to the horseman who was now stopped abruptly beside the coach. He caught the hat before holding it up to read the tag inside. His head jerked to me.

"You're the wealthy one, are you?" the thin man said into my ear from behind. "You won't be fooling us. Surely you have more to give than a fistful of coins."

In answer, I thrust my fist backward, feeling the wet, disgusting contact of my knuckles with his teeth.

His grip loosened and I scrambled toward the coach. The thick, short man had his pistol trained on me. I had nowhere to run. From the corner of my eye, I saw the horseman move forward, tightening his heels against the horse. They would kill me now. They would kill me or abduct me for my lack of cooperation. I could hardly breathe.

The man on his horse was approaching fast, and the other men backed away in confusion. The horseman bent over, reaching one arm down toward me, prepared to abduct me. When I realized his intention, I screamed again, turning away. But as if I weighed nothing, the horseman bent over, hooked his arm around my waist from behind, and hoisted me up onto the back of the horse with him. I gasped, landing on my side, scrambling to pull myself upright on the wide saddle. The horse was starting a full trot now; if I tried to jump off I would be trampled or—

Two shots cut the air and I ducked instinctively. Why were the others shooting at us? The horse veered to one side, throwing me off balance. I stole a fistful of the rider's jacket to right myself before thinking better of it. I was being abducted! My heart hammered with a mass of emotions. I wanted to cry and scream and knock this man off the horse.

I looked behind me where another gunshot sounded, followed by the low scream of a man. The horseman slowed abruptly, turning his horse back toward the scene. I could see nothing over his wide shoulders. He froze for several seconds before turning us away again and setting his horse in quick motion.

Had the coachman been shot? I felt the small meal I had eaten at the inn threatening to spill all over the highwayman in front of me. Perhaps then he might release me. I swallowed hard, my hands shaking. "Let me down!" My voice could hardly be heard through the brisk air that tore into my lungs as we raced away from the coach.

The highwayman ignored me, leading his horse off the path. Glancing behind me, I gasped. As a small shape in the distance, one of the men was in pursuit, moving much faster than us with only one rider. Another shot pierced my ears—this time it was aimed toward us—and I leaned down.

We were approaching a copse of trees now that opened into a wider area that was heavily wooded. The trees were dense, and with one wide leap, we bounded into the woods and weaved through the trunks and under the branches. Little moonlight filtered through the leaves, and my view was even more distorted of this strange man that had abducted me. I choked on a surge of fear. Would I ever see my family again? I didn't dare think of this man's intentions.

I had ridden a horse several times, but never like this. I had always dreamed of riding with such speed and risk, but not in a situation so dangerous. Even if I did manage to push this man off the horse (which was far from likely) I would have only the slightest idea of how to ride myself. I did not know the temperament of this sleek black horse.

My mind raced, struggling to formulate a plan of escape as we rode deeper into the woods off the path. A branch caught in my hair and I ducked to avoid the rest. I tried to swallow but my throat was too dry. Suddenly we slowed down, and the man glanced behind us to ensure we were no longer being followed. I needed to sound strong.

Perhaps it would show this wicked man that he was not dealing with a compliant abductee.

"I demand to know where you are taking me." My voice was firm. I was quite proud of it.

The night was silent except for the sound of the horse tromping through the weeds and the blood pounding past my ears. The man didn't answer. I took a moment to study him from behind, noting the wide shoulders and short brown hair. A gasp of realization started deep inside my chest but never made it past my lips.

"Don't make a sound, Lucy." The man glanced over his shoulder, straight at my face. He stopped the horse in a small clearing tucked behind a thick covering of trees. With one hand he reached up and pulled the Venetian mask from his eyes.

My head ached. *How?* How was this Nicholas? His eyes were deep and rustic brown, shadowed by the twilight. I could not comprehend it. Perhaps I had injured my brain at some point in my journey.

"I cannot believe it's truly you. Lucy Abbot."

I shook myself of my shock, letting anger tighten my jaw. I had dealt with quite enough from him for one night. "Nicholas!" My palms slammed into his back, off-setting his balance. He caught himself from falling off the horse. But only just.

"What are you doing?" My voice was a sputter. "You are—you are a highwayman! A *highwayman*?"

He seemed unaffected by my outburst, straightening on the horse and glancing over his shoulder. He extended my hat to me with one gloved hand. I hadn't even realized that he still had it. I snatched it away and put it on my head, avoiding his gaze.

His eyes flicked over my appearance in quick glances. "It has been years. I cannot believe I didn't recognize you at the inn." My cheeks burned under his study. Half his mouth lifted in a grin. "I'm afraid I must contradict your claim that you are uglier than the back end of a horse."

How dare he act so amused, so surprised to see me, when he had just kidnapped me and assisted in the robbery of my traveling coach? Anger kindled within me, sparked by the years of uncertainty and heartbreak that had come at his hand.

"That does not matter. I demand an explanation for this." It was easier to speak to him with his head facing forward, where I didn't have to see the grin of amusement on his face and be caught in his brown eyes.

He exhaled, long and slow before swinging his leg off the horse and dropping to the ground. Lifting his eyes up to me, he extended his hand. Betrayal stung me to the bone, hardening my fortitude. Ignoring his hand, I flattened myself against the horse and slid to the ground, trying not to appear desperate as I clung to the pommel of the saddle for support instead of Nicholas's hand. I worried that if I touched him I would fall in love with him all over again.

My skirts slid up my legs as I dismounted awkwardly, and I rushed to the ground to adjust myself. My hair had fallen over my eyes. I cleared it with a puff of air.

Nicholas was standing two feet away from me, half his face brightened with moonlight and the other half dark and unreadable. My heart skittered.

"Nicholas—" It felt so strange speaking his name. My words faltered when he took a step closer, tipping his head down in curiosity. A breath caught in my chest and I swallowed hard.

"You've grown taller since I saw you last," he whispered, his voice brimming with laughter.

My eyes traveled to his waistcoat, to the long row of buttons. There were several, and I had to look down at them all but the top one. It was difficult to believe that I had once reached only the second to the last. Despite how fascinating that revelation was, I found my attention focused on the broadness of the muscle in his chest and shoulders instead, the way his form tapered down to a trim waist, a pistol and sword at his belt. The years had definitely served him well. I shook myself. *Compose yourself, Lucy.* I forced my gaze up, to where I found his top waistcoat button to be level with my eyes, his cravat just at the base of my hat. "Or you have grown shorter."

Nicholas dropped his head with a chuckle—one that melted the shell of defense from off my shoulders, where it tingled me all the way to my toes. But then came the pinching, the betrayal, the reminder that he was married, that he had lied to me. He had not yet even offered an explanation for my kidnapping. My hands found a firm place on my hips.

"I believe you have an explanation to offer . . . ?"

In the distance I could hear shouting, followed by another gunshot. Nicholas gripped my waist from behind.

I gasped. "What do you think you are do—"

He was stronger than even I had calculated in my recent study of his muscles. I tried not to let my face burn as he lifted me onto the saddle and jumped with ease up to settle in front of me. Thank the heavens for the darkness. I couldn't let him see the way he had colored my cheeks.

"What gives you the airs to assume you can hoist a lady onto a horse without express permission?" I grumbled. My voice was louder than I intended.

"Do you wish to be killed?" he whispered harshly. "Don't make a sound."

Setting the horse to a slow walk, we weaved between trees, the commotion still raging on the streets beyond. What had become of my traveling companions? I shuddered to think that any of them had been hurt. I had so many questions for Nicholas, scratching against my head like broken glass. What did his wife think of all this? I could not even begin to imagine the business he had dealing with highwaymen. He did not dress like them. He dressed like any respectable man, aside from the weapons and mask, but lacking the brass buttoned cloak and other lavish accessories the highwaymen bore. What had brought him to these circumstances? Kitty had mentioned in a letter that he had abandoned his family. I had wished then—desperately hoped—it was for a noble cause. I did not want my image of him to be tarnished.

I studied the back of his head, the slope of his shoulders, even the shape of his ears I recognized. Where was the mild-mannered, caring boy I knew?

He had left that day at his garden. The day everything had changed and he had broken my heart.

"One of them has been shot," Nicholas said in a heavy voice.

I was confused at his tone. "That sounds like a wonderful happening to me. Those devilish men deserve to be punished for their crimes. I should like to know what you were doing in such company. Had I not been there would you have still interceded? I think not."

We stopped abruptly. Nicholas's back stiffened. "You know nothing of me. It seems you are forgetting that I have potentially saved your life. It would serve you well to—"

"Keep my thoughts to myself? Hold my tongue?" My voice was mocking; my ears burned with anger. "I will not be led to believe something that is not true. Not again. I am not the same naïve and foolish child that you remember me to be. And you are not half the same as I recall."

"You are more vexing than I recall," he said.

I opened my mouth to offer a cutting retort, but another gunshot from the distance led me to grip the back of Nicholas's jacket instead. I dropped my hands immediately, trying my best to balance with minimal contact with Nicholas. It served to clear my head and enable me to focus on the issues at hand.

"Where are you taking me?" I glanced over my shoulder. The trees swayed behind us, a crisp chill penetrating my traveling cloak.

"A safer place." His voice was barely a mutter, almost impossible to hear above the whistle of the wind. I had never been in the woods at night, much less alone with a man. If we were seen by any person of status or interest, my reputation would be ruined.

"Do you care to elaborate?" I asked through the darkness.

"No."

With a huffed breath, I turned my attention to the sky, studying the constellations. One of them was shaped like a hat. My hat. The one Mr. Connor had so kindly given me and invested hours of delicate work in. Certainly the hat-constellation was a delusion, but it awakened a sense of dread—I had lost all of my belongings to the highwaymen. All that remained was the hat and a reticule half full of small coins. How was I to find my way to Rosewood now? And what when I arrived? I had nothing to wear but the clothes on my back. My eyes burned with tears and a slew of deep emotion boiled in my chest. Anger burned a hole through it all. If not for Nicholas and his accomplices, I would have found my way to Dover without complication. I could have achieved something on my own. Nicholas had proven my parents right. How dare he presume to keep me out of danger now, when he had been the sole reason I was in danger in the first place?

"Please take me to the nearest inn," I said.

"That would not be a safer place."

"How so?"

He let out a long, slow breath, and I suspected he would say nothing at all. "How might the innkeeper react as you, a respectable lady, arrive disheveled as you are, on the back of a horse with a man in the middle of the night. You do see how your reputation could not survive such an appearance, do you not?"

My pride flared. "Would you prefer that we be seen emerging from the trees at dawn in the same situation by the people of the nearest village? I daresay the latter would cause more of a stir." I bit my lip against saying anything more.

He seemed to be contemplating my words. I pushed a low, drooping branch away from my side as we came around another tree. A bead of water met my cheek, then another on my arm. Rain was the last thing I needed to make my night complete. It served as a prompt reminder of my misfortune.

"I have little money, no possessions, and now I have been abducted."

"Rescued," he corrected.

If I had known my mischief would lead me to this moment I could have spent another year in Craster without complaint. If only my chance at a season had come a year before, when the things I cared for most were dancing, fashion, and handsome gentlemen. Handsome, *single* gentlemen.

"To my knowledge highwaymen do not rescue. They steal, hurt, and endanger innocent people. What could have possibly compelled you to participate in such a nefarious practice?" The horse buckled as we crossed a hole in the ground. I lurched forward, gripping Nicholas's shoulder with a screech. I flicked my fingers over his jacket as if I were clearing a bit of dust, rather than clinging for my life. A crack of thunder pulsated through the air, calling both our eyes heavenward. Lightening cut the sky into two jagged lines of dark glass. Soon the trees joined the chorus of rain, rustling their leaves with the weight of thousands of drops.

"Are you all right?" Nicholas cocked an eyebrow over his shoulder. Water soaked through his hair and droplets hung from his lashes. I ducked down, pulling my hat lower on my head. My dress was soaked in a matter of seconds, and the dirt from my cheeks washed down my neck despite the partial shelter my hat offered. My lack of response seemed to be enough, for Nicholas turned his head forward. "The Lucy I once knew also had a propensity for begging information from me that I didn't wish to give." He raised his voice to be heard above the storm. The horse moved faster.

My face tingled with heat despite the rain as I thought of the moment Nicholas was surely thinking of. I had once begged him to tell me the name of the girl he fancied when he was fifteen, even to the point of promising him a week of my desserts.

I shouted through the rain, "When you keep information inside you it will only grow and spoil and one day you will spew it out to the person you least hope to confide in. In your case, a clergyman, perhaps?"

Nicholas stiffened, but relaxed into a chuckle. The depth, richness, and charm of his laugh seemed to pull every last scrap of spite from me like flames wicking moisture from the air. How wonderful a fire sounded at this moment. I shuddered with the cold. We had no other option now but to stop at an inn. My heart thumped. What a hobble I had gotten myself into.

"I understand, Lucy, that my actions appear wicked, but you don't know where I have been, what has led me to those men. I am not proud of it, but for my purposes I find nothing to regret. At this moment, I simply need you to trust me."

"What does your wife think of all this?" I blurted.

It took me a moment to realize that the horse had stopped walking. Nicholas had turned to face me fully. "That bit of gossip has reached your side of the country, has it?"

I nodded as another shiver took hold of me. I tried to appear non-chalant, as if the news had not affected me the way it had.

His eyes brimmed with laughter. "It isn't true."

My heart leapt. "What?"

"I am not married." He leaned forward and eased the horse to a trot. I almost didn't hear him between the water in my ears and the shock. I thought I heard him chuckling, but I couldn't be certain. "Does that come as a relief or a disappointment?"

My mouth dropped open and I gasped, nearly inhaling a mouth-ful of rain. I spit to the side and shook my head although he couldn't see it. "I am disappointed that you would create such a ruse!" I boiled with anger. Did he know that I had suffered over that news for weeks?

"You're relieved."

"I am most certainly not."

"You are going to catch a cold," he said. "Please, say that you'll trust me."

There was a square of light ahead through the trees, far to the right where the main road curved. The rain blurred the image, but as we neared the square of light, I could make out a rustic brown sign. Unmistakable marks of an inn. My stomach tied itself in knots.

Nicholas turned his head to look at me again. I expected to see a look of teasing or an impish grin of some sort, but his eyes were clear, inviting, begging me for certainty that I didn't feel. My mind spun.

"Why should I trust you?" My voice was colder than I intended—too full of hurt. I couldn't let him hear it.

"It is time your adventurous spirit be used to your advantage. But allow me to speak when we enter the inn, and do not protest."

Much to my dismay, the rain fell harder once free from the trees. Nicholas led the horse to a post. Before he could offer his hand to me again, I slid down to the ground, stumbling over the weight of my soaked skirts as they tangled between my ankles. I pushed a mound of dark curls away from my eyes and gave what I hoped was a charm-ing smile. But the smile Nicholas gave me wiped it straight off my face and set my heart racing. Why could I not keep my head with the sight of him? It vexed me to no end.

He quickly removed his jacket and shook out the water before extending it to me. I hesitated, but the shiver that rolled over my shoulders made my decision much easier. I wrapped myself up, grateful that the rain had washed away his scent from the jacket.

He looked down at me, a hint of amusement crossing his eyes. "You should be grateful it's rain and not horse water in this instance."

Part of me wanted to defend my twelve-year-old honor, but the other side was quite flattered that he had remembered such a trivial thing. I stayed silent, the worry of the situation catching me by the heels.

After depositing Nicholas's weapons in a sack with the horse, he took his small trunk of belongings from the side of the horse as well, and we started toward the front doors. Keeping close with his long strides, I followed him to the entrance of the inn, where he pulled the door open and motioned for my entrance. Warm, deep wood covered the parlor on all sides, illuminated by the candles and fireplace. I breathed the smell of fresh baking. My body cried out in exhaustion. I wanted to curl up by the fire and sleep until Kitty and her family grew worried and came to find me here themselves.

My senses were captured by the sound of a kind greeting. A man had approached behind the bar, eyes crisp and sharp as they took in my disheveled appearance.

"Welcome. I am Mr. Allington." He extended a nod without dropping his gaze for a moment. He seemed to cringe at the mud and water that dripped from my skirts onto the clean floors. I peeled my hat from my head and held it at my side, letting the warmth of the room envelop me. The man's eyes traveled down to the hat in dismay. A heavy dripping sound led me to realize that my hat had collected a fair amount of water that had now spilled onto the floor. "Oh. I'm very sorry." I took a step to the side as if that would help the situation.

The man slowly turned his attention to Nicholas, who gave the man a nod. "What a blessing it was to come by such a fine establishment after that spell of weather we encountered."

"Oh, yes, a fine, mighty storm that is, to be sure. The pair of you look as though you have been through quite the ordeal. Please let us see to your comfort. How may I make your acquaintance?"

Nicholas slid his gaze to me. There was that question of trust again, but also a spark of mischief. "My manners have deserted me." He chuckled, flashed a devilish smile at the innkeeper, and said, "We travel from the North, making way to Dover. Mr. Bancroft and Mrs. Bancroft, pleased to meet you."

# SIX

*I*f seeing Nicholas at the previous inn had been a shock, then there was not a word to describe how I felt at this moment. *Mrs. Bancroft?* My throat was as dry as parchment as I choked out a gasp and threw my gaze to Nicholas. He warned me with a look.

Nicholas flaunted a smooth face, hiding any remnant of his deception. How many lies had he told? Surely such a performance required practice. It was disconcerting—the way he spoke with such ease and charm, as if his wayward ways came naturally. And how dare he ensnare me in this lie? It affected me and only *me*. Nicholas was indeed Mr. Bancroft, but I was most certainly *not* Mrs. Bancroft. But to deny it now would only lead to further questioning, and further ruin. How dare he create such a ruse without informing me?

There was a spark of humor in Nicholas's eyes when the innkeeper turned his back. My teeth gritted and I promised him with the darkest look I could manage that he was in for an infamous scolding from me. I imagined how I must have appeared, large eyes narrowed, hair matted and wet, short nose flaring in anger. Why could I not appear fierce and intimidating when I needed to?

Nicholas just answered with a lift of both eyebrows. If Mr. Allington had not been standing five feet away, Nicholas might have burst into laughter. His lips pressed together before he smiled and cleared his throat. "Have you someone that might attend to my wife?

She is quite in need of washing," his voice fell to a whisper, "and the comfort of a warm fire will likely ease her nerves."

I huffed a breath of annoyance.

Mr. Allington threw him a look of heartfelt understanding. "Of course." The innkeeper's thin lips twitched into a forced smile, eyes wide with concern.

"I would like to purchase two rooms for the night. My wife will need a plentiful rest." He leaned closer to the man, his voice again dropping to a whisper. "As will I. She often speaks in her sleep. Endlessly. It is not pleasant."

I rolled my eyes even as Nicholas flashed me a secretive grin.

Mr. Allington nodded. "Yes, of course. Allow me to fetch Mrs. Allington. She will assist you in cleaning and dressing and show you to your room." He was speaking to me now, I realized too late.

I tried to swallow, but my dry throat turned it into a cough. "Thank you, sir."

"It is my pleasure, Mrs. Bancroft."

The name grated against my heart like a rough, jagged stone. It was who I had always wished to be. But the name was not mine. This was not real. I flashed my gaze to Nicholas and my stomach sunk to my knees. He had always been the one to censure me for my misbehavior, but it seemed our roles had reversed. My anger burst like a steel bubble in my chest. If he thought he could come away from this unscathed, then he was mistaken.

My eyes darkened in his direction one last time before a woman rounded the corner behind the bar. Her hair was silvery gray, pulled into a severe bun at the top of her head. Even her stoic expression could not be held with the sight of me. Her brows lifted in disdain.

Introductions were made, and I was led by the arm up a narrow staircase and into a bedroom. Mrs. Allington did little to hide her disapproval of my supposed husband.

"My, how could a man presume to drag a lady through such a storm? If Mr. Allington had done such a thing I might have stuck him in the leg with my knitting needles. I do traveling when within the confines of a carriage, but to take such a journey by horseback? How absurd!"

At first I was surprised by her outspoken behavior, but found myself quite enjoying the conversation when it came at Nicholas's expense. Mrs. Allington puffed a breath of frustration as she dipped a towel in a basin of warm water and soap.

"He is a buffle-headed niddicock." I shrugged. "I did not marry him for any measure of intelligence, that is for certain." I wished Nicholas was near enough to listen. "He has little to recommend him at all. He is dirty and horrendous and when he is not, he is simply ridiculous." I tried not to smile at my insults.

She wrung out the towel and I took it to wipe off my face. She shook her head and lifted one finger to scold me. "He will not always be handsome, you know. His warts and gray whiskers will come faster than the rain fell from the sky tonight and you will have no place to hide and no brooding eyes, smooth skin, and charming smiles to save you."

My jaw seemed to unhinge and drop to my chest. I cleared my throat, trying to recollect my thoughts. "Not to worry. I did not marry him simply because he is handsome." *I did not marry him at all,* I wanted to add.

Her hands stilled in the water and she raised her brows for me to continue.

"Well, I—" My mind was tired. I searched for the things I had once loved about him, but it brought with it a piercing reminder that those days were past. "I find him to be a wonderful friend—even when it does not suit him to give me his time, he always does. He listens to me. He challenges me and makes me feel like I am worth . . . more than I feel I am. He makes me laugh." I wanted to deny it all, but I knew every word was true. Whether he wanted it or not, I needed Nicholas back. The former Nicholas.

Mrs. Allington gripped my wrists and dunked my hands into the water. Then she stood and came behind me to pull the pins from my matted hair. "I see."

I expected more of a response, but she seemed intent on keeping silent.

When my hair was combed and I was dressed in a borrowed nightdress since mine were gone (much to Mrs. Allington's dismay), I thanked her for her hospitality and climbed beneath the covers of the bed that was tucked against the wall. The moment my eyes closed, my eyelids seemed to be anchored to my lower lashes. I had not an inkling what tomorrow would bring, but at the very least I would have a refreshed mind. I tried my best to look forward to that. What an impossible night this had been. I shook my head against my pillow and attempted to forget Nicholas and the terror of the highwaymen and the cold of the rain. Especially Nicholas.

Perhaps he would be gone in the morning—perhaps I would never see him again. I opened one eye and smiled, the effort difficult with my cheek pressed to my pillow. *Perhaps I had never seen Nicholas at all. Perhaps this was all a dream.* I turned toward the wooden wall and closed my eye again with that flowery, happy thought.

"Please assure me that you have grown out of your snoring."

Both eyes flew open this time and I jerked backward, falling off the other side of my bed in a tangle of blankets, the sound cutting the air in a loud thud. The moment I hit the ground, I bolted upright and stared at the wall from over my bed, hand pressed against my chest. My heart skittered like a trapped mouse. I stared at the wooden wall with wide eyes. Had the voice come from within the wall? It had sounded so clear and close.

A familiar chuckle came from between the thin wooden boards of the wall. "What the devil was that?"

Nicholas! My cheeks flared with heat. My eyes flashed to the doorway to ensure my room was closed and locked. What sort of man would try to make conversation with the person, likely asleep, through a wall in the room next door? I squinted at the wall, still unable to believe his voice sounded so clear through it. There were several small gaps between the panels.

"Did I startle you?" The deep richness to his voice hinted at amusement.

My voice untangled itself from my racing heart enough to speak. "Based on the noise you just heard, I can assume you know the answer to that question."

"I am sincerely sorry, Lucy."

But there was nothing about his tone that implied he was sincere at all. In fact, he sounded quite the opposite.

"How dare you laugh at me?" I stood from my tangled place on the floor and brushed dust from my knees before sitting on the edge of my bed, just far enough from Nicholas's voice for my heart to feel safe. There was nothing more torturous than listening to that charming laugh and smiling voice echo through the dark when I was trying my hardest not to fall for him.

"There was a time you seemed to do little else but laugh." His voice was softer now, not as easily heard through the wall between us. I found myself leaning closer to the wall to hear it. I pulled my blankets back up and pressed my ear against the wall in the dark. "Now you seem to do nothing but . . . scowl."

His words struck me like daggers. "Not so. Only when I'm with you."

"It was not always that way. Something has changed you."

*Yes, something has changed me*, I wanted to scream. *You.* Did he not see it? Did he not remember the things he said to me the last time we parted ways? I had pushed my feelings aside for years for the sake of appearances; I had worn my smile well. My friends and family had distracted me, even my dear friend Mr. Connor and all the hats I ever wanted to wear. I had started to forget, my heart had healed. But then Kitty had told me of Nicholas's marriage, and I had fallen apart again. And for nothing. He had only lied again.

"Something has changed you as well," I rasped. "I wish you would tell me why you have such . . . wayward habits. I want to understand."

Everything was quiet. It was his turn to say something but I wasn't sure if he knew how. I eased back down onto my pillow, nestling the covers under my chin and stared at the ceiling. It was too dark to see more than that. I waited, wondering how he would respond to such a statement.

The silence persisted until I couldn't contain my curiosity. "Have you fallen asleep?" I asked. A faint rustle met my ears. I needed an answer. I knocked my fist against the wall. "Nicholas?"

"I'm undressing."

It happened again. I jumped, but caught myself from falling all the way to the floor. My head crashed against the headboard, creating another loud thud. I gasped. My instinct to run from anything frightening or rather uncomfortable was heightened tonight, it seemed.

"I would understand that reaction had you been on *this* side of the wall." He chuckled.

I started to imagine him standing there, shaking his head in amusement, but stopped when I realized at this moment he was not entirely clothed. I squeezed my eyes shut and turned my back to the wall, as if I was in danger of seeing through it. "I did not require explanation beyond a simple, 'no, I have not fallen asleep.'" I made my voice loud and clear so he could not mistake my words.

The chuckling continued, and I folded my pillow to cover my ears.

A muffled sound told me he was speaking again.

"What?" I snapped, turning back toward the wall.

"Thank the heavens I paid the innkeeper for two rooms. I told him you needed a plentiful night's rest. Don't make me a liar. Off to sleep with you."

"You've already made yourself a liar, Nicholas. You don't need my assistance," I said in a grumble.

He gave an exasperated sigh. "Your reputation is safe with my lies. Imagine if we had introduced ourselves not as husband and wife."

"Imagine if our deception is discovered. That will be far worse, I daresay."

He was quiet for a long moment. "Then I suppose you will have to trust me."

There it was again—that dreadful request. "You will need to explain yourself first. I cannot have you keeping secrets from me. You have quite a lot of trust to earn."

He was quiet. Surely he was remembering the time when keeping secrets from me was fun, not nearly so serious as it was now.

"I'll try," he said finally. His voice was hoarse and firm at once, as if the words had taken effort but were now engraved in his soul with determination.

I stared at the faint glow of the white of my fingernails in the dark. "You may begin by telling me how you became involved with those highwaymen." I clicked my fingernails together in anticipation. My entire body was tense, counting the seconds before his voice would cut the air.

Five seconds of silence passed in excruciating length before he offered a curt, "No, I would rather not."

I scowled, rolling to my other side. I deserved to know; it wasn't fair that he taunt me like this. He didn't seem inclined to continue the conversation, so I tried to close off my mind and heart and get the sleep I desperately needed.

It was bright outside by the time I peeled myself from the bed. How long had I slept? I wished I had a maid to help me dress, but all I had were my clothes from the day before, folded neatly on the scrubbed floors by the door. I hurried over, scooping up the pale yellow dress and my other unmentionables. They were soft and warm and smelled of fresh soap. My heart bloomed with gratitude. That gruff Mrs. Allington had done such a service for me. The fact that the clothing was warm told me it had been out in the sun drying for quite some time. How late had I slept?

After making myself somewhat presentable, I made my way down the stairs, combing my loose hair with my fingers. Despite Mrs. Allington's brushing, it had still tangled together in tight curls. When I reached the parlor from the night before, I found it to be empty besides an elderly man and his wife, as well as two small children and the innkeeper.

I approached Mr. Allington with a smile, shifting my eyes around the room one last time. "Pardon me, but have you seen Ni—er—my husband?" Last night I told myself to hate calling Nicholas my husband, but with every childish dream so etched on my heart I knew that wasn't true.

"Ah, yes. He is out with the horse."

I tipped a nod before spinning around and stepping out the front entry. My palms sweated and my heart thumped a little faster. So Nicholas had not deserted me yet.

There he was, standing beside that sleek black horse in the late morning sun. He wore a different shirt, waistcoat, and jacket from the day before. Clean and neat. The brightness of the day marked strands of golden blonde in his brown hair, reminding me of the flecks I remembered seeing in his eyes. He was focused on the horse's face, running two fingers down its muzzle reassuringly. The horse's ear twitched and piqued as Nicholas whispered quietly in its ear. He bent over to look at its front hoof. The horse tensed, faltering back. He reached up and patted the horse's side.

I realized how long I had been staring at him and quickly dropped my gaze, allowing myself to glance up at him from under my lashes. I hoped Nicholas hadn't noticed me staring. My hair was far too disastrous. I almost jumped. He was watching me, a little smirk lifting his lips. One eyebrow cocked in appraisal, making that crease mark his forehead. I could see him more clearly now that it was day, no sheet of darkness, rain, or a wall dividing us. I walked forward with miniscule steps, scolding my heart for quickening with each one. "Good morning."

He narrowed his eyes before standing upright and fixing me with a look of concern. "You are in terrible danger."

My face fell and my stomach pinched with dread. What could he mean? Had the Allingtons discovered our ruse? Was my reputation already in shambles? My eyes widened and I wrung my hands together. "What? What has happened?"

He breathed out a long sigh and drew closer, the top half of his face blanketed in shadow, bringing his eyes to a darker brown. "It is difficult to say . . ." he looked away from my eyes and rubbed his jaw, ". . . but word of your horrendous snoring has already spread throughout all of England. You will never find a suitable place in society now."

"Nicholas!" I crossed my arms. "You cannot frighten me so!"

He laughed, returning his attention to the horse. He stole one more glance in my direction. I didn't mean to, but my mouth slipped into a wide grin. The laughter on Nicholas's face faltered and his gaze lingered on me. He seemed to be studying me, a gentle awe in his expression. "I had forgotten that mile-wide smile of yours."

I pressed my lips together and looked at my feet. "I had forgotten it too."

He watched me, the concern on his face disarming. I pretended to smooth an invisible wrinkle from my skirts. He was still watching me.

"What is next on the schedule?" I asked, changing the subject. "Shall we walk to our next destination? Or is this the place we part ways?"

I lifted my chin, trying to appear more confident than I felt. I was still miles from Rosewood. The only person that knew of my situation was Nicholas. As much as I hated to admit it, he was the only one who could help me.

"I'm not letting you loose alone out on those roads again." He shook his head.

"Will you take me to Rosewood?"

His jaw tightened. "I thought you were bound for London?"

"That was not entirely true."

He gave a half smile before growing serious again. "I haven't been to that part of Dover for months."

"That does not mean you shouldn't." I rose on my toes to be closer to his height. "Please, Nicholas."

"Perhaps I should just return you home."

"No!" I shouted in alarm. "I mean—no, I will not go home. I have scheduled my arrival with my relatives at Rosewood. If you will not accompany me, then I will go there myself. I must."

His face grew serious, a deepness clouding over his eyes. "I will take you to the front gates, no farther. We must be intelligent about our expenses as well . . . I have little left to spare."

I raised an eyebrow. I almost asked where he had acquired such money, but thought better of it.

"We cannot be more than two days away from Dover. Three at most." I pleaded with my eyes.

"Jack is injured," he said, nodding toward the horse. "It doesn't appear to be too consequential, but he will need to rest before we can take him."

"But *will* you come with me? If you do not, then I will go alone whether you like it or not." It was only a slight lie. I lacked the money or possessions that it would require.

He released an uncertain breath, refusing to look in my direction. "Very well. I will take you to Rosewood." He gave a nod, but the narrowing of his eyes told me that he didn't quite trust his traveling companion. That made for two of us.

"We have little to carry. Perhaps we might travel on foot to the next inn, then await the mail coach."

He ran his hand over his hair and turned back to the horse. He leaned close to Jack's face. The horse's wide brown eyes seemed to stare straight into Nicholas's. "I cannot leave him like this." His voice was resolute. "He must rest first."

My shoulders slackened in defeat. There would be no arguing with him on that matter. I knew how Nicholas loved his horses from the hours he spent caring for them each summer. I glanced at his face as he stroked the horse between the eyes. Surely it required a large, kind heart to be so attached to animals. Watching Nicholas now, it seemed that nothing had changed. It startled me and warmed me to my toes at the same time. I pictured him standing by the horse with slightly narrowed shoulders and a much lankier build, messy hair and an untucked shirt.

"Very well. We shall leave as soon as Jack is well rested," I said in a quiet voice. "If you still wish to accompany me." Perhaps he would change his mind and refuse to assist me.

He gave me a sideways smile. "It is the proper thing to do. And of course, I would never object to spending a few extra days learning what has become of my childhood friend."

A sudden warmth spread over my shoulders and into my cheeks, threatening my lips with another smile. I shook it away, stepping backward and into the shade. "When you are ready, I will be inside."

Nicholas was still smiling. I think my reaction to his charm was his form of entertainment. It always had been.

He nodded, bending over once again, focused on comforting the horse. That warmth in my chest caught fire with admiration. He had once teased me about caring for a small, injured bird I had rescued from the gardens at Rosewood. I had kept it in a box under the shade of a tree, letting it heal until it could fly. Nicholas had laughed at me but then he had helped me, and when the bird had recovered, we both had released it into the sky. I smiled a little at the memory. Seeing him today, with the horse, reminded me of another day, one that had taught me one truth about Nicholas—something he tried so hard to hide. He had a soft, caring heart. I had never forgotten that.

# SEVEN

SUMMER 1813

*I* strung the last ribbon around the crown of my bonnet, ending it in a wide, draping bow. It was bright yellow like the sun, edged with blue to match my day dress. It was my first week at Rosewood for the summer, and I had been filling my days with endless embroidery and creative use of ribbons. Nicholas would be returning home soon from his stay with his friend in Bath. I wanted to prove that I could behave like a proper lady, and that I was beginning to look like one too.

"What do you think of the mauve?" Kitty asked. She sat beside me on the settee, leaning over the tea table with her bonnet. One single strand of ribbon encircled the top. Rachel sat beside her. She offered a nod of encouragement.

"Is that all?" I shook my head. "Add at least three other colors and pin some flowers to it and you will have a start."

She giggled. "I prefer a simple accent. You know that."

I chewed my lip, threading a needle through a bundle of rose buds I had picked from the garden. "If that is what suits you, then I like the mauve very much."

Kitty smiled contentedly and set to work stitching the ribbon to her bonnet. I secured the flowers to my hat and set to work with a string of white thread to embroider an L for Lucy on the last cherry red strand of ribbon. When the flowers died I would replace them with the perfect arrangement of bows. I almost squealed with delight. Some of the delight was brought on by the hat, but much of it was inspired by the sound of a knock at the door. I tried to appear composed. Kitty and Rachel liked to tease me about caring too much for Nicholas.

"Could that be the Bancrofts?" I whispered to Kitty.

She shrugged one shoulder and continued with her stitching. Both Kitty and Rachel seemed unaffected by the prospect of Nicholas returning. Both their lips were pinched in tight smiles, focused on their decorating.

My eyes flicked to the doorway of the morning room when I heard the butler welcome the visitors. I bounced with excitement.

I heard Mama's voice, followed by Aunt Edith's. A third woman mumbled something quick and harsh, followed by a shuffling of feet toward the morning room where I sat. The voice sounded like Mrs. Bancroft. I had not seen her hardly at all the previous summer. Mama had told me she was ill.

"Oh, dear." A pause. "What shall we do?" It was Mama's voice outside the door.

"The poor boy. We must inform the girls so they should not be so dreadfully disappointed at his absence this evening."

An agreement seemed to be reached between them, and the morning room door swung open. Mama smiled, but her eyes twitched in Aunt Edith's direction. I searched the hall for Mrs. Bancroft, but she was gone.

"Where are the Bancrofts?" I asked, setting down my hat and needle. Concern filled me and I realized my legs were shaking.

"Mrs. Bancroft is unwell . . . she has returned home with her family. Nicholas however, has received a bit of dreadful news." Mama stepped forward and placed her hand on my shoulder. "His horse has died in his absence and he is quite upset over the matter. I expect he will not be joining us for some time. You know how he cared for that horse."

I was puzzled. I could not picture Nicholas upset. He was always so joyful and lighthearted.

I threw my gaze to Kitty and Rachel who seemed hardly affected by the news, carrying on with their stitching as they half-heartedly listened to Mama. I blinked. Why could something so simple as a horse keep Nicholas from greeting us after a year of absence? Disappointment surged inside me. "Where has he gone?"

"I haven't the slightest idea, my dear. I do hope he will be recovered soon from his grief." Her eyes softened with sympathy. "The poor boy."

Nicholas? A poor boy? He had always been so collected, I could hardly imagine him in any other state. I was worried and utterly confused, wringing my hands together and chewing my lower lip. "Please excuse me."

Turning away from Mama and the girls, I ran out the door and out the back of the property. I swept my gaze over the lawn, running along the outer edges near the bordering hills and gardens. When I reached the small stables where the lawn switched to the Bancroft's property, I stopped, trying to quiet my breathing.

There was a hushed sound, a broken sound, something so raw and feeble that I felt momentarily immobilized by it. I leaned my head closer, too afraid to walk toward the sound. A sniffle and a muffled sob came from behind the stables. I couldn't breathe. I took one step, dragging my hand against the outside of the stables, but stopped again.

What was I doing? If this truly was Nicholas, surely he would not appreciate me, a simple girl, bothering him at such a dreadful time. But my heart was captured in awe at this strong boy sounding so weak. It seemed impossible, but here it was, and I was a witness. I felt much like an intruder. If he had hidden himself away, there must have been a reason for it.

I made my decision to turn and run back in the direction I came. My heart pounded as I raced over the trimmed grass. But then I stopped again. I looked over my shoulder back at the stables. How could I be satisfied with my decision to leave him when he needed comfort? I was not very skilled at offering comfort, or at least I had never been tested in the matter, but it was necessary that I try. I took three large, shaking breaths, and . . . I still didn't move.

After several minutes I gathered the courage, soaking it in slowly, like individual droplets of warm rain. When I was within twenty feet of where I had heard Nicholas, I slowed my pace. He was still there; I could hear him.

Before I could lose my resolve, I walked closer to the sounds.

The sunlight beat down on my face, sticking strands of hair to my temples. My legs carried me with purpose toward the front of the stables. Perhaps it hadn't been Nicholas at all. Perhaps it was just one of the children. As the thought crossed my mind, a head of brown hair came into view from around the edge of the stables. One wet eye saw me before turning away in a flash. A strong jaw clenched against tears. I was breathless. I could hardly comprehend it.

"Nicholas?" My voice was barely a whisper. What would he think of me? Surely he would toss me aside and tell me to leave him alone. But had he ever done such a thing? I could think of no such instance. But I had never seen him like this. Anything was possible.

I walked with soft feet to where I could see him clearly and he could see me. But he didn't look up. He knew I was there.

At the age of thirteen, I had never experienced such a penetrating heartbreak. Never had I considered how such a thing might feel, or how it might come to be. It struck me that if heartbreak were to be personified, it would be this boy in front of me. Knees tucked to his chest, head stooped, shoulders quaking, eyes closed against the world.

I had absolutely no idea of what to do. Of all the moments in the past year I had envisioned our first meeting of the summer, I had not considered this. Not one bit. Nicholas was the strong one, the brave one, the smiling face and the even countenance. He always had been. I had been the one to show the things I felt, embarrassingly so.

Looking at him now, it seemed that even the strong ones felt deeply, perhaps even more.

And here I was, being weak and afraid.

Filling the final three steps, I moved to his other side and sat down, several inches away, never letting my gaze stray from his face—the half that wasn't hidden from me. Nicholas was silent, just a remnant of the crying I had heard when he had thought he was alone. Several minutes passed before he turned his head toward me. His eyes were wet but his cheeks were dry, flushed with red. His brows tipped downward, not in the playful quirk I had come to know. The creases of laughter were replaced with lines of sorrow—lines that were much too deep to have been molded in this moment alone. He had grieved before. His father had died when he was very young.

"Good morning," I sputtered. My cheeks immediately burned. "I am sorry. It cannot be a good morning. I didn't intend to suggest that a morning filled with such devastation might be a good one."

*He was still looking at me, the golden flecks in his eyes blended with the brown, the thick lashes wet and dark. It felt as if it had been many years since I had seen him, not just twelve long, boring months.*

*"I am very sorry to hear of the passing of dear Ginger. If ever I were charged to name my favorite horse, it would be Ginger. It would require little consideration. None at all, in fact."*

*A shadow of a smile twitched the corners of his eyes, but it was brief.*

*"I did not know him well, but I know that he must have been quite special." Why was I still sputtering on like a ninny? Surely I was capable of speaking with more eloquence. I pulled my knees to my chest so I could hide my face in my skirts if I needed to.*

*"Did you love him?" I asked.*

*He glanced at me, as if the answer were obvious, like it was something I should have known. But I wondered—more in that moment than ever—that if Nicholas could love a silly old horse, then maybe he could love me too.*

*One side of his mouth was smiling now, just a pinching at the corner. "I did." His voice sent a shiver of familiarity over my shoulder blades, marred by a touch of sorrow that wasn't familiar at all. "Do you remember when my Papa came home from the continent with two new horses?"*

*I nodded.*

*"He gave Ginger to me as a gift. He taught me to take care of the horse, to take him as my responsibility. I had never been trusted with such a thing before. Papa was proud of how I trained him and looked after him." There was a faraway look in Nicholas's face, a wistful longing that rattled my core. "When Papa fell ill I took Ginger on longer rides, I brushed him for hours, I never left him alone, because I wasn't allowed to see Papa for the chance that I would catch the fever too." His words were fading. "Ginger was my last piece of him."*

*It ached and ached to see the hurt in his every motion, every word. I waited, thinking long and hard about my reply. Finally I said, "I suppose the reason God has taken Ginger back is so your papa may now have a piece of you to keep near."*

*Nicholas met my eyes, a sort of wonder and awe in them. He swallowed, and ever so slowly, a faint grin pulled at his mouth. "You're a wise one, little Lucy."*

*I tried not to grin too much. I couldn't have him thinking that I appreciated being called Little Lucy. But his endearment sent a warmth flooding my chest, like drinking a cup of chocolate in the early hours when the fire hasn't yet been lit.*

*"Thank you."*

*Embarrassed, I brushed my hair away from my eyes and shrugged.*

*Then came that warmth again, rolling, building, catching fire. I looked down, grateful for the rush of the coming wind to drown out my pounding heart.*

*He breathed out the last of his tears and put on a smile I hoped would stay forever. "Welcome home, Lucy."*

# EIGHT

There were three things I had learned about the new Nicholas Bancroft. Firstly, he laughed more than the average man, and often at my expense. Secondly, he held his secrets as weapons, preparing to surprise me with them at any moment. Lastly, he held his smiles the same, tossing them at my heart like pebbles at the ocean, easy, light, but with enough force to break through the surface.

We stood outside a nearby coaching inn, one that Nicholas had claimed received mail at this hour. The three-mile walk had been filled with dust and heat and more of those uncalled-for smiles. Given the daylight, Nicholas had agreed to travel with me by mail coach, keeping Jack in the capable hands of the innkeeper, the cost of which he would pay the innkeeper upon retrieving his horse after I was safe at Rosewood. I chewed my lip and wiped the sweat from my brow as I surveyed the area. There was not a coach in sight. I tugged my hat down farther on my head to shade my face.

"I am sincerely sorry, Lucy. I presumed that it was you that possessed the expertise on the topic of mail coaches and their time tables." Something in his eye told me he was indeed sorry, but still not *sincerely* so.

He looked down at me with one of those smiles, right at the moment I wished to give him a thorough scolding.

"I was certain that you and your dear highwaymen friends might have traversed these roads on some occasion and would know when to expect the coach." I eyed him with a frown.

He turned toward me, a dark shadow looming between me and the sun. "You are mistaken about them being my friends. They are far from earning such an endearment from me."

"If that is so, then . . . why were you involved with them?"

Nicholas crossed his arms. "It is a long story. And I am not certain you will understand."

I drew a breath, fighting the frustration building inside me. "I can assure you, I am capable of understanding the English language. And since we have missed the coach, we have plenty of time in which you can tell me this 'long story.'"

He simply shook his head—a faint but firm movement. There would be no swaying his resolve. At least not today. I squinted at him through the sun. "Very well. What shall we do now? It could be hours before we find passage onward."

"You were correct on one matter. I do know these roads well. There is a village up the road one mile." He met my eyes and his lips twisted in a grin. "You enjoy perusing the shelves of shops, I gather."

He was right. But for an odd reason I didn't want to venture to these unknown shops today. I missed the quaint millinery shop of Mr. Connor. A cloud crossed the sky and the brightness faded to gray. For a moment I was reminded of home. Craster. What were Mama and Papa thinking at this instant? Surely they were not thinking that I had been through such an ordeal. I had written Kitty that I would be arriving in two days, on the twenty-fifth. Such an accomplishment seemed impossible now. My body ached with the walking and the rooftop seats on the coaches. My mind was weary. Under the gray sky in this unknown town, it felt very much like the depressed hours I had lain in bed at home, wondering if I would ever again see the sun. Emotion clenched my throat so hard I could barely breathe.

Nicholas must have seen the depth of my thoughts in my expression because he moved toward me, looking down at me with concern. It only took one look. My lip quivered, my chin wobbled. I begged myself not to cry. But I was so far from home and so far from my new destination. Torn between two places, my heart ached. All I could do was cry to the person that had always held it.

But I turned my face away, pressing my hands over my eyes so Nicholas wouldn't see how weak I truly was. Only a few seconds passed before I felt Nicholas's hands on mine, pulling them away so he could see my face. Perhaps he wanted to tease me for crying. He hadn't seen me cry since I was fourteen. Even so, his administrations were the same.

His eyes were filled with worry, but his mouth gave a soft smile. His fingers caught the tears before they could fall far, and when my cheeks were dry he pressed his thumb to my chin to stop the wobbling. My skin tingled where he touched. I was utterly embarrassed and comforted at the same time. Utterly confused.

"What is the matter?" His voice was gentle, and it unraveled my emotions all over again.

I choked on a quiet sob. "This has been the strangest week of my life." I looked up at him through a thick layer of tears, squinting to keep them in. Nicholas looked distorted through my teary lens, the top half of his head narrow and the bottom half wide and long. His head was shaped very much like a pear fruit. I erupted in choked laughter, blinking to see him clearly.

He stepped back, one hand on the back of his neck, eyes wide with concern and a bit of fear. His head had returned to a normal shape, but the image was stuck in my mind. And so the laughter continued.

"What is it?"

I shook my head as my giggles faded, wiping my cheeks free of moisture. "My spirits have been much revived."

He raised one eyebrow and made a sound that was half relief and half surprise. "You are a strange little gir—woman, Lucy." He seemed confused at his own words.

I looked down at my boots, resting my forehead in my hand. My smile refused to slacken. He was correct; I was strange—in every sense of the word. When I composed myself enough to glance up again, Nicholas was still watching me, this time with a solemn expression, one of deep study. I caught a look of awe, of quiet admiration in his eyes that surprised me. I wondered if I had only imagined it.

"Since you have recovered from that . . . extensive emotional display, shall we take the remainder of the walk to the village? By late afternoon we may travel back to this location and will be much more likely to catch the coach at a later hour." He flashed a smile, trying to convince me with his eyes. "What say you, Mrs. Bancroft?"

I gave him my most unimpressed look, swiping the moisture from under my nose with a sniff. "I should hope that you are not using that name as a way to win my favor. It will cause quite the opposite."

He dropped his head against a smile. "I'm disappointed."

"As you should be. After all, if I were married to you, I would much prefer to be called simply 'Lucy.' Perhaps 'my dear' or 'love' every so often. 'Mrs. Bancroft' is much too formal." I bit my lip before I could continue. What was wrong with me? My cheeks surged in heat. I was spilling all my dreams out for him to see. Someone needed to sew my lips shut.

Nicholas was not speechless like I expected. In fact, he had *plenty* of speech. "Very well, Lucy. Take my arm and we shall take a walk to the village." He took my hand, wrapping it over his elbow. "Are you cold, love? I should hate for my dear Lucy to be uncomfortable in the slightest." His eyes turned down to mine, hiding a smile. "Are you quite comfortable, my dear?"

I looked straight ahead, pulling my lips tight. But Nicholas saw the grin. "I change my mind. 'Mrs. Bancroft' will suit me just fine."

He chuckled and moved closer, guiding my hand to curve tighter around his arm. I didn't dare look up at him, knowing how close his face would be to mine. "I agree, the name does suit you well." There was an edge to his voice, a teasing that stabbed at my heart. He would never seriously consider courting me. This would never be genuine. There would never be a real chance to be called *Mrs. Bancroft* by strangers and *love* by Nicholas. It hurt. But I couldn't let him see that. And I hated that it hurt. He was a dangerous, wicked man for all I knew.

I smiled instead. "But I do believe 'Miss Abbot' suits me the very best."

When no response came, I stole a glance at the side of his face. He was staring straight ahead. His jaw tightened, but he put on a smile before I could wonder what it meant.

The village was in sight before long, and I marveled at the quaint beauty of all the shops and the width of the streets. The heart of Craster was half the size of this, with a much more lowly and broken population.

As we walked down the path toward the first of the shops, I watched in masked envy as women passed in fine clothing and wide bonnets. I felt like a character from a novel, taking hold of adventure with a handsome man at my side. Despite every reason not to, I felt safe and secure with Nicholas. I would make it to Rosewood. I would be happy.

"Where shall my notes and coins find themselves first?" Nicholas held up a small leather purse, dangling it in front of me.

Surely he was only jesting. "Money should not be spent on frivolous things," I said as my eyes strayed to the millinery.

He slowed his pace. "Hmm. Do I recall correctly an extravagant hat adorning your head?"

I touched the brim of my hat. "I did not purchase it," I said in a quiet voice, leaving out the fact that I had intended to purchase it. "The milliner in Craster is a dear friend of mine and, much to my surprise, he offered the hat to me, free of charge. It is a gift I will never forget. After all, it is the only possession I managed to keep from the highwaymen."

I expected Nicholas to laugh at me, but he looked down at me with that same expression I had been trying to decipher—the mix of curiosity and something I couldn't name. "I am very sorry you lost your trunk."

"It is not your fault. Not entirely, at least." I bit my lip.

His jaw tightened again, and frustration pulsed in his eyes. He wasn't looking at me, and I thought I felt a distance growing between us, all in a matter of seconds. "It is. You lost much last night. You must have been very afraid. I should not have led those men to you. I—I do not know what I was thinking." He was almost mumbling to himself now, anger strung between every word.

I stopped walking. "What do you mean when you say you . . . led them to me?"

We stood in front of an alley that divided a bakery and cordwainer's. An outcropping from the bakery shaded us, and I shivered against the darkness of the alley and the drop in temperature from the shade.

Nicholas pulled his elbow away from my hand, rubbing one side of his face. "I am not a noble person. I am not honorable." His eyes were cast down, the lashes crumpled when he squeezed his eyes shut.

My immediate reaction was to comfort him, to contradict him somehow. But chills tingled over my arms and the back of my neck. I needed to hear more. I reached forward and touched his arm. Nicholas's eyes opened, a flash of anguish that surprised me. What was he hiding? I wished I could see it there behind his eyes, but all I saw were shades of brown and secrets. From where I stood, Nicholas was split between dark and light, the light touching just one side. I wondered if his soul was the same.

"Tell me. Please," I said. My heart pounded with anticipation—with dread.

He gave a sad smile. "I mean precisely that. I led them to you. I led them to the wealthy woman in the hat from the inn. I had no idea it would be . . . Lucy Abbot."

"Why?"

He dropped his gaze again, as if he couldn't bear to look at me or at the disapproval in my eyes. "I don't know."

But he knew. He simply didn't wish to tell me. I wanted to be upset and hide away my heart, but something told me that was precisely what Nicholas needed. He needed a little more heart. He needed to see sense. If there was anything I knew to be true in the world it was that Nicholas Bancroft was indeed a good person. Perhaps the good had only been hidden beneath these secrets and burdens that he carried all these years. Determination flooded through me as I watched his downtrodden features. I would find a way to learn the truth. I would find a way to change him for the better. Surely I wasn't qualified or invited to do so, but I certainly needed to try.

"When you do know, please inform me," I said. "I wish to help you."

Nicholas seemed even more frustrated at this. He looked down at me as if I were an unfamiliar creature sitting on his shoe that he desired most fiercely to flick away. My logic was strange, but the look in his eyes could not lie.

"It may be best if I ordered a carriage for you." Nicholas spoke in a firm voice. "We could hire a companion to accompany you to your destination."

My heart sunk in my chest and my throat was dry. He did not want me. "I cannot ask you to withdraw such an expense," I choked.

"But it would make everything much simpler for me. And less dangerous for you." He was leaned against the brick of the bakery now, falling more deeply into the shadow of the alley. People passed on the opposite side of the road, glancing with a lazy eye in our direction before moving on.

"I know you cannot afford the expense, Nicholas." My voice was getting softer. It had been just a day and I already dreaded letting him leave. "Why is it so unreasonable that I might be able to help you?"

There was a fire in his expression I had only seen once before. It shocked me and made me take a step back. His face fell in regret and he filled the space I had made. "Lucy . . ."

"I am not afraid of you," I blurted. "If that is what you think, I will say it again; I am not afraid of you. I am not afraid to tell you that I don't approve of you being a highwayman, but I am also not afraid to tell you that there is an unsteadiness in your character that I am indeed afraid of. I cannot trust you completely. And I despise secrets." My chin lifted higher and my cheeks flushed.

Nicholas's chest rose with a breath, his face tightening with emotion. He opened his mouth to speak, but I stopped him.

"You may find me at the millinery when you have 'calmed your nerves.'"

Then I turned and marched away, as quickly and with as much dignity I could muster on my small legs. My curls bounced as I walked, and I wished my hair had a softer wave like my sister's. Rachel's hair never bounced, affording her a much more sophisticated walk. Hair like mine couldn't help but bounce.

My mind spun with conflicting emotions. Nicholas made me angry and happy and confused all at once. Did he truly wish to be rid of me? I had spoken in truth. I was not afraid of him. Did he think I was in danger from *him*? But he had rescued me. Just this morning he had planned to accompany me to Rosewood. If he had truly been away from his family for so long, would he not be anxious to return? I thought of Mama and her apparent fear and dread at the thought of the Bancrofts and the neighboring Rosewood. What secrets could be hidden there? What had my youth sheltered me from these past years? Mama was a sensible woman, steadfast and thoughtful. It struck me that perhaps she had more than a simple dislike of the place to keep us away for so many summers.

I had been walking for several minutes, far past the millinery now. Lost in my thoughts as I was, I didn't hear the chaise approaching from behind me until it was too close. I turned around to find the horses just a few feet from me. I gasped before something solid collided with me from the side. I stumbled off the road, nearly crashing into the stone wall of the shop beside me. My hat fell from my head and skidded across the cobblestones. The chaise rattled past, and I blew the hair away from my eyes. My heart raced.

"Pardon me." A man—the one that I assumed had just pushed me to safety—was gripping my arm, looking down at me with concern. "Are you all right?"

I exhaled shakily. "Yes, thank you. I—I should learn to be more attentive to my surroundings." I tried to smile, but the effort was painful.

"A pretty woman such as yourself can afford to be in danger. There are often a multitude of gentlemen waiting to assist at any sign of trouble," he said.

I would have been taken aback by his words, but the charming smile that followed made his boldness acceptable in an odd way. He was very handsome, with wavy dark hair and striking blue eyes. I was suddenly very aware of his hand on my arm. I steadied myself and he dropped his hand.

"I don't see a multitude of gentlemen."

He glanced behind his shoulder. "Then I suppose I was more fortunate than most."

I laughed politely. "I was the fortunate one. If not for your assistance I might have been run down. I sincerely thank you . . ."

"Mr. Parsons." He tipped his head in a polite bow.

"I sincerely thank you, Mr. Parsons. My name is Mi—" my voice trailed off. Nicholas was crossing the road between us, carried by long strides. I cleared my throat. "My name is Miss Abbot." I made my voice louder than necessary, hoping Nicholas would overhear. "A pleasure to meet you."

"Oh, the pleasure is mine," Mr. Parsons said in a cheerful voice. He spotted my hat sitting in the road and scooped it up, handing it to me. He didn't make a sardonic comment on it, which I quite appreciated. Nicholas had stopped walking, looking at Mr. Parsons with narrowed eyes. When Nicholas saw me watching, his expression placated. Had I seen jealousy? The thought made me smile.

"I must be going," I said. "I cannot thank you enough for your service to me."

He seemed uncomfortable with the flattery, giving a bashful smile that was quite endearing. "When might I see you again?"

He was indeed a bold one. I enjoyed the attention. Or rather, I enjoyed that Nicholas did not enjoy it. Something devious inside of me giggled with triumph. "I am bound for Dover at the moment, planning to visit my aunt, uncle, and cousins at their estate, Rosewood."

"You cannot be earnest." His eyes widened. "I live just outside of Dover near Canterbury. I will be returning home in a week! How interesting that we should meet here at this time—and how auspicious that I might know where to call upon you when I arrive. Rosewood is a very fine estate. It neighbors many other fine homes, does it not? Stanton Manor and Willowbourne?"

"Yes—I believe it does. I look forward to our reunion." I clasped my hands together and gave a quick nod before squinting in the direction Nicholas had been. He was still watching, the same tightened jaw and narrowed eyes.

Mr. Parsons gave another charming smile. "As do I, Miss Abbot. I wish you the safest and most comfortable of journeys."

I glanced at him again from beneath my eyelashes. He truly was striking, and very kind. We bid our farewells, and he walked away. I turned toward Nicholas where he stood across the road, forcing myself to keep my smile at a reasonable size. With one hand on my hip, I raised an eyebrow. "Have you calmed your nerves?"

He brushed his hands against his breeches uncomfortably, walking toward me. Finally he tipped his head back with a smile. "Yes, Lucy, my nerves are quite calmed." He didn't seem inclined to address the issue of Mr. Parsons and his flirting. I was just relieved that Nicholas was not still angry and unsociable.

"Do you still plan to send me off on my own way?" I asked, dreading the answer.

He was standing several feet away, and a duo of well-dressed women bustled between us on the road. When I could see him again, my heart gave a firm leap. He was looking at me in that odd way again—the look I couldn't name. It was unfamiliar and unnerving, and it made my breath catch.

"I'm afraid I cannot do that."

Relief pounded through me. "And why not?"

He exhaled fast in an attempt at laughter. And then his eyes met mine again with a humble smile. "I need you."

My knees seemed to buckle in shock. I licked my lips, avoiding his eyes. *Nicholas needs me. Nicholas needs me?* Had I heard him correctly? I was certain it couldn't be true. I needed him; he never needed me. I fiddled with the ribbons of my hat that I held, forcing myself to act composed. I frowned in confusion, willing him to explain.

"I need you to help me," he said. "I—I have lost sight of . . . everything. You spoke frankly of my character, and I needed to hear it." His voice was uncertain, shy—a sound I never thought I would hear in my life.

It took a moment, but I composed myself enough to speak clearly. "Of course." I breathed deeply, deciding whether or not I should say the next part. "You—you have helped me many times throughout my life. It is the very least I can do."

He looked confused. "How have I helped you?"

I shrugged, trying to appear nonchalant. "You always gave me something to look forward to. Every month of the year I was in Craster I looked forward to the adventures I would have in the summer with you." I fluttered my hands around the air to give dramatic effect to his name. "Nicholas Bancroft." I grinned as he laughed. "But . . . I will gladly serve another platter of scolding if that is what you need me for. I am at your service." I gave a low bow, earning a chuckle from Nicholas.

His hair was falling over his forehead and I wished I could brush it away for him. If only I were brave enough. Or tall enough, for that matter.

Nicholas moved closer, a smile still stretched across his lips, and he tipped his head down to look at me. I determined that I could certainly reach his hair if I wanted to. If I rose on my toes high enough then I could even kiss him. Just with the thought my cheeks burned. His eyes studied my face, growing more serious. The unspoken conclusion he reached with his study made him smile even wider. "You should wear your hat again."

I touched my head. "Why is that?"

"We cannot have hair so enchanting as yours free for men like Mr. Parsons to see." The way he said *Mr. Parsons* sounded as if the name had been coated in sour milk and forced down his throat. It made me smile. He turned on his heel to the direction of the millinery, glancing over his shoulder with a sly grin, extending his arm. "Come now, Mrs. Bancroft."

I pressed my smile down, keeping my reaction dignified as I set my hat over my hair again. I could not squeal with delight and have Nicholas assuming that I cared for his flattery.

When we reached the door of the millinery, I glanced inside, tingling with excitement. The shop was much larger than the one in Craster, with taller ceilings and many more hats. Women worked at the edges of the room, stitching ribbon to bonnets and trimming hats. I watched in admiration.

The milliner was quite unlike Mr. Connor in both manner and appearance. He was aloof to say the least, throwing color suggestions without a glance in my direction, twisting his finger over his thin beard and speaking in French to the women in the room when I asked him a question. Nicholas stood by in amusement as I tried on the plainest bonnets and then the most extravagant hats. It was a welcome way to spend an afternoon.

When we exited the shop, I blinked fast. The sky was streaked in peach, and the moon was visible as a translucent sphere. "What is the time?"

"I didn't wish to interrupt you. You seemed to be enjoying yourself." He laughed as he pulled a small watch from his jacket.

"I was." My eyes moved fast over the cloudless sky, taking note of every color in the sky. I didn't want to forget this day.

"The mail coach," Nicholas said. My gaze tore from the sky to his face. He was squinting at the watch in his palm. "I'm afraid we must hurry if we wish to catch it."

I had nearly forgotten. My stomach sunk with dread.

"Are you fond of running?"

My eyes widened and excitement thrummed in my chest. There was a wild thing inside, stretching its bound wings. I was fond of it, but I didn't remember when I had last done it. Brisk walking was the extent of my speed. "Are you suggesting we run to the inn?" I scoffed. "How utterly ridiculous. I am a lady, do you remember?"

"I remember quite well."

"How could my short legs keep speed with you?"

Half his mouth quirked in a smile. "I am slow. Do you remember?"

I did remember. Quite well. Nicholas had always let me win in our races across the Rosewood property. But I hadn't known it then, and that's what made the memory so special to me now.

We set at a rapid walk in the direction of the coaching inn. I had never been very skilled at mathematics, but I was intelligent enough to know that three of my strides, perhaps two and one half, matched the equivalent of one of his. I grimaced, straining my legs as I tried to keep up.

"I fear we won't make it," Nicholas said.

I could not endure an additional night and day in this dress. "We must," I choked. Short on breath, I added a spring to my step, soaring past Nicholas in a run. When I saw the surprise on his face, I couldn't help but laugh. My hat slipped over the top of my head, but I placed my hand on top of it to keep it from blowing away. Nicholas was there beside me in a matter of seconds, but just a few inches behind, like always. I wondered how fast he could really run.

My throat burned with exertion and laughter, but my feet moved and the wind stole my breath and Nicholas laughed beside me. My hair bounced, and I didn't mind it one bit.

We approached a hill, a steep, rounded, grassy top before it sloped down toward the road that would take us to the inn. I could see it—candlelight glowing from the windows and cutting the dimming air. And then my heart sunk. There was the mail coach, and there were the passengers claiming their seats on the back and on the rooftop, two women climbing inside. The coachman took his place in the box. We were too far.

I stopped, bending over to catch my breath. I put my hand against my damp forehead. Would my fortune ever turn? I was beginning to doubt I would ever make it to Rosewood. Disheartened, I turned to Nicholas. He had stopped too, craning his neck to see the inn far in the distance. He appeared so composed, hardly a drop of perspiration on his face, his hair windblown but even more handsome for it.

"Not to worry. We will catch it tomorrow." He put one hand on my shoulder, sending a thread of warmth all the way to my fingertips.

I couldn't hide my disappointment. What would Mama and Papa think of me now? I had tried to prove my maturity by taking this trip alone, but instead I had found myself in an unbelievable and rather forbidden situation. What had they thought when they read my note? Surely Papa had not taken it lightly. I was under his protection, and he took that responsibility very seriously. I had taken it for granted. I was under Nicholas's protection now.

"Let me see that smile of yours."

I glanced up. Nicholas had one eyebrow raised, that curved crease above it on his forehead, an inquisitive grin on his lips. My heart flooded with familiarity and comfort. Perhaps under Nicholas's protection was not such a horrible place to be.

I sighed, wiping my palms on my skirts with finality, and mustered the smallest of smiles. "I suppose I am very tired. Another night of rest sounds wonderful at the moment."

Nicholas looked relieved as he stepped forward and curved my arm around his. We walked down the hill in the direction of the inn.

"Off we go, then," he said. "But you must promise me one thing."

"What?"

His gaze rested on me for a moment before shifting to the road ahead. "That you will keep the snoring to a minimum."

I giggled, slapping my hand over my mouth to hide it. "I cannot control it!"

"Then I will pray that this inn has denser walls."

I laughed, turning my face up to the sky, watching the stars come to light. If I finally did make it to Rosewood, then surely the intrigue and excitement wouldn't be half what I had experienced in the past day. The thought filled me with a sudden ache that reached through my ribs and stabbed at my heart.

I was reminded of a gift Nicholas had once given me—a box of pearls that he had convinced me were wishes. I didn't have it with me, for I had already used all the wishes inside. I didn't want Nicholas to leave. If I still had that box of wishes, then I would certainly have used it to wish that this journey to Rosewood with Nicholas could last forever.

# NINE

SUMMER 1813

*T*he stones in front of me formed a path, a jagged one with spaces between. I lifted my skirts and hopped over each stone. There were ten. When I reached the end, I turned, catching my breath, and beamed at my accomplishment. And then I bent down, pushing the stones so they lay even farther apart, and moved to the first stone once again.

The woods were quiet today. Kitty sat at the base of a tree nearby, sketching the birds that perched on the branches above her. Every so often she gave an angry remark about how they simply couldn't hold still. I fancied myself to be much like the birds, always hopping, moving, untucking my wings from my sides. Surely if I were a bird I would take every opportunity I had to fly. How daft to not use wings if you are given them.

I bent my knees to jump again, swinging my arms for added momentum. My right foot hit the ground, half on top of the stone and half on the dirt. I stumbled, hitting the ground with my elbow first. Laughing, I brushed myself clean. "Too far," I breathed.

Kitty glanced up, a smile playing across her soft features. She had always been a conservative girl, keeping the rules and behaving like a lady. I tried, but at times it was simply too tiring.

As I pushed myself off the ground, I spied a round ivory ball not one quarter inch in diameter, sticking out from the dirt. My heart sparked with excitement. I had always hoped I might find a piece of buried treasure.

*With eager fingers I dug at what I now recognized as a pearl. As the dirt fell away, I found a strand of them. I held it up, counting the pearls. Five. They were darkened with age and grime, but I smiled as I held them to the sunlight. "Kitty! Look at what I found."*

*She squinted from across the clearing, giving into curiosity and coming for a closer look. She grimaced, dipping her head to see them from a different angle. "They are dirty."*

*"They have been living in the dirt, Kitty. How else might they be? You live in a clean house, so it would not be acceptable if you were to become dirty. These beautiful pearls had no choice in the matter." My voice was rambling on, but I was hardly listening to myself. I studied the pearls as I held the end of the strand pinched between two fingers.*

*Kitty laughed. "You are living in my very same clean house, yet you are dirty."*

*It was true. My hands were lined in filth. Kitty reached down to pluck a twig from my hair. Cradling the pearls in my palm, I stood up. "Where shall we keep them?"*

*Leaves rustled behind us and I jumped as a figure emerged.*

*"Nicholas! You cannot sneak behind us like that!" Kitty shrieked. As predictable as clockwork, my heart ticked a little faster as I turned around. I hadn't seen Nicholas all week, and I had begun to worry he was avoiding me after I had found him behind the stables at his most vulnerable moment, crying over his horse. The image was burned in my mind, so when I saw him standing there, I was surprised to see his wide grin.*

*"How else could I approach two unsuspecting people than by surprise? It is much more entertaining." His eyes shifted to me, an unspoken greeting in them. Then he winked.*

*"I found a buried treasure," I said in a quick voice, trying to dispel the feeling that burned through me with that wink. My cheeks reddened with embarrassment. A buried treasure?*

*I wanted to bury my face in my hands instead. Certainly my expression wasn't a treasure.*

*Nicholas's smile only grew, and his eyes lit up with interest. "What is it?"*

*I looked down at the toes of my boots, tightening my fist around the strand of pearls. Why must I be so painfully shy? It was uncharacteristic of me. Something had changed that day by the stables. Nicholas wasn't indestructible. He wasn't the face of perfect strength and ease. He was cracked and broken. He not only laughed but he cried sometimes too. He was much like me.*

*Nicholas walked closer, and I noticed that his hair was combed today, tucked behind his ears and pushed back from his face. His eyes were open and clear, and my heart skittered when they looked down at me with a question. "Where is this treasure, Lucy?"*

*I pressed my lips together, planning my words carefully.*

*"Ah. I believe I've found it," Nicholas brought his hand up to my head, pulling a short twig from between my curls and holding it in front of my face. I swatted his hand away, a smile breaking over my cheeks. How many twigs were in my hair?*

*Nicholas laughed, and Kitty shook her head in disapproval, but her lips were pinched in a grin too.*

*It was remarkable, the strength of laughter to break down barriers and clear the mind. With a deep breath, I opened my hand, hoping Nicholas didn't notice the dirt beneath my nails. "It is only these pearls."*

*He was quiet as he surveyed them in my palm, tapping each one with his finger.*

*"They are quite unremarkable," I muttered. I didn't want him to think that I had been so excited over a dirty strand of pearls.*

*"Not in the slightest." Nicholas shot his gaze to mine. He was playing with me, but I was curious what this game might entail. "Anything can be remarkable if you make it so."*

*Kitty had reclaimed her spot by the tree. I knew her current attentions were held by a boy that frequented the local village. She didn't care for Nicholas like I did. But my attention was captured wholeheartedly by the boy in front of me. I tipped my head up to look at him, scrunching my brows in confusion.*

*Reaching inside his jacket, he withdrew a small wooden box. It could only have been two inches long and one inch tall, with small carvings at the edges. The wood was misshapen, striped in pale tan and brown. "I made this today. I finished my chores early." He held out his hand, gesturing that I hand him the pearls. With wide eyes, I obeyed. He lifted the strand to his mouth and bit the knot at the end, breaking the pearls* free. Pinching the strand, he tipped each pearl into the box and capped the ill-fitting lid.

"This is not an ordinary box now, Lucy. This is your dream box, and these pearls are wishes."

I shifted my eyes to the box, my imaginative side quaking with excitement but my logical side questioning every word. But if any person possessed magic, it had to be Nicholas. My smile stamped out the logical side in one firm stomp. "How does it work?" I whispered.

He didn't hesitate, but placed the box in my hand. It fit perfectly in my small palm. "Each pearl is a wish or a dream. You may use them at any time, but when you do, you must wash each pearl clean of the dirt and throw it . . . in the fireplace. If you do this, and if you never give up, your dream will come true." He smiled with half his mouth, little crinkles marking the corners of his eyes.

I stared in awe at the tiny box filled with my dreams. Then I looked up at Nicholas, gratitude surging through me in one overwhelming wave. He was my biggest dream of all, I supposed. My face blossomed with warmth and I looked down at my toes again. "Thank you."

"Keep it safe," he said.

I nodded, curling my fingers over the gift—this present I would never forget. I would keep it very safe.

# TEN

*I* dreamt that I still had my pearls, that I hadn't used them all yet. In my dream I wished that I hadn't left Craster alone, that I had bid my parents a proper farewell, that I hadn't been stopped by those highwaymen. I awakened before I could use my fifth wish.

We had made it to the inn with little trouble the previous night, Nicholas conveying the same explanation as he had in the last inn. I was Mrs. Bancroft. He loved me. But it was only a story, and my heart was growing tired of hearing it. These days of travel would end. Nicholas would leave, and I would be helplessly sad because of it. It would be best that I arrive at Rosewood as quickly as possible. It wasn't sensible to wish for any more time with Nicholas.

To my relief, a mail coach was arriving that morning for an early delivery, opting to travel during the day because of suspected storms that would reach us in the evening. I squinted at the skies when we stepped outside, and was reminded by the gray clouds of the sky I had left behind.

When he stepped out beside me, I observed that Nicholas had combed his hair. His face was shaved too, clean and smooth. I couldn't help but smile as I looked up at him. He was too handsome for his own good. But I couldn't let him see that I was admiring him.

Tearing my gaze away, I marched toward the halted coach. Boots crunched in the grass behind me. I tried to make up for my tiny strides, but Nicholas was there in an instant.

"You look beautiful," he whispered into my hair as he passed. A shiver rolled over my shoulders and I caught my breath.

"Do not ever do that again." My eyes widened. I hadn't meant to say it aloud.

He raised his brows, making the molasses sugar of his eyes spark with amusement. "I thought you were going to help me with my wayward habits. Offering flattery is never a nefarious endeavor."

I huffed a breath. *It wasn't the compliment. It was the whisper. The much-too-close whisper.*

"You are wrong. Flattery is most frequently offered with insincerity. How many times have you searched to offer praise upon someone simply because they praised you first? Insincerity is a nefarious thing."

We reached the coach and found the narrow seats outside on the back of the coach to be unclaimed. Nicholas stopped in front of them. I expected him to extend a hand to guide me up, but instead he gripped my waist with both hands, setting me on the narrow outcropped seat. I pushed my hair back from my eyes, embarrassed, as he took his place beside me. The seats were quite close together, and my feet dangled above the dirt ground. My shoulder pressed into Nicholas's upper arm, and my leg bumped against his repeatedly as the passengers unsettled the coach as they climbed atop it and inside. I looked to my left, hoping there would be room to slide over, but there wasn't an extra inch to spare unless I wished to fall off the coach. I swallowed hard. Nicholas shifted to face me. I knew his face was too close when I could see the gold streaks in his eyes.

"I don't believe that to be true. My flattery was sincere, I assure you."

His eyes bore into mine and I snapped them away, feigning interest in the embroidery on my skirts. I was embarrassed by my behavior; he hadn't meant to make me uncomfortable. Or maybe he had. "Thank you," I said in a quiet voice. "You are very kind."

He gasped. "What a nefarious thing to say! I shall not believe a word of that insincere praise."

I pinched my lips and shifted just my eyes to look at him. Nicholas chuckled before draping his arm across the metal piping that rested just behind my shoulders. "I have always hated coaches," he said, changing the subject. "I always find the ride monotonous and uneventful."

I couldn't stop thinking about his arm directly behind me. I wished he would wrap it around my shoulders instead. I banished my thoughts and swept my gaze over the surrounding landscape. If I looked at his much-too-close face then I would lose my head. I certainly couldn't endure another much-too-close whisper.

"There must be a way to make this ride more enjoyable," I mused. "We cannot have you dying of boredom."

"That's unlikely with you here, Lucy."

I flashed my gaze to his face, one quick glance before turning forward. "Why do you say that?"

"You are the most unexpected person I know." His head was tipped down closer to mine, begging for my eyes. I dared another glance and wished I hadn't. My heart thumped at the look he was giving me, at the unmistakable admiration that shone there. His smile was so close. I wanted to kiss him—but I knew I would never survive such a thing. My heart was already in pieces from a simple look.

I pushed my curls back from my face, tucking them under my bonnet. "How am I unexpected?" Perhaps he was referring to our unexpected reunion.

He shrugged one shoulder. "The things you say, the things you do. The things you love."

"Did you not expect me to love hats? Or fashion?" I grinned up at him.

"I fully expected that." He smiled, but it faded into a question, a puzzled look. "I expected you to be the same little girl from years ago. I didn't expect a woman with opinions and boldness and spirit. You hide the things you feel. I never had to question your thoughts or your emotions before. You couldn't hide anything from me even if you tried." He gave a little smile and I felt my cheeks warm. He paused. "I expected you would still care for me."

I caught my breath. My words were stuck in my throat. What could I say? I *did* still care for him, much more than I should. But I was afraid of the things he made me feel. I stuttered for a second before Nicholas stopped me with a casual smile. "I like unexpected things. They keep me alert. They remind me I cannot have everything I want."

His words lingered in the air and rang in my ears. His eyes were cast down at his lap, a shyness that didn't seem to fit. Did he want me to care for him? His feelings could not have changed within two days of seeing me. But something warned me that perhaps he wasn't completely indifferent.

But maybe he was.

The coach had been moving for several minutes now, and I focused on the trees and plants that we passed, soaking in the silence that had fallen between us. We traveled for most of the day, stopping periodically for a new team of horses. For the first hour we didn't speak much. I made the occasional remark and Nicholas gave a brief response. But as the day went on, I found my smile returning. We talked of easy, light things, and I laughed over and over again. I recited children's stories I had never forgotten from my nursery days, and Nicholas reminded me of summer events from our childhood that I had forgotten. The hours passed like minutes, and I wanted them to last forever.

I found myself studying him—looking for further indication that he might feel what I felt for him. But it was a mystery. He smiled, he spoke with animation, and he looked at me like he might look at any other lady. There was no flirting, just joyful conversation carrying on without effort, comfortable in the silent moments. But still, my heart ached with each of his glances in my direction. I was every bit in love with him as I had been six years ago. I couldn't deny it. No matter how troubling his past, how many secrets he held, he was still Nicholas. He could still make me smile at any moment he pleased. He could still pluck out every emotion inside me and play them like a pianoforte.

I thought of a porcelain doll my grandmother had once given me. As a child I had played roughly with it, throwing it in the air and letting it fall onto the soft grass where it couldn't break. I carried it by the leg, swinging it by my side everywhere I went, never thinking of the dangers of doing so. I loved the doll. Then one day I had walked too close to the fence, swinging the doll without looking, and cracked off several pieces of the face against the picket. In a panic I had tried to fix it, enlisting my father to help me. With the new pieces crookedly in place, I had set the doll on a high shelf in my bedchamber. I didn't throw it or swing it. I didn't touch it. I hadn't understood how fragile it was until it was broken. I didn't want to hurt it again.

Nicholas had once played dangerously with my heart without knowing it. And I hadn't seen the potential harm that would come from caring so much for him. My heart was now the cracked doll, high up on a shelf where I was too short to reach it. But Nicholas was tall. He knew where to find it, and how to swing it and throw it until it was beyond repair.

My eyes squeezed shut and I built another shelf, a much higher one this time.

We were just outside of London when the coach stopped for the night, depositing us outside of the last country inn before we would be in the center of town living. The air was crisp under the blackened sky, making the tip of my nose tingle with cold. Passengers climbed out from within the coach and were assisted from the top. They bustled around us, moving toward the inn's entrance, stretching their backs and legs. Nicholas helped me down from the coach and smiled down at me, a twinge of mischief in his expression. His hand lingered on my waist for a bit longer than necessary. I noted it.

"Have you enjoyed your time spent as Miss Lucy Abbot?"

"Am I not still Miss Lucy Abbot? I'm not Mrs. Bancroft until we walk through that door. Even so, I wish such deceit weren't necessary." I pressed my lips together and tried not to smile, looking up at him through a sheet of lashes.

He stared down at me. I could see the details of his face from the flickering windows of the nearby inn. "Be careful."

My brow furrowed.

"You can never know what sort of men would be tempted to kiss you when you give them a look like that."

I felt my cheeks flame. Perspiration gathered in my palms and I wiped them on my skirts. My eyes were planted firmly on the patched grass at my feet. "And what sort of men are they?"

"The sort with eyes. The sort that have heard that voice, that laugh, and all the intelligent and silly things you have to say." His voice held a smile as he nudged my chin up with his knuckle, cold like the tip of my nose. His eyes searched my face, and when his hand touched my cheek I felt my face burn further. "Ah. Your face is warm. Thank you . . . my hands were cold." He chuckled and cupped his hands, breathing into them and rubbing them together.

I released the breath I had been holding, willing myself not to shake. Nicholas had taken that exchange—whatever it was—so lightly. Deep, stinging emotion throbbed in my chest.

"Shall we go inside?" My voice was too quick and harsh. The people around us had dispersed, and I couldn't stand being alone with Nicholas for another moment.

He watched me for a second longer, a question hovering in his eyes. But then he pressed his mouth into a firm line and nodded. "Very well."

I turned on my heel and marched toward the entry, not waiting for Nicholas. The inn wasn't nearly as welcoming as the other I had visited. It smelled musty, and there were only a few candles to light the parlor. Nicholas caught the door before it could swing shut behind me and stepped closer, giving me a confused look.

I kept my eyes forward to where the innkeeper was speaking with another traveler. He was tall and thick with a roughly shaven face covered in pockmarks and sweat. His gaze fell on me in a sweeping motion, a darkness in his eyes that disturbed me. I looked away but determined that his eyes had not strayed from me even a minute later. My stomach dropped. There was something very wrong with that look.

I turned my face over my shoulder, searching for Nicholas. My hand shook, but I took his arm anyway. The anxiety melted from my shoulders and I could breathe again.

"Is there something wrong?" Nicholas asked.

He looked down at me with concern, brows drawn together, then searched the room. I saw his gaze land on the innkeeper. He pulled me closer and tipped his head down to whisper, "Don't be afraid."

I nodded, flicking my eyes back to the horrifying man. He was still watching me through half-lidded eyes, no shame in the prolonged stare. He stepped around a cluster of travelers and approached us. He had plenty of unsettling smiles for me and plenty of frowns for Nicholas. "Good evening. May we interest you in a hot meal?" Half the time he spoke to me he met my eyes. The other half his gaze was . . . elsewhere. I shifted and gripped Nicholas tighter.

Nicholas stepped forward, his face even. But I could feel the tension in his arm. "Yes. My name is Mr. Bancroft and this is my wife. We thank you for your hospitality."

The innkeeper watched us as we turned toward the parlor, and Nicholas glanced over his shoulder. "Perhaps we have chosen the wrong inn tonight." He smiled down at me, and I thanked him with my eyes. I thanked the heavens too for sending him here with me. That innkeeper was unsettling in every way.

We took a place by the low-burning fire in two soft chairs with a short table between us. I sunk into the cushion, fully prepared to fall asleep within seconds. Nicholas sat across from me, his face glowing with amusement.

"What?" I sat up straighter.

"You're so little."

Out of old habit, I crossed my arms with a huffed breath. "I am fully aware of that fact, Nicholas."

He chuckled, leaning his elbows on the table and resting his chin on his fist. His lips were lifted in half a smile, and his hair had fallen softly on his forehead. The flames performed a dance over his face, light and shadow. He looked so endearing in that moment that I couldn't help but smile back.

When we received our food, I realized how hungry I was. My stomach rumbled as I enjoyed the ham, bread, and soup. Nicholas finished my bread after I insisted that I was quite full. I glanced at him over my cup, imagining what it might be like to share a meal with him every day of my life.

It was strange. At times I thought I knew him well, and at others he felt much like a stranger. He had no occupation that I knew of. He was a thief and a scoundrel. Was he not? I rubbed my head, trying to make sense of it. How could I care so much for a thieving scoundrel? What would Mama and Papa say to that? Of course I could never marry him. No matter that he hadn't made any serious indication of the sort, but he was living a secretive life with no reliable or honorable income. I was tempted to ask again—for the truth. But I didn't want him to close himself off again. I enjoyed spending time with the light, happy Nicholas.

He was holding his open wallet in front of him, a look of consternation on his face. "We may be in a slight quandary."

My stomach dropped as I eyed the leather in his hand.

"When I paid the coachman I didn't realize the expense. We have little left, not enough to pay for the meal. Certainly not two rooms. Or one for that matter." He rubbed his hand over his hair, glancing behind him where the innkeeper stood. I followed his gaze but immediately wished I hadn't. The innkeeper met my eyes and set foot in our direction. Nicholas jerked around in his chair. Our gazes locked, and he stood to face the horrifying man heading in our direction. I stood too, standing several feet back.

Nicholas gave a brief nod. "Good sir, I regret to say I have fallen short on my means. I am immensely sorry. The very moment I have the funds to pay you for your service I will return here promptly. I will leave you with the location of my residence." He spoke with an apologetic charm that would have convinced the mantua maker to send him with an entire shop of dresses, free of charge. But this man was not a mantua maker.

The innkeeper's face reddened and his teeth formed a straight line. "You mean to say you'll be leavin' without paying? Everyone must pay."

"For the inconvenience I will send your pay in double forthwith."

The man stepped closer to Nicholas, and I was astonished at the similarity of their height. The innkeeper was just an inch or two shorter. His nostrils flared and a stream of sweat fell down his temple. "You 'spect me to take you for your word?" He shook his head. "Why not your lovely wife? Give me her and you are free to leave." He laughed, shifting his eyes behind Nicholas. Without thinking, I gripped the back of Nicholas's jacket.

He stood straight, but I saw his fists tighten at his sides. His jaw clenched.

"A tempting armful, she is." He sneered, and tried to glance at me from around Nicholas, but Nicholas shifted to hide me. Reaching back, Nicholas held my wrist, and I stepped close to his back.

"Don't speak another word of her." His jaw was tight when he turned to the side, pulling me along beside him. I walked fast, but not a second later a large hand clamped over my shoulder.

I shrieked, reeling back in disgust as the innkeeper leaned close to my ear. His breath reeked of port. His hand slid down my arm and I slapped it away. Nicholas took one stride, extended both hands, and thrust the man against a nearby table. The parlor was nearly empty, except for the couple that stood in the corner, watching with alarm. The innkeeper recovered for a short moment before launching himself at Nicholas, swinging his fist and making contact with Nicholas's cheekbone.

I gasped, stumbling back as Nicholas returned the gesture, knocking the man to the floor this time.

Nicholas turned to face me, and I could already see the start of a bruise on his cheek. "Run," he said, grabbing my arm.

I gladly obeyed, and he pushed his way through the front door until we were outside again. Nicholas slipped his hand around mine and pulled me along as we ran down the road. His hand was warm and safe, and I tried to calm my racing heart. What had just happened? The wind pushed my hair back and capsized my bonnet, but I caught it before it could spin away.

Nicholas led us to a narrow path that adjoined the one we had taken on the coach, but farther up the road from where we had come.

There was a square of public gardens, edged with topiary and rose bushes. Hills rose and fell, marked with simple benches and rocky pathways. We ran until we were hidden safely behind the trees behind the gardens. The grass grew sparsely here and branches closed in from all sides. We stopped to catch our breath, but Nicholas didn't let go of my hand.

"Are you all right?" he asked in a gentle voice.

I tried to speak but could only nod. Was I all right? Nicholas was the one who had received a firm facer from a horrific man.

He held my gaze with concern for one more moment before exhaling in a shaky laugh. I snorted into laughter, pressing my hand to my mouth to muffle it. I bent over, leaning my hands on my knees and continued to laugh in disbelief. Nicholas threw his head back, joining me. When my giggles finally subsided, I felt an enormous sense of release.

"I am very sorry," he said.

"I am too."

He raised one eyebrow. "What can you be sorry for? You cannot be sorry for being—how did he put it?—a tempting armful."

I cringed as a shiver rolled over me. "Do not ever speak of that again."

He smiled, but there was a seriousness in his eyes that disarmed me. "Are you certain you're well?"

"I'm as well as I can be for a woman who hasn't changed her dress in multiple days, nor had a warm bath, and who is many miles from her home and family, not knowing when she might arrive at her destination or how many other levels of madness she may encounter on the unpredictable journey." I bit my lip. "I suppose when you consider all of that, I am faring quite well."

Nicholas burst into laughter, shaking his head.

"Have you paused to consider your own state?" Without thinking, I rose on my toes and squinted through the dark. And then I reached up and touched his cheek—the place the innkeeper had struck him. My hand froze there. I was so surprised at myself that I didn't know what to do. Soft as a feather, I traced my index finger over the bruising skin. My eyes met his in the dark, and the traces of his smile were gone. His eyes searched mine, but I looked away, dropping my hand to my side.

He had defended me. Surely that was not a sign of a dishonorable person. It was impossible to know what to believe. But this could be all an act, an effort to deceive me. He could be stealing my trust and my affection only to tear it away. He had done it before, why should he not do it again?

I crossed my arms, standing uncomfortably in front of him. "I don't know what has come over me. I suppose I am much too tired to function properly." I laughed, but it was dry and dull.

I sensed a great battle in his expression, over which emotion to portray. He looked . . . frustrated. Guilty. Ashamed.

Opening the large canvas bag at his side, he unpacked several shirts and a jacket, laying them out on the ground at the base of a tree. Then he slipped his own jacket off and gestured at the line of shirts on the ground. "I'm afraid that is all I can offer you for a bed."

I smiled down at the neat shirts and almost laughed again. "Are you certain I can use your . . . clothing?"

"I know it is not proper and certainly not comfortable, but you need to rest. At least for a few hours."

I was shaking my head, and Nicholas stopped. "How did you know that I have always wanted to sleep out of doors? Mama and Papa never allowed me to do so as a child."

I expected him to laugh, but I only saw that look again—the frustration and the guilt. He shook it away before I could consider what it meant. "Rightfully so. I will stay nearby and ensure that you are not seen."

And there he was again, protecting my reputation, protecting me from harm. With careful movements, I knelt on the first piece of fabric and rotated back until I was flat on my back under the tree. I set my bonnet beside me and smiled up at Nicholas, laughing between breaths. "I feel ridiculous."

Bending down, he draped his jacket over me, tucking it over my shoulders before moving to sit several feet away. He didn't look at me.

The ground beneath my back was hard and covered in bumps. I shifted so I faced away from Nicholas, self-conscious at the thought of him watching me sleep. Despite all the things I didn't know about Nicholas, I felt safe and secure even in my current situation. Several minutes passed and I was still completely awake. I listened to the sound of crickets and night breezes trickling through the branches. In the middle of it all came Nicholas's voice.

"Lucy?"

My eyes opened. I stared at the nearby trees on the other side instead of rolling over to face him. "Hmm." My heart picked up speed in the silence that followed.

"Have you ever wished you could reach inside a person's head and pluck out any memory you wanted and hide it from them forever?" His voice was hoarse and quiet.

I puzzled over the odd question. "Yes."

He paused. "I'm sorry for hurting you."

My throat clenched with emotion. His voice rang in my ears and I held perfectly still. By the time I composed myself enough to speak, the words wouldn't come. Too much time had passed to respond, so I held his jacket more tightly around myself, squeezed my eyes closed, and tried to sleep.

# ELEVEN

SEPTEMBER 1814

*I* hadn't spoken more than a few words in the last week of our travel home from Rosewood, and neither had Mama. Rachel knew why I was sad, but neither of us understood why Mama was distant. She told us that all was well. She smiled and patted our hands. Papa held her close and played with her hair.

The day we finally arrived home, our house was cold. It wasn't cold like snow or ice, but cold like desertion, darkness, and broken things.

I stayed in my room the entire day, trying not to think about Nicholas. He had occupied my thoughts for too long already. It was unfair how people changed and grew. Some grew faster than others, and some were waiting for the right opportunity to make them grow. Nicholas had grown out of being my friend. He had grown out of being kind to me. He had grown far past the possibility of ever loving me. He had said it in the clearest possible way.

Tears stung the corners of my eyes and I swallowed. Crossing the floor of my bedroom, I lifted the lid of my trunk. My things were packed hastily, but I knew where to find the item I sought. Emotion tore through my lungs as I breathed until I gasped for air. I wrenched the tiny engraved wooden box from the trunk and placed it on my palm. Nicholas had given it to me over a year ago. I hadn't wished away any of my pearls yet—nothing had seemed important enough. Until now. Through blurred vision, I pinched the clasp between my fingers and lifted the tiny lid. There were *my pearls, all five rolled to one corner of the box. I chose one carefully, withdrawing it into my fist and setting the box on my writing desk.*

*I cleaned it free of all the dirt until it shone. Then I held it to my chest and whispered my first dream.*

*"I wish that Nicholas will never forget me."*

*As I walked through the drawing room, I tossed the pearl into the fire. Mesmerized, I watched it within the flames. And then I tried to forget about him.*

The first hint of light that bled through my eyelids shocked me, and I felt the unevenness of the ground before opening my eyes. It was still dim, and for a moment I forgot why I was here, sleeping on a pile of shirts under a tree. Never in my life had I imagined I would find myself in such a situation. And that didn't even include the fact that Nicholas Bancroft was sitting five feet away, watching me with a thoughtful expression on his far-too-handsome face.

I sat up, blinking fast, and rubbed my eyes. Nicholas laughed.

"What?" My voice came out harsher than I intended. I didn't even want to imagine how I must have appeared at this moment. My hair hadn't been washed or combed in days, likely sticking out at strange, curly angles, my eyes puffy, and my dress dirty.

He dipped his head and glanced up at me from under his dark lashes. "You must have been dreaming."

"Why?" I dropped my hand from my face. My eyes widened in horror.

"I have never seen so many expressions cross one face in such a short time."

I was mortified, to say the least. "You cannot be serious! I do not remember having a dream of any sort. I hardly remember falling asleep at all." I bit my lip, stopping my own words. I recalled what Nicholas had said to me just hours before. He had apologized and I hadn't given him any response. But it was a new day, renewed by my short few hours of rest. And Nicholas seemed to have recovered from his strange mood, so I counted myself fortunate.

"Shall we get you to Rosewood by nightfall?" Nicholas stood up and brushed the dirt from his trousers. Had he slept at all? I forced myself to stand on my aching legs and scooped up Nicholas's shirts that had functioned as my bed.

I stretched my back. "But we don't have money to pay for a coach."

"Then we will walk."

I studied him for a moment, his strong shoulders, open face, smiling mouth, and friendly eyes. Never would I grow tired of seeing him. I would never grow tired of speaking with him or laughing with him, of knowing that he was beside me.

But for a reason I didn't know, he didn't want to be at Rosewood. After today, he could be gone again. But he wanted me to help him, did he not? He was determined to change his ways. If he left me I wouldn't have the chance. He would go back to the highwaymen and forget me. If only I could convince him to stay.

There was something that kept him away from Rosewood, that had also kept my mother and father away for so long. There was too much I needed to still discover about Nicholas. I wanted to learn as much as I could. There was no possible way I was letting him deposit me at the gates and ride away. *Ride away?*

"Nicholas? Have you forgotten Jack?" His horse was still at an inn miles behind us.

He took a few steps closer to me, breathing out a sigh. "No, I haven't forgotten him."

"How will you—how will you pay the innkeeper for looking after him?"

He dropped his gaze to the ground, rubbing his boot in circles in the dirt. It reminded me of something the younger Nicholas would have done, at moments when he hurt but didn't want to show it. "I hope the staff will take care of him while I'm away."

My brow furrowed. "But when you do return for him, how will you pay the man?"

His eyes flashed. "I haven't a sixpence to scratch with, Lucy. I know it. But Jack will be just fine. It is you and your safety that I am most concerned for." He sounded frustrated as he always seemed to be when I mentioned money. My stomach sunk at the thought of him among those dreadful highwaymen. He could not go back to them. I refused to allow that to happen.

"Please promise me, Nicholas," I blurted. "Please promise me you will stay at Rosewood with me, just for one week."

His chest rose and fell with a slow breath and he rubbed his forehead. When he looked at me, his eyes were heavy.

"Please. Are you not indebted to yourself? Think of how you will feel if you return home and mend your relationships—or whatever it is that has been troubling you. I can see it."

His eyes locked on mine, and he was silent for several seconds. "Have you any other motive for me staying? Or is it strictly for me and my . . . troubled spirits?"

I shifted, avoiding his gaze. "Well, er—I . . ." He couldn't possibly discover that I wanted him there because I would miss him.

When I finally dared a look at his face, he was smiling, just a devilish quirk of his lips. He quite enjoyed making me uncomfortable.

"I'll tell you this," he said. "I will not stay unless you admit something to me this very instant." His feet made tracks in the dirt as I watched them walk closer to me. I couldn't look at his face when he was smiling in such a way, or speaking with that deep, taunting voice. He stopped. "Please look at me, Lucy."

I huffed a breath of annoyance that I hoped he could hear and lifted my face, staring him straight in the eyes.

"I need you to tell me what it means when you refuse to look at me. Tell me what it means when you smile uncontrollably and a short moment later frown and refuse to speak to me." He stared down at me in earnest, not letting me escape. "Why do you want me to stay at Rosewood?"

The leaves rustled around us, and the sun had begun its ascent into the sky. My heart fluttered with the contrast of the beauty around me and Nicholas's strange question. "I don't wish to tell you."

"Why not?"

I felt my posture tighten, my firm look grow firmer. "Because you already know." I shook my head. "You cannot pretend that you do not."

Nicholas's smile was gone, replaced by a look of deep thought, regret, and confusion all at once.

I clasped my hands together, the resulting sound much louder than I intended. "But enough of this. I need you to tell me if you are staying or not. At any rate, Mr. Parsons will be in town and I should hate for him to not become further acquainted with you."

I grinned inwardly as Nicholas's jaw tightened—and not merely because I enjoyed the sight of his jawline. He smoothed his expression, but I had seen it. He had given Mr. Parsons the same look after Mr. Parsons saved me from that awful chaise.

"Very well," Nicholas said. "I will stay for one week."

I accidentally jumped and released a squeal of delight. Nicholas laughed, staring down at me with a wide smile that made my heart jump as well.

He smoothed a wayward curl from my forehead, sending tendrils of warmth through my face. "Off we go, then."

I closed my eyes and smiled. "Off we go."

I had never walked fifteen miles in one day before, and it was not an experience I wished to repeat. However, as I pondered on the matter, I decided that if I were to have Nicholas walking beside me, talking and laughing and teasing me, then I would walk twice that distance every day if it meant he would be there.

It was a troubling thought. It put the extent of my feelings into harsh perspective. If Nicholas made walking for hours in the dust with blistering feet and sore legs enjoyable, then I must care for him far too much.

I scolded myself over and over for allowing him back into my heart, for allowing him to weaken my boundaries.

Nicholas was my childhood, the very thing I was trying to escape. He came from the days of weakness and naïveté. Yet here I was, even more weak and more naïve than ever. But I couldn't blame him for it, no matter how much I wanted to.

As we walked the final mile to Rosewood, I tried to imagine everything I could remember of the place.

Rosewood sat at the end of a very long road, behind a set of wide gates edged in rose bushes. The Bancrofts' home sat just to the left side, shrinking in comparison. The Rossingtons and Bancrofts had always been close friends, the relation extending back for several generations when the current families came into residence. Rosewood was one of the largest estates in all of Kent, especially the Dover area, second only to Willowbourne. I closed my eyes for a brief moment, trying to picture it. The bright stone, wide windows in perfect rows, immaculate gardens. The smell of courage and adventures and joy. Surely those things didn't have a scent, but if they did, it would be the scent that came through Rosewood's property on the wind.

Nicholas nudged my arm. I opened my eyes, unable to hide my smile. The road was turning to the right, where I knew Rosewood was standing beyond the trees. I always loved the journey there because you couldn't see the estate until you rounded that final corner. The anticipation overtook me every time.

I felt Nicholas's hand curl around my arm. "There is something you need to know."

Confused, I looked up at his face. His eyes were heavy.

"You have been away for a very long time. There are certain things that have changed."

I scrunched my brow. "Kitty did not mention that anything was out of sorts. You have been away for quite some time as well."

"I haven't been away for six years. I don't want you to be disappointed."

I pushed my curls away from my forehead and wiped the dust from my cheeks. "How would I be disappointed?"

He looked ahead with a solemn expression, and I followed his gaze. We started walking again. Dread made a pool in my stomach, making each step heavier as we approached the corner. What did he mean?

I looked at him over my shoulder; he was lagging behind. "Are you afraid?" I asked in a quiet voice.

He caught up to me, taking large strides that I could hardly keep up with. "I'm not afraid."

I smiled up at him, but he didn't smile back. He looked slightly ill.

My stomach fluttered with excitement as we came around the curve of the path, and I momentarily forgot Nicholas's foreboding words and his obvious discomfort. There it was. Rosewood. It looked precisely as I remembered it, perhaps even more beautiful.

The sky was clear today, bringing a brightness to the neatly trimmed lawns and making the copper brick of the estate's facade radiate warmth and the gray stone around the windows shine like silver. My legs ached in exhaustion but I hardly felt it. I could only imagine the warm bath and clean clothing that likely awaited me upon my arrival. Perhaps a hot meal with my favorite roasted vegetables. And I positively could not wait to see Kitty and tell her every detail of the last several days. She would never believe that I had traveled so many miles with Nicholas Bancroft. I remembered the late evening gossip we always shared during my visits. There would be much to tell. My smile spread wide before I could stop it.

The leaves rustled at my feet and Nicholas stepped up beside me. His face was firm and taut, turned not toward the lumbering estate, but toward the quaint manor a short distance from it. He had grown up there. Something had driven him away. Without thinking, I reached over and touched his arm. My fingers made light contact, so light I wasn't sure if he felt it. His eyes lowered to mine. He tried to hide the emotion in them. But I had seen it.

"Shall we go?" I gestured at the path ahead, the one leading to the wide gates and rose bushes.

Nicholas rubbed his jaw, turning his boot in circles in the dirt once again. "I would suggest that you take what remains of the walk alone. Enter the house, tell the family that you have traveled here alone. I will come back later tonight, seemingly by coincidence, but will stay in my home with my family. I will inform you in some way that I have arrived."

I puzzled over his plan with suspicion. Was he trying to deceive me? Did he plan to leave instead and not stay the week he had promised? One of my eyebrows arched. "Why not come with me now?"

"As I said, there are a great many things that have changed here, of which you are unaware. If we were to arrive together, unchaperoned after an extensive journey, we may not be received so . . . affectionately." His eyes cut into mine.

I was torn between staying and leaving. Part of me believed that if I left Nicholas here in the trees he would be gone. I would wait for hours and he wouldn't arrive. I didn't know what to believe. I trusted him. But I also *did not* trust him. My mind ached under the pressure of the contradiction.

"Please, Lucy." His voice was a half-whisper.

I chewed my lip and wrung my hands. Why was this so difficult? Even if Nicholas could not be believed, I hadn't come here for him. I had come for Rosewood. For Kitty and Mrs. Tattershall and her son, William. So why was it so difficult to walk to that path and through those gates if Nicholas wasn't there too? The risk of losing him was more frightening than being away from the safety and security of a home and familiar people. The realization made my heart pound a little faster.

"Go on, Lucy. I will be there soon."

"Do you promise?" I blurted.

He stood by a short tree, the branches brushing over his shoulder when he shifted to face me more fully. He hesitated. "I give you my word."

I looked at him in panic, my legs rooted where they stood. Why couldn't I turn around and walk to the gates? My feet refused to move. It was as if I faced him now like I did six years ago, begging him to understand something he couldn't.

Begging him to love something he couldn't.

He smiled down at me. "Why are you so concerned? I will come back, not to worry."

It was the look that always set my heart racing—the look that made me burn and crumble inside and fill with strength all at once. It bothered me that he assumed I was so reliant on him. It might have been true, but I couldn't let him think that.

"Only come back if you wish to. I don't want you to feel as though I am forcing you to stay. It was never my intention to force you to do anything you did not wish to do."

"I'm staying because of you," he said.

My words spilled out. "Yes, I know. But truly, I don't want to be any more of burden upon you, so you don't need to stay simply because I asked you to, and—"

"No." He stopped me by stepping closer, so close that I could see the gold in his eyes and the fine lines and deep smiling creases of his face. "I'm staying because of you." His words were slower, as if he needed to emphasize his meaning. "I'm not ready to part from you just yet."

Understanding dawned on me. Had Nicholas just confessed something? Were his feelings toward me as I suspected? I tried to speak, to say the same thing to him, but the words were lodged in my throat by the look on his face, the weight of his gaze, and the smile on his lips. So instead I clapped my hands together, sending a shock through the air and making him take a step back in amusement.

"Very well. I will see you tonight," I said as I backed toward the path. "I will pretend it has been years rather than hours since my eyes have beheld you."

He smiled, taking another step backward into the trees. "And I will pretend that I don't think you are as lovely as I truly do."

My eyes widened and my cheeks burned.

Nicholas laughed, likely at the shock in my expression, and gave me one more smile, the softness in his eyes enough to crush me. Did he mean it? Did he think I was lovely? I didn't know what to say, so I turned on my heel to hide the redness on my face, said goodbye over my shoulder, and stepped out of the trees.

I thought I heard him laughing behind me, but I couldn't be sure. All I knew was that if he didn't come back, I would find him. I would find him and I would strike him firmly in the face, and I would kick him in the back of the knees for good measure. He simply could not call me lovely and disappear for the remainder of my life and get away with it. There were dozens of mysteries that involved Nicholas, but the mystery of that 'lovely' would haunt me the most.

My mind spun so quickly that I forgot exactly what was happening. I was here! I was at Rosewood. Exhaustion had yet to catch up to me, but I knew it would be coming soon. For now, my heart fluttered with long-awaited belonging. The gates were open in front of me, flanked by their signature rose bushes. I paused there, taking a breath and letting my gaze sweep over the property. It appeared the same as I remembered, but the trees and bushes seemed taller, and the air seemed a little colder. September was nearly complete, and soon the leaves would turn yellow and red and golden orange. I had never seen Rosewood in autumn.

My heart pounded as I took my first step through the gates. The Bancrofts' small house was there, directly beside the property. But there were trees planted now that hadn't been there before. Young, small trees, creating a curved line between the house and the rest of the Rossingtons' property. As I came closer, there was the unmistakable line of a neat picket fence. The vegetable garden was on the inside of that fence.

As puzzling as it was, I couldn't pause to think on it. The doors of the estate were coming closer, and I needed to plan my explanation for my lost belongings and haggard appearance as to not worry Kitty too greatly.

The sun beat down on my head, making my curls stick with perspiration to my forehead. Despite the chilled air, the sun was warm. When I reached the door, I released the breath I had been holding and knocked three times.

It felt like an eternity before I could hear footfalls within the house. I strained my ears and tapped my foot partly with impatience and partly with worry. At last the door was swung open in front of me. An unfamiliar butler stood in the doorway. His slim face held perfectly straight while his eyes traveled down to look at me. I stared straight up at him, expending all my effort to not gaze into his alarmingly large nostrils as he greeted me.

I cleared my throat and forced myself to speak. "Good day, sir. I am here by invitation of the Rossingtons." My voice shook.

His brow tightened. "I beg your pardon."

I thought I had spoken clearly enough. "My uncle and his daughter, Kitty . . . they have invited me here." Had my uncle refused my welcome? Had they forgotten that I would be coming to visit? Mr. Rossington had never seemed to like me. He had always been a quiet, mysterious sort of man.

With one more masked look of concern, the butler ushered me inside, where he seemed to take notice of my haggard appearance. His nostrils flared wider above me. "Please make yourself comfortable in the drawing room. If he is not otherwise engaged, Mr. Rossington will be with you shortly."

I gave a nod, my lips closed tight. How strange. With the butler walking away, I paused to admire the interior decoration of the home. It had been redecorated since I had been here last. The paintings were still there, and the colors of the walls the same, but the furniture was now in the Greek style, and the bookshelves were much more sparse in the drawing room. It ached me to see it. Aunt Edith had always loved books.

I took a seat on the edge of a red sofa, keeping my spine straight and my knees pressed together. My eyes flicked to the doorway every two seconds. Mr. Rossington had never been a favored uncle of mine. He had certainly not been a contributing factor to my desire to visit Rosewood. My mother had never seemed to like him either. Or perhaps it was distrust that I had seen in her eyes each time she spoke of him.

A figure appeared in the doorway and I jerked my gaze away from my lap. I stood, turning to face Mr. Rossington and the butler, several paces behind him.

My uncle was a sight to behold. I had to blink twice to fully absorb the appearance he flaunted. He had always been a man of conservative dress, but now he was dressed in an intricately embroidered waistcoat, with a cravat so frilled I wondered if it would engulf his entire face should he move his neck more than one inch at a time. His breeches were pale ivory, flush with his plump form, creating a bulge at his knees.

I tore my eyes away at once.

"Miss Lucy, my niece! I did not know we should be expecting your arrival." His voice was raspy and deep, edged with a friendliness that I couldn't recall ever hearing before. It seemed false, hidden behind annoyance and anxiety at my presence in his home.

I squinted out the front window at the trees, wishing Nicholas were here with me. Surely he knew more than I did about this strange figure-flaunting man in front of me. I forced a smile to my face and willed my eyes not to travel to that awful lower half again.

"I thought Kitty had received your permission to host me. I'm sorry."

"Do not apologize! You are quite welcome." There was something in his voice that contradicted his choice of words.

"I am glad to hear it. Thank you. Where is Kitty?"

"Kitty is with her husband in town today but will be returning for dinner this evening. Kitty would never have taken the day trip should she have known you would be arriving at this moment."

My eyes narrowed as I watched him speak, the buoyant tone of his voice too much for what I remembered of him. There was much about this new Mr. Rossington that unsettled me. I suspected he wore his friendliness like a mask, hiding something he didn't wish to be seen. I studied the tile floors, lost in thought.

"Lucy, dear?"

I didn't know what frightened me more—that my eyes landed directly on Mr. Rossington's much-too-fitted breeches or that he called me 'dear.'

He stopped as his eyes traveled to the window. "Where is your coach? Have my footmen already taken your trunk?"

He hadn't the slightest idea just how strenuous the journey had been. "I'm afraid my belongings were stolen from me in my travels. I barely managed to make it here."

Mr. Rossington exchanged a baffled look with his butler. "How did such a horrific event come to pass?"

"Highwaymen."

"How unfortunate," was all he said on the matter. "I will have a room prepared for you. My sister, Mrs. Tattershall, will assist you from here."

I had met Mrs. Tattershall many times before. As Mr. Rossington's sister, she had often visited during the summers the same weeks as my family. William was her son, and not related to me by blood, though I still fancied calling him my cousin. Though I had seen Mrs. Tattershall much over the years of my childhood, I couldn't recall a time I had spoken to her alone. Mrs. Tattershall entered the room behind Mr. Rossington. She was tall and thin, with sharp cheekbones and warm brown eyes, just as I remembered her. Her hair was pulled back softly, with dark curls streaked in silver at her temples. She did not have the inviting countenance of Aunt Edith. I stood and followed her to the familiar guest hall, and tried to let the feelings of belonging and long-awaited excitement enfold me again. It didn't work. Nicholas's words echoed in my ears. *Rosewood has changed.*

Mrs. Tattershall was a woman of few words, I learned, as she quickly deposited me in my room and introduced me to my maid. My thoughts refused to slow down, so I hardly noticed her departure.

The maid assigned to me was short like me, but with bouncing blonde curls instead of brown. She appeared to be a bit older than I was, likely in her mid-twenties. Her smile did little to console me. Working quickly, she assisted me in changing into a clean dress—likely an old one of Kitty's, and brushed my hair and styled it in a simple knot. I could hardly speak enough to thank her.

When she left the room, I stood, walking from corner to corner. Dinner could not come soon enough. I wanted Kitty here. Surely once she arrived it would feel the same again. Perhaps Mama had been correct in her fear of the emptiness of the place without Aunt Edith here. But I was still happy to be at Rosewood. I was at Rosewood at last. I took a deep breath and tossed my misgivings aside.

To pass my time before dinner, I penned a letter to my mother and father.

*Dearest Mama and Papa,*

*I am sorry for leaving. I should have listened to you. Although I regret working against your wishes, I am also glad I did.*

*As promised, I am writing to inform you of my safe arrival at Rosewood. The journey was quite interesting and invigorating. I am happy to be here. Please do not worry, and please write often.*

*With much love,*

*Lucy*

When I was called down to dinner, my feet hardly touched the floor as I hurried to the drawing room. Kitty and her husband had arrived only moments before, and I was anxious to see her. My wild, dark curls had partially escaped the knot my maid had styled it in, and my cheeks were flushed by the time I reached the drawing room doorway. I could see Kitty's face from around the barrier of the door, and when our eyes met around the footman's shoulder, she screamed in delight.

"Lucy!" She ran forward and threw her slender arms around my shoulders, burying my face in muslin. She pushed me back by the shoulders and studied my face. "You have grown so beautiful! Oh, my! You look precisely like Aunt Helen!" I smiled, taking a moment to study her appearance as well. I had been told I looked like my mother before, but Kitty had never looked more like her mother than she did now. Aunt Edith was there in every blink, every shift of a feature.

"I've missed you," I said, forcing my eyes to remain dry.

"You should have come sooner." She raised a playful eyebrow before her face broke into a smile.

"Why must I always travel so very far? You might have visited Craster."

She shook her head, scrunching her nose. "Not that blustery place. How did you describe it? Cold, dark, and depressing? Gray and wet? Besides, I despise long drives. I trust your journey suited you well?"

I choked back a laugh. My smile stretched wider.

"What is it?"

"I will tell you later this evening. I have *much* to tell you."

She squealed again, a quiet, secretive sound. "I cannot wait to hear it." Kitty moved back a step and took her husband's arm, pulling him forward to greet me. "Might I make known to you my husband, John Turner. And this is my dearest cousin, Lucy Abbot."

I gave him a polite nod that he returned. Mr. Turner gazed down at Kitty with such raw adoration it made my heart skip with joy. I wished Nicholas were here. Perhaps he would look at me in the same way. I quickly stopped my thoughts and clasped my hands together in front of me.

We were led to the dining room where William, the once little boy, was seated. He was much older now. The last time I had seen him he had been ten years old. Now he was hardly recognizable, a sturdy sixteen-year-old with raven black hair and sharp blue eyes. His face was smooth like a child, marked with pink cheeks and his familiar dented chin. He was shy and observant, like he had always been.

"William, how you have grown!" I stepped behind him and almost pinched his cheek before thinking better of it. He stood and gave a shy smile, dropping a nod.

"Come, now, William. I am not nearly so frightening as I appear." I squeezed his arm and stepped around him to take my seat.

I was seated beside Mrs. Tattershall and across from the odd Mr. Rossington. Again, he seemed far too boisterous and loud. And he smiled far too much. There were many people in the world that smiling suited quite nicely, but when a face that one has never seen smile grins so constantly, it becomes worrisome rather than pleasant. And his laugh could flatten even the most postured woman to the ground in shock. I cringed as another booming laugh cut the air. It wouldn't have been so disconcerting if I had ever heard him speak a word before. In social gatherings Aunt Edith had always donned a kind smile, gentle words, and soft laughter, much like my own mother. My uncle had sat beside her, dull, uninterested, and quiet. What I saw now shocked me so much that I didn't hear him address me.

"Pardon me?" I asked, lowering my goblet.

"How is your family faring?"

"Quite well." I didn't want to share any further details—not of Rachel's marriage, not of my father's occupation, not of anything.

He raised a chunk of bread to his mouth and said, "I am glad to hear it," before taking a large bite that he had to wash down with a swig from his cup. My eyes skipped over to Kitty, who watched her father with a look that surprised me. Caution, annoyance . . . distaste. She caught me watching her and quickly thrust her fork into her beef, avoiding my gaze.

"I am anxious to see the Bancrofts again upon my visit here. How have they been these years? I trust they are well?"

A hush fell over the table. My fork froze. Mr. Rossington straightened in his chair and Kitty and William exchanged a glance. Mr. Turner whispered something in Kitty's ear.

"They are quite well," Mr. Rossington said in a blunt voice.

The party resumed eating and fell to silence once again. My brow furrowed. What could have passed between the families? I recalled the fence and line of trees between the houses. They had never been there before. I thought of Nicholas again and frustration filled me. Why must he keep so many secrets?

I cleared my throat. "I suppose I will have to call upon them while I am here."

Mr. Rossington muttered a few words under his breath that I couldn't hear. He raised his face from his plate with a pleasant smile. "They will be happy to receive you, I am sure."

His sister threw him a hidden look of annoyance. But I saw it.

"I hear that Nicholas has been married in the recent months." I took a spoonful of soup to my lips, keeping my complexion even as Mr. Rossington gave a firm nod.

"Indeed, he was."

Ah. So the rumor had not been dispelled yet. Why had such gossip started at all? Nicholas had created quite the ruse, and I wished I knew the reason behind it. What would he do when he arrived here? How would he explain himself? My heart beat with dread. It was growing dark. If he had not returned home by now, he likely never would.

Nothing was right in this house. The entire property was filled with an air of dishonesty and shifting eyes. It was heavy and quiet, dark to the soul but still bright as ever to the eyes. If I hadn't treasured this place so much, I might not have noticed the difference in the aura. And there Mr. Rossington was, smiling away in the center of it all.

When the meal was complete, the ladies withdrew to the drawing room while the men stayed behind for port. I took Kitty's arm with urgency, mumbling my excuses to her aunt, Mrs. Tattershall. I needed to speak with Kitty. I lacked the patience to wait another moment. She laughed as I pulled her down the wide hall and stopped beside a candle so I could see her face.

"What is so urgent?" She straightened her elbow-length sleeves, raising her delicate eyebrows.

"What the devil has happened here?" I whispered. My voice echoed in the halls. Kitty's eyes widened. "I have been kept in the dark. What has happened between your family and the Bancrofts?"

Kitty chewed at her fingernail in silence.

"Nicholas Bancroft is not married," I whispered.

She met my eyes in shock. "What do you mean? Of course he is married. He abandoned his family for it."

I shook my head. "He told me himself. But do not suppose he hasn't been up to mischief; he most certainly has."

She looked over her shoulder and grabbed my wrist, pulling me farther down the hall until we reached a small study. She lifted a candle from a nearby sconce and pushed open the door. Inside, the room was small and crowded with three wooden chairs, a desk, and a single shelf of books. Kitty lit two candles on the desk and motioned for me to sit. "When did you see Nicholas?"

I swallowed. "In my travels here. He and his accomplices apprehended my coach on the road, robbing me of my belongings. Nicholas rescued me after he recognized me and assisted me in what remained of my journey."

She gasped, covering her mouth. "He is a highwayman? You cannot be serious! What could compel him to behave in such a way?"

"I have been thinking on that for quite some time." I sighed. "He would not explain. I hardly knew if I could trust him."

"How did you trust him? You could have been in great danger!"

"I know." My head clouded with questions and confusion. "But somehow I knew I could trust him. He would never harm me, Kitty, I know it."

"Do you still fancy him?" She raised one eyebrow in reprimand.

"Of course not," I lied. "I never did." My cheeks reddened against my will as I thought of our last encounter—when he had called me lovely and walked backward into the trees.

She scoffed. "That is not true."

I gave up my ruse. "I once did, but not now. I forgot him years ago."

She eyed me with suspicion. "You mean to say that you traveled alone for days with him? Your reputation could have been vastly tarnished."

"We took the proper precautions, I assure you. I am grateful for his services to me. I will always be grateful. I was never afraid of him. He seemed intent to change—to turn his life to that which is honorable once again. We mustn't give up on him. Please know that what I am sharing with you I am sharing in confidence. Do not tell a soul, I beg of you." I pleaded with my eyes. "I do not know why he created a false marriage and resorted to such wicked ways, but please do not tell anyone."

She gave a slight nod. I knew I could rely on Kitty. "Where is he?"

"I do not know." I chewed my lip. "He told me he would return tonight."

"To his home?" Her eyes flew open.

"Yes."

She brushed her hand over her hair in an effort to appear nonchalant about the matter. "How wonderful."

"Kitty." I willed her eyes down to mine. "Please tell me what has passed between your family and the Bancrofts. I can see there is something amiss."

"I don't know enough to tell you. I have been kept in the dark as well." She stood from her chair and offered a forced smile. I knew she was lying. "I am very happy that you have come to visit, Lucy. But please do not worry yourself with things that are not of any consequence to you. I will be in the drawing room with my family if you wish to join me."

I slumped in my chair in defeat. With closed lips I nodded, but didn't move an inch. With one more glance over her shoulder, she exited the room, leaving the door cracked open. I stood and pulled it shut, returning to my chair. I put my face in my hand. What was I doing? I had come to Rosewood with the intention of finding joy and entertainment and freedom. I would not find such things in a dim, lonely room. I felt uninvited, unwelcome here. I needed Nicholas. I was reminded of another day my last summer here. Another day I had been alone in a room behind a closed door at Rosewood.

# TWELVE

*N*o matter how many times I told myself not to cry, I always did. My tears were like an uncooperative child, much like what Mama had called me this morning. I was only fourteen years old, therefore it wasn't smiled upon to have me in attendance at an organized ball. Rachel was old enough to go. Many other girls from the town would be in attendance. That was why I needed to be there. It would hurt to see Nicholas flirting with the older girls, but at least I could intervene if absolutely necessary.

I wiped my cheeks and forced my crying to stop. I was such a pathetic watering pot, crying over something that I had endured for years already, and that every other girl had to endure. It was a social rule, nothing more. But I was afraid—very afraid that Nicholas would fall in love with someone else. I would feel much more sad than I did now. Much more.

Sniffing one last time, I sat down in the empty morning room and watched as the carriage took everyone else to the ball. William was upstairs and Kitty was sick in bed. I would have no one to play with. I closed my eyes and tried not to imagine Nicholas with his arms around anyone. Anyone but me.

Something had changed since the previous summer. Nicholas saw me differently. He didn't treat me so much like a child. I was growing *up, little by little. But he also didn't play with me as often as he used to. He was growing up too.*

*My family had been at Rosewood for two weeks now and with every passing day my heart leapt a little higher, my face burned hotter every time Nicholas looked my way. He didn't know any of this, of course. And I intended to keep it that way. How embarrassing it would be if he discovered how I felt. My heart leapt just with the thought. He was too old and too handsome and kind and perfect to notice me. He did notice me, but not in the way he noticed the older girls.*

*The sort of girls that would be at the ball tonight.*

*I had a suspicion. I asked Nicholas often who he fancied in town and his cheeks always turned a deep shade of pink. He refused to tell me. But Miss Sarah Hyatt was tall and beautiful with long blonde hair, and she most certainly fancied him. I wondered if she would be there tonight, batting her lashes across the ballroom and gliding toward him, practically throwing her dance card at him. My hands gripped a tight ball of plum satin from my gown. If only I had been allowed to be there, just to see if he did dance with her. She was seventeen. He was nineteen. I was fourteen. Much too young to be noticed. Much too young to attend a ball and look pretty. The rebellious tears pinched my eyes again and I sniffed.*

*Three taps sounded on the door and I bolted upright in my chair, hastily swiping at my cheeks. I glanced at my reflection in the brass sconce on the wall behind me. My cheeks were still splotched in red. "Who is it?" I rasped.*

*"Guess."*

*My heart jumped and I scrambled to my feet. Nicholas? Why was he here?*

*"Are you still there?"*

*I forced myself to speak. "Yes." I didn't feel like playing a guessing game tonight. It was ridiculous to pretend I didn't know who stood behind that door. I would recognize Nicholas's voice anywhere.*

*"May I come in?" His voice held a smile.*

*"Not yet."*

*"Why not?"*

*I couldn't let him see that I had been crying—and crying in part over him. My eyes caught on the inkwell on a small desk in the corner. "I—I am writing a secret note." I bit my lip.*

*He paused. "A secret note? How interesting. Let me see it."*

*"No!" My eyes flicked to the door. It was still closed. I breathed a sigh of relief. "You cannot see it."*

*"And why not?" He repeated, even more amused this time.*

*"Because it is written to you." I scrunched my face and pressed my palm to my forehead. What was I thinking?*

*I could hear a muffled laugh, as if he didn't intend for me to hear it. "For me? Now I'm really curious. Open this door."*

*"You cannot have it," I said in a resolute voice. "But I suppose you may enter."*

*The door eased open and Nicholas peeked tentatively around the frame. He was smiling a charming half-smile and his hair was combed neat and dark. First his head, then his shoulders and torso came through the door. He was dressed in black with a snowy white cravat. His shiny boots stepped through the door and he crossed his arms. My heart skipped with admiration. He was very handsome tonight. But I knew that no matter how he looked, I would still admire him, even if he looked like a slimy toad. And I despised all toads.*

*His smile faded and he eyed me with concern. "What is the matter?"*

*He knew. He always knew how I felt before I admitted one word of it. "I wasn't allowed at the ball and I am acting very much like a child about it. That is all." I dropped my gaze and ignored the way my heart pounded as he walked closer across the room. "Why are you here? Did you not dance with Miss Hyatt?" I bit my cheek. Why could I not control my own voice?*

*"I did dance with Miss Hyatt," he said.*

*My eyes shot upward. He was grinning down at me and I felt my cheeks flush. A weight settled in my stomach. "She is quite beautiful, is she not?"*

*Nicholas chuckled, and I watched carefully to see if his cheeks darkened. They did.*

*"So are you," he offered.*

*I didn't believe him for one moment. "That is not why you are here."*

*"Why do you suppose I am here?"*

*My words came spilling out without permission. "Because you danced with Miss Hyatt all evening and had a wonderful time. She is quite pretty and eligible as I'm sure you know, and before the town could form their gossip, you decided it would be best to leave and visit her in secret at a later time instead, lest you find yourself trapped in an engagement brought about by the public eye and the fluttering gossip of her mother and her companions for afternoon tea." I took a deep breath.*

*Nicholas raised both brows, pressing his lips together in an apparent effort not to laugh. "That is precisely what happened. Well done, Lucy."*

*My face fell before I could stop it. I wanted him to deny all of it.*

*He broke into laughter, tipping his head back. "I am sorry to disappoint you."*

*"That is not a disappointment. It's very much the opposite. I daresay you and Miss Hyatt would be a lovely couple." I tried to make myself sound composed and mature.*

*Nicholas rubbed one side of his face, breathing out a long sigh. "Unfortunately she does not share your sentiment."*

*My ears piqued. I knew he fancied her. I knew it. As glad as I was to be right, the sting in my heart overturned any feeling of accomplishment. The light out the windows was dim, bringing the candles in the room to their full potential, making Nicholas's features more prominent and more handsome. I looked at the floor. "Is that why you left?"*

*"I left so I could dance with you."*

*My eyes shot up, wide and uncertain. He was grinning down at me. He was only teasing. But my heart thudded all the same.*

*"I believe I taught you a short few years ago." He winked.*

*"You are a horrendous dancer," I said. It was impossible not to smile now.*

*His eyes wrinkled at the corners when he smiled back. "I was only sixteen then."*

*"But I was only eleven and you must confess I was quite graceful and talented in the art of dancing." I placed my hands on my hips, cringing at the way my tight curls bounced as I did so.*

*He held out his hand and bowed deeply, glancing up at me from under his dark lashes. "We will see about that."*

*I pinched my smile tight, staring at his outstretched hand. My eyes flickered to the wide-open door. How embarrassing it would be to be seen dancing with Nicholas in the morning room all alone. "Shall I stand on your boots?"*

*"That is not the proper way to dance." He smiled down at me.*

*I took a breath and placed my hand in his. It was strong and warm, just like the time last summer he had helped me up after I had fallen and twisted my ankle in the grass.*

*"We have no music. How shall we dance with no—"*

*He put his hand on my waist, and lifted my hand up in his. He was smiling, a laugh dancing across his cheeks. But I was far from laughing. I was much closer to fainting.*

*"Are we waltzing, then?" I asked in a shaky voice.*

*He took one step, guiding me with him, then took another, swaying to an unheard instrumental. He laughed, likely when he saw the sheer horror on my face. "You need to learn to waltz. One day you will be at a ball and a very eligible gentleman will sweep you away for a waltz and you simply cannot make a fool of yourself."*

*I didn't want an eligible gentleman to sweep me up. As I stared up at Nicholas, at the laughter in his golden brown eyes, the creases in his cheeks, the neat hair still falling over his brow, I decided that I didn't want any gentleman and certainly not an eligible one in the way Nicholas implied. Nicholas's family was not wealthy. His mother was ill. They lived in a small manor beside the expansive Rosewood, and Nicholas worked hard to maintain it. He did not attend university, and likely never would. He took care of his family instead.*

*My heart hammered with all the admiration I had been hiding, the realization that I would never see any boy as I saw Nicholas. His light was too bright. I wasn't a fool. I knew my own heart, and I knew it was unalterably his.*

*I forced my mind to focus. "You know I will make a fool of myself no matter what you teach me. If this imagined gentleman cannot love me as a fool then he cannot love me at all."*

*Nicholas laughed again, turning and stepping faster. I followed each step, smiling down at our feet—his large boots and my tiny slippers. I wanted to freeze time in this moment. I wished with all my concentration that I could, but it was impossible.*

*At last we stopped turning, and Nicholas placed one hand on my shoulder, looking down at me as a brother might look at a sister. It shattered every hope I had that he might have been earnest—that he might have left the ball for me. "You deserve the very best sort of man one day, Lucy. And I mean that. Do not let anyone steal your heart that is not worthy of it."*

*My bones ached. "The very best?"*

*He nodded.*

*Nicholas was speaking of himself. He was the best. He simply didn't know it.*

*"I thank you for this dance." He dropped a bow, throwing me another wink and flashing a teasing smile.*

*My hands twitched at the fabric of my gown and my eyes wandered away from his. "Thank you for coming to my aid. I was quite lonely here by myself."*

*"I will always be here should you need a friend at any moment." I felt his eyes on my face, and dared to look up.*

*He was my friend. My best friend. The best of all the best. My heart squeezed with emotion and I clicked the toes of my slippers together. When Nicholas took his leave, I shut the door behind me again, letting the silence of the empty space soak through my skin. I sat at the small desk in the corner, and wrote a secret note to Nicholas, one he would never read. My words scratched across the page.*

*Nicholas –*

*I know I am small and foolish and silly and many other unfortunate things. I know my hair curls much too tight, and I know I am much too short, and I know I am only fourteen years of age. But I am quite in love with you, and wish to know if you will ever feel the same. I will grow older soon. In fact, I am growing older even as I write these words, and even as you read them (but you will never actually read them because I am disposing of this note at once). Even if you never love me, please stay beautiful. Stay kind and honest and good. You said that I deserved the very best, but the only best I can think of is you.*

*~~With kind regards,~~*

*With all my heart,*

*Lucy*

*But when I finished writing I didn't dispose of the note. I tucked it inside my glove where it would be safe. One doesn't simply go disposing of their heart. They keep it safe and nearby in case they ever find the strength to let it be seen.*

# THIRTEEN

*T* was surprised to find a short note at the base of my door when I awoke the next morning. It had been the most restless sleep of my life, and I arose early, arranging my hair in a simple style and wearing another of the dresses that had been lent to me by Kitty. It was far too long, so I gathered the fabric in my hands as I stepped into the hallway. Scooping up the mysterious parchment, I retreated back into my room and closed the door.

I unfolded it and read the words.

> *I've arrived as promised. Meet me at the trees on the west side of Rosewood at noon today.*

It wasn't signed, but I knew who it was from. My heart flooded with relief. Nicholas was here. And he wished to see me. I closed my eyes and pushed my hopes down with a firm hand. I had felt this before. I had allowed myself to feel as if I were important to him. It always made rejection more painful when you weren't expecting it. Or even when you were expecting it, but had even the smallest drop of hope. Hope made expectations soar to dangerous heights.

I tucked the note away and checked my reflection in the mirror. But Nicholas *had* called me lovely. I puzzled over that encounter over and over in my mind. He wasn't prepared to part from me, he had said. My stomach erupted in fluttering wings of excitement. What could he have meant with those words?

After breakfast, the morning passed slowly. Mrs. Tattershall tried to convince me to join her and Kitty in the music room to show-case our talents, but I had very little musical talent and I was too distracted to listen. I kept my eyes fixed on the clock, pacing the halls and my room when I couldn't sit still. At last noon came and I secured my bonnet to my head and rushed out the door to the back property.

The west trees were the ones bordering the Bancroft's home—the new ones that met with the fence to form an obvious barrier. As I approached them, I could see Nicholas stretching his head around one of the small trees, motioning with his hand for me to hurry. When I stopped in front of him, he smiled as if he couldn't help it.

"What?"

"If I know you at all, I am wagering that you will trip on the hem of that dress before day's end."

I looked down and lifted the dress, clicking the toes of my shoes together. "Might I remind you that I am a fully grown lady now? My days of ungainliness are in the past."

His eyes brimmed with laughter, but I could also see a weight in them, an uncertainty and weariness.

"Are you well?" I asked in a quiet voice. "How is your family? And do not tell me all is well because I can see by your face that all is not well. I am tired of being lied to."

He gave a sad smile. "My mother's health is declining still. She is very ill of the mind. I should not have left."

"Why did you leave then?"

He was staring straight ahead, his brow firm. He looked down at me and my heart skittered at the raw emotion in his eyes. "I thought they needed money more than they needed me."

It felt like the day his horse had died, when I had come across him and hadn't known what to say. "There are other ways to earn wages, Nicholas . . ."

"I know." His eyes snapped into mine. "I never intended to do what I did. Since my father died we have struggled to pay expenses.

I maintained our grounds on my own, but Mrs. Rossington always ensured that the Rosewood staff assisted me. She was very kind to us."

"My aunt Edith," I whispered. He nodded, pausing on the sadness that was likely showing in my expression.

He stepped forward, taking my arm and securing it around his. Stepping into the trees, we walked along the white fence until we reached a stone bench that rested against the side of the small house. He gestured for me to sit and took his place beside me. I tried to ignore the way his leg pressed against mine as he turned to face me. "My mother's health had been growing worse, and due to a set of terrible circumstances, it deteriorated faster. I took her to a specialist in London, but the bills were too great. I promised the man money that we didn't have, and now I am struggling to repay that debt as well as feed my family and maintain the household."

I remembered the strangeness of Mrs. Bancroft's behavior. I had heard whispers of the late King George and the madness that had claimed his life. The illness she had was a condition of the mind as well, and I couldn't help but picture the way her face had been that night I had seen her in her armchair six years ago. Her eyes had been glazed and her face sullen. She had lunged at me and Rachel, telling us we were not welcome there. The memory had been buried deep and for a good reason.

The pieces of Nicholas's story were falling into place; my head was beginning to make sense of them. "But what led you to the highwaymen? Why did you convince so many that you were married?"

The moment I finished speaking, the shattering of glass caught my attention from above where we sat. Before I could comprehend what was happening, a large pot was falling from the window near the top of the house. It was too fast. My eyes followed it for a brief moment before I jumped away from the direction it appeared to be falling. From the corner of my eye I saw Nicholas stand in alarm, moving as if to shield me. I ducked out of the way just as the pot shattered on the bench where I had been sitting.

I gasped, jerking my gaze to the window. What looked like a hand retreated behind the curtains. Had it been Mrs. Bancroft?

My heart raced as I squinted at the window. The hand had appeared too small and frail to belong to her.

"Lucy, are you all right?" Nicholas had both his hands wrapped over my shoulders, pulling my gaze back to his.

"What was that?" My voice swam in the air, making me feel as if my head were encased in glass rather than a straw hat.

"He doesn't know how to behave."

My ears sharpened. "He?" Nicholas had a sister, Julia. And his mother. There was no *he* to speak of. "Is there someone else living in your home?"

"No. I'm sorry, I meant to say *she*. My mother." His eyes shifted away from mine as he spoke.

"But the hand that I saw . . . it looked very much like a child's, Nicholas." I had recovered enough to fix him with a look of suspicion.

"My mother has grown quite frail." His voice was blunt. I didn't quite believe his explanation, but I didn't want to argue with him.

"May I see her?" I asked. He shook his head, holding me steady as we walked away from the house. We stopped at the place we had met, at the edge of the trees between the two properties.

"You cannot see her, I'm sorry. At least not yet. She doesn't take well to visitors."

"Has she been receiving any medical assistance? Surely there is a doctor that may perform tests and administer antidotes of some sort that will not create the same cost as the specialist in London."

Nicholas breathed out, long and slow, and rubbed the side of his face. He didn't need to answer. I knew he couldn't afford it. If Aunt Edith knew of the situation, surely she would help. But she was gone. I couldn't imagine Mr. Rossington, flaunting his riches as he was, being willing to sacrifice any money to assist Nicholas. Or that he would in any case, given their secret dispute.

I wanted to reach up and comfort Nicholas in some way, but I didn't know how. My heart blossomed with understanding. At least I knew why he had convened with such wicked men, even if I didn't know when and how. He had been desperate for money—not for greed—but for the purpose of maintaining his family. He regret-ted every moment, I could tell, and it hurt me to see it. My throat tightened for his sake, and I reaffirmed my commitment to help him. To show him that he was indeed good and kind.

"Perhaps you should go back to the Rossingtons. They will wonder where you have gone." Nicholas's voice was hoarse and soft. "I will walk you back."

I nodded in understanding. "Will you join us for dinner this evening? The Rossingtons are not aware of your return."

Nicholas bristled. "I cannot imagine anything worse than spending the evening with Mr. Rossington."

I threw him a puzzled look that made his expression smooth over. He had spoken too frankly and he knew it.

"Please, Nicholas. Because I, too, cannot imagine any worse way to spend an evening. If you are there we may share the discomfort and it will not be so severe." I smiled in an effort to lighten the expression on his face. I was still not accustomed to this brooding, serious side of him.

"I assure you, if I am there your discomfort will be quite the contrary."

I planted both my hands on my hips. I had taken quite enough of the deception and secrets. "Tell me what has passed between your family and the Rossingtons! I must know."

He took a step backward, but I followed. My own confidence surprised me.

"Lucy . . ." He shook his head. "It is better that you not know. At least for now."

My cheeks flamed with anger. "Is it because you think I am a child? That I cannot bear any troubling news or—or that I cannot possibly comprehend the consequences of quarrels and scandals or whatever this may be? I am not a child." I shook my head. "Not anymore. I wish you would see that. I might have been a *foolish girl* the last time I was here, but time has passed and I have changed. I am tired of being protected by lies. Lies build barriers and break hearts."

In this moment, Nicholas looked very much like a child himself, being scolded for a wrong he already realized he had committed. I had pulled the very words from his mouth from all those summers ago. *Foolish girl*. He remembered them as well as I did. They were scarred on my heart and I could see them on his. He had apologized to me, two nights ago when I had slept under the trees. But I had pretended to be asleep. Perhaps I truly had been. It wasn't enough.

I stared up at Nicholas, my breathing fast and angry.

"Lucy, I wish I could tell you, but I can't, not yet."

I uncrossed my arms and smoothed my dress. "Thank you for coming back. I suppose I will see you again when you are prepared to be entirely honest with me." I gave him a nod, and as I turned my back to walk away, I saw him scuffing his boot in the dirt, tracing frustrated circles.

I found Kitty in the morning room, and she was eager to take me to the nearby village to have me fitted for a small new selection of clothing. Until I returned to Craster, I would have nothing to wear. As we walked, Kitty spoke of the generosity of her father. He had insisted that I be equipped with proper dresses and other pieces of clothing that fit me correctly, taking the bills upon himself. The walk seemed short in comparison to the walking I had done in the last week. We were approaching the cobblestones of the town roads. Green leaves were just beginning their transformation to warmer tones. I tried to imagine how beautiful they would be in a few short weeks. The golden red, orange, and yellow of autumn.

"Would your father not consider using the funds they are allotting to me for a different purpose instead?" I asked.

Kitty loosened her grip on my arm and turned toward me. Her hair had blown over her face and she pushed it away. "What is this alternative purpose you speak of?" Her left eyebrow arched in question.

I took a breath. "To pay a doctor to look after Mrs. Bancroft. Her health is very poor."

Kitty gave an exasperated sigh. "I cannot imagine that would be allowed."

"By the Bancrofts?"

"No, by my father."

I watched my feet as we walked, disappointment dropping through me. I was tired of asking questions, so I just accepted her words. At least for the moment.

The village here was much larger than the one in Craster and even the one Nicholas had taken me to in our travels. The shops were taller, the roads wider, and the people passed in greater numbers. Through the crowd of passersby, a familiar face made me stop.

"Kitty!" I pulled her back the step she had taken ahead of me. "Do you see that man standing by the tan horse? The one holding the hat? Oh, he just put it on his head. Do you see him?"

I watched her eyes land on Mr. Parsons. "Yes, who is he?"

"I met him on my journey here in a village much like this one." My mind wandered back to that day, when Mr. Parsons had pulled me away from the oncoming chaise. He had flirted with me, and Nicholas had seen it. Mr. Parsons had indeed told me that he lived in Dover.

"He is very handsome," Kitty observed. "Are you going to speak to him?"

I studied him standing there by the horse. "No . . . it was rather embarrassing the circumstances in which we were acquainted. I would rather not speak to him." I turned my feet to the opposite direction but Kitty stopped me.

"You are speaking to him. I will not allow you to flee."

I gasped at her and she laughed. "He sees you."

"He does not!" I jerked my eyes in his direction and met his eyes immediately. Drat. He had certainly seen me.

Forcing a smile to my lips, I took several steps forward to meet him as he approached, dragging Kitty beside me. "Mr. Parsons," I nodded, "I thought we might see one another again."

His eyes truly were striking as he glanced over my face. "Miss Abbot, I have not forgotten you. I sincerely hoped to see you again."

Kitty poked a gloved finger discreetly into my ribs. The faintest giggle came from her lips; any observer might think it was nothing more than a breath, but I knew her too well. "This is my cousin, Miss—er—Mrs. Kitty Turner."

He gave her a polite greeting and turned his attention back to me. "I am glad you have arrived to Dover in safety."

"You as well."

He smiled.

"Mr. Parsons," Kitty cut in, "we would be honored if you would join us for dinner at Rosewood this evening."

I twisted my head to give her a look of dismay that only she could see.

"The honor would be mine, Mrs. Turner. I was just now thinking that I had no engagements to speak of for this evening and would likely sit in my solitary chair in loneliness all evening."

Kitty laughed. "We will welcome you at six."

"Thank you." He shifted his gaze to me again and offered one final charming smile. "I will look forward to seeing you again."

I was baffled by his attention. Rarely had men ever given me attention, especially one so kind and charming. It was strange, but I quite enjoyed it. If only Nicholas were here to observe such behavior. "And I you."

When Mr. Parsons took his leave, Kitty turned to me with her mouth gaping open. "He is quite smitten by you, I daresay!"

"Do not dare to say it one more time, Kitty."

"I will. He is smitten by you!"

I couldn't help but smile. "Keep your voice down!"

"And he is coming for dinner." She wiggled her eyebrows and threw her head back in delight. "Do you know of his family? Background, station?"

I shook my head. "We only spoke briefly. I know nothing besides his appearance, charm, and that he seems to be somewhat agreeable, although I cannot claim to know his character further than that."

"And we know he seems to fancy you," she added.

I bit my lip, waiting for the excitement I expected to come. I was flattered, but found myself not caring as much as I wanted to care. He was not Nicholas. Would any man ever compare? My steps were heavy as we went about our business in town. I found several simple dresses that would suit me well until I returned home to Craster.

ASHTYN NEWBOLD

Since arriving in Dover I had missed my family more than I thought. I wished so badly to speak to my mama and papa about the mysteries of Rosewood. I didn't quite understand why they had kept away for so long, but I was beginning to, which also made me more and more aware of my guilt. How childish and disrespectful I had been, running off alone against their wishes.

The note I had written wasn't enough. It wouldn't arrive for nearly a fortnight. Mama would sit and worry until then. I thought of Mrs. Bancroft and Nicholas. His devotion to her was admirable. He would risk his life and reputation to acquire money to help her. I didn't condone the circumstances, but he was desperate and he loved her. How could a heart not forgive that? He had seemed regretful to the highest degree, and intent to change. I wished there were a way I could help their situation, but I didn't know how. I wanted to visit Mrs. Bancroft, but I was afraid. Perhaps all she needed was a female companion to fill her life with gentleness. Nicholas was loyal and loving but not the epitome of gentleness.

I puzzled over the idea as I walked home with Kitty. She was speaking endlessly, telling me of her courtship with Mr. Turner, but I could only listen with half an ear. I imagined myself in Mrs. Bancroft's position, living alone with her young daughter and relying on her son to provide when he was nowhere to be found. Kitty had said that Nicholas had been away for years, but it could not have been possible. He must have sneaked back often to tend to the grounds and take care of his mother and younger sister, Julia.

Julia had always been shy. I had nearly forgotten that she lived there. Why had she not made an appearance? The last time I had seen her she had been only nine years old. How lonely she must feel.

By the time we arrived at Rosewood, I made the quiet decision that I was going to see the Bancrofts whether Nicholas liked it or not. The entire family needed a friend, a supporter, someone to love them. If the Rossingtons would not do it then I must.

If Nicholas would not be honest with me, then why should I be honest with him? I would visit his family and not give him one word about it. I remembered the pot that had come from the window, nearly falling on my head. I would certainly have to exercise caution.

My heart hammered with anticipation. Tomorrow I would go. I would be brave and learn for myself the mystery of the Bancrofts.

# FOURTEEN

*I* hadn't noticed the clock for several hours. I had perched myself in front of the west windows, staring into the window of the Bancrofts' home, hoping to catch sight of anything peculiar. My efforts had not met success. With a sigh, I uncurled my legs from beneath me and stood, stretching my back. Mr. Parsons was coming for dinner. The thought filled me with dread. I didn't know why.

My feet felt as if they were tied down with chains as I moved across the house to my room. I needed to look presentable whether I wanted to put forth the effort or not. The only person I wanted to see was Nicholas. I didn't care if he told me the truth or not. I just wanted to speak with him and laugh with him. I was weak, and I hated myself for it. Rubbing my eyes, I tried to shake my mind free of him. It didn't work.

After dressing in a peach dress with white-lace-trimmed sleeves, I flounced my hair in the mirror and pinned it back in a simple bun at the crown of my head. Without intending it, several curls escaped the knot and fell at my neck and forehead. I studied the array in the mirror, deciding it looked better that way.

I was late arriving downstairs, so I skipped down the stairs, turning the corner of the drawing room door with a smile. The room was quiet and heavy. My eyes scanned every corner and stopped.

Nicholas sat in the settee by the fire, engaged in quiet conversation with Mr. Turner. My heart jumped in surprise. I thought he had refused to come! What had changed his mind? My eyes lingered on him until I felt the weight of Kitty's shocked gaze on my face. I looked around the room. Mr. Rossington appeared as if he wished for nothing more than to catch on fire and turn to a pile of ash on the floor. I caught Nicholas throwing looks of disgust and dislike at Mr. Rossington every so often. Mrs. Tattershall cleared her throat and stepped away from William's side to approach me. "Did you extend an invitation to Mr. Bancroft?" Her voice was clipped. Her eyes were pinched. "And where is his wife?"

"I—er—" I had nearly forgotten about his false wife.

Kitty shuffled forward. "It was me, Aunt Susan. I knew he had just returned from extensive travel and thought it prudent to offer him a place at our table. And Mr. Bancroft's wife . . . she was unable to attend with him. I extended the invitation to Mr. Parsons as well." She gestured at the left side of the room. Heavens, I hadn't even noticed the man standing there. He seemed to be straining his head toward us, trying to eavesdrop on the conversation.

"Kitty, dear. You know how this upsets your father. He—" Mrs. Tattershall seemed to remember I was standing nearby. She closed her lips and took a breath through her nose. "I confess I am shocked that Mr. Bancroft made an appearance at all. What purpose could he have in being here?"

My gaze traveled across the room to Nicholas. Mr. Turner had left his side. It was just Nicholas, looking back at me with a suppressed grin in his eyes. He had been correct. Having him here would make things vastly more uncomfortable. My mouth split into a grin that I tried to hide. Nicholas arched one devious eyebrow at me. I had to look away before I exploded into inappropriate laughter.

I felt the weight of Mr. Parson's gaze watching the interaction. Before I knew what happened, he was across the room at my side, dropping a bow. His blue eyes appraised me before he offered an intentionally loud remark. "I must say, Miss Abbot, you look quite stunning this evening. You have chosen your colors wisely."

I laughed awkwardly, my eyes shifting to Nicholas. There was that look again—the annoyance and . . . was it jealousy? I tried not to let myself hope that it was, but I had certainly felt jealousy before, and I had certainly given someone that very look before.

A certain girl named Miss Hyatt, to be precise.

My cheeks warmed. It wasn't very difficult considering that two handsome men had their eyes trained on me. "I thank you, Mr. Parsons. You look very handsome this evening as well." Out of the corner of my eye, I saw Nicholas stand.

"I am glad you were able to make it here," I continued, flustered. "I hope you enjoy your time at Rosewood. I certainly do." I tried to keep the conversation moving along before Nicholas could reach us. In all honesty, I didn't care one bit about speaking to Mr. Parsons. I scolded myself for encouraging him with any measure of flirting.

"I am certain I will. It is a very fine house filled with very fine people."

Nicholas was coming closer, but I didn't allow myself to look at him. I had already smiled at him, which was something that I had trusted myself not to do. Our last encounter had been less than pleasant. My face burned at the thought of the things I had said. I had told him not to see me again until he was prepared to tell me the truth.

Nicholas stepped up beside me. His closeness alone made the rate of my heart increase and my palms sweat.

"Mr. Parsons, I don't believe you have met Mr. Bancroft," I said, my voice too quick.

Mr. Parsons eyed Nicholas with a hint of disdain that bothered me. "Good evening, Mr. Bancroft." His nod was brief before he turned a look of adoration on me. "I was just telling Miss Abbot how attractive she is in peach. Do you not agree?"

I dared a glance at Nicholas. His expression was rankled, his arms tense as he watched Mr. Parsons. Then his eyes fell down to mine and his face smoothed over. I was trapped in his gaze—in the sudden softness that filled it. "I'm afraid I must disagree with your assessment."

My heart sunk and I looked away. Pain radiated in my chest, stinging out to my fingertips.

"I would call her breathtaking."

Before I could absorb his words, I felt his hand wrap around mine. I almost gasped but couldn't find the air. My eyes shot to his. His hand was warm and strong, and although I had touched his hand many times before, it felt different this time. Combined with his words and the depth in his gaze, it was painful—the effect it had on my heart. It was stabbing, squeezing, wrenching, but it was also empowering, safe, and certain.

I didn't know hands could feel so much.

He dipped his head and kissed the top of my hand. A faint smile touched his lips as his eyes met mine again. He turned to Mr. Parsons, keeping my hand in his. "Any woman can be attractive, but it's the woman that takes away your breath that is dangerous. She steals the words from your mouth and speaks them in a way you never could but always wished you could."

My eyes were trained on our hands. Mine was too small, but it fit perfectly.

"She steals your breath in laughter, in exasperation, in sighs. She takes your breath in all the words you expend to impress her. In stepping into a room in a peach dress." There was a pause. I couldn't help but look up again. Emotion pulsed through me and I begged myself not to care for the words he was saying. I had promised myself that I would be strong, but being weak was much easier. Nicholas smiled, and for an odd reason I felt the threat of tears in my throat. It was too sweet. He was too handsome and too wonderful.

My arm was shaking as he released my hand. It fell to my side and I forced my fingers to move—to put myself at ease that they still could function. It would take me all evening to recover from what had just happened. I looked around, remembering that most of the room believed Nicholas to be married. What would they think of that display he had just made? To my relief we seemed to go unnoticed by all but Mrs. Tattershall. Her thin lips were curved in a frown.

Mr. Parsons appeared more vexed than ever. When he caught me watching him, he straightened his posture. "Yes, Mr. Bancroft, I agree with your assessment entirely. There are few women that possess such a quality."

I thought Nicholas would speak again, but instead he nodded in silence. I wished Mr. Parsons would leave so I could speak to Nicholas. I wanted to know what had compelled him to come here after he had first refused. But I would have to wait.

In the dining room, the meal passed much like the one the day before: in awkwardness. Mr. Rossington and his sister spoke only to Mr. Parsons, Mr. Turner, and Kitty. William ate beside them with his eyes cast downward, never speaking a word. Nicholas was seated beside me, but much like William, we didn't speak at all. Periodically I glanced over at Nicholas, and often caught his gaze fixed on Mr. Rossington, eyes narrowed as he chewed his food. Nicholas looked as if he wished to take the man outside for a duel. I added the menacing stare into my list of clues. I felt quite like a detective as I tried to puzzle out the mysteries at Rosewood. One thing I had gathered from my work was that Nicholas was always in the center of it all.

When it was nearly time to move to the drawing room, Nicholas leaned his head close to mine and whispered, "I need to speak with you."

I shifted in my chair. "Why?"

The other two ladies stood up, and I followed. Nicholas turned toward me where no one else could see his lips move. "Meet me at the stables tonight." His voice was almost impossible to hear, but I understood.

I gave a miniscule nod and followed Mrs. Tattershall and Kitty into the drawing room. Within two minutes, Mr. Rossington and the other men entered the room. Apparently the awkwardness between Nicholas and Mr. Rossington had been impossible to bear. As I surveyed the room, I could see that there was a bit of discomfort between Nicholas and Mr. Parsons as well. Unfortunately Nicholas had been correct about his prediction for an uncomfortable evening.

It wasn't long before Nicholas excused himself from the party. He had been talking with William in the corner. I watched him stand and met his eyes. When did he want me to meet him at the stables? And more importantly, why? We couldn't speak privately here; I couldn't have the Rossingtons suspecting that there was anything between Nicholas and me. Mr. Parsons hadn't left my side all evening. He was not one to be intimidated by competition it seemed.

Nicholas picked up the book he had been holding and took several large strides toward me. Mr. Parsons shot him a look of contempt.

"I believe you will enjoy this book. You do appreciate poetry, do you not?" Nicholas extended the book to me.

I raised one eyebrow. "Yes, I do. Thank you, Mr. Bancroft."

He smiled, just a lifting of the left side of his lips. "You are very welcome, Miss Abbot." I half-expected him to call me Mrs. Bancroft. As eager as I had been to arrive here at Rosewood, I found it strange that I missed the days of travel with Nicholas. It was different now.

But why had he given me a book? As he left the room, my heart raced with a sudden idea. I turned closer to the fire where I sat so Mr. Parsons couldn't see and opened the book. It fell to a page with a slip of parchment wedged in the crease between two pages.

*I will be at the stables. Meet me there.*

I slammed the book shut and held it firmly between my hands. Mr. Parsons raised his brows and leaned closer to me. The fire made shadows beneath his cheekbones and deepened his eye sockets. "This evening has been quite invigorating."

I hardly heard him. *Nicholas left me another note.* "Are you certain? I have always thought my topics of conversation to be boring."

"Conversation with you would never bore me."

I accidentally smiled to myself as I smoothed the cover of the book in my hands, which led Mr. Parsons to lean even closer. Kitty watched from across the room, grinning deviously.

"What are you doing?" I tilted my head away from his approaching face.

"I want to be sure you know my intentions toward you. I would very much like to learn more about you, Miss Abbot. You are quite fascinating."

He was very handsome. And from the things I had overheard at dinner he seemed to be very wealthy and eligible. But something about him filled me with unease.

"I'm not fascinating."

"You are."

I took a breath and scooted away a few inches in my chair. "I am flattered, sir." My voice was dull. I didn't want to encourage him, but I didn't want to hurt him either. I knew how it felt. "Please excuse me."

I stood and approached Mrs. Tattershall. She stood by the pianoforte as Kitty sat down to play a piece. "I do not feel well. I'm afraid I must excuse myself for the evening." I bit my lip, awaiting her response.

Her face was perfectly still. Her nose twitched. "I suppose. I hope you feel improved by morning."

I gave a nod and moved toward the door. It had only been minutes since Nicholas had left. After retrieving my shawl from my room, I sneaked down the stairs and walked out the back door.

The moon was a small crescent tonight, and the sky was filled with clouds. I couldn't see the stars. I shivered, pulling my shawl tighter around my shoulders. I felt mischievous and vastly improper for sneaking away to meet a man in the dark. Alone. How inappropriate. But I trusted Nicholas and we had much practice in the art of not being seen together.

I could see the stables—they were just a dim outline on gray against the dark background. The trees behind them rustled with the crisp wind, swaying back and forth in unison. As I came closer, I saw the yellowing leaves spiral off the branches and fall to the ground. It had only been ten of the clock when I exited the drawing room, but it felt much later and much more haunting now that I was outside in the dark.

"Nicholas?" I hissed through the blackness. The stables loomed closer, and for a moment I wondered if he had already gone home. I walked on the tips of my toes, trying not to make loud sounds with my movements. If Nicholas was not here, then my imagination would fill my mind with an array of other people or creatures that could be here in his place. I swallowed. "Nicholas?"

"Lucy?" His voice cut through the air and I breathed a sigh of relief. He stepped around the opposite side of the wooden walls of the stables and walked closer to me. I remembered the day I had found him when his horse had died. He had been sitting on this side of the stables, leaned against the walls with his head down. I had never seen something so broken. I felt a pang of guilt when I remembered his horse, Jack, that he had left behind at an inn several miles away. He had told me he would reclaim him when he had the money, but I doubted he ever would. Why would he make such a sacrifice for me? It didn't make sense.

Nicholas stood in front of me, and his head tipped down to look at me from several inches above. The difference in our height was a gap that I placed between us. I pretended that was why he had never found me attractive.

But he found me breathtaking.

Despite the cold, my cheeks warmed at the reminder of the words he had said to me tonight. Had he meant them?

"Do you remember what I said tonight?" he asked. His voice was rich and low, sending a shiver over my arms.

I nodded, but decided to act as if I didn't know he was referring to the moment he had held my hand and called me breathtaking. "I remember a number of things you said." He was drawing closer, and my heart fluttered dangerously. I needed to change the subject. "I also remember the things you said earlier today. You did not finish explaining."

He sighed and rubbed one side of his face. He knew precisely what I meant. He had begun telling me what had led him to the highwaymen but he hadn't finished. "Are you certain?"

"I have only asked you several dozen times."

I thought he would chuckle, but instead he shifted, scuffing his boots and feigning interest in his hands. Nicholas was not the sort to become nervous.

"You know why I did it. You may not understand, but you know why. The Rossingtons thought that I had been away for months. I created the ruse that I was married in order to explain my absence. I was traveling during those months, but I returned home often in secret to look after my family. I paid the London doctor with the money the highwaymen gave to me." He took a heavy breath. "My responsibility was to find the wealthy travelers. So I moved from inn to inn, giving my employers their next target. I followed as they robbed each coach and then they paid me."

Although it was dark, I could see the shame in his eyes—I could feel it touching my own heart.

"I met them on my way back from visiting that London doctor, when I had been begging for more time to pay him. I was angry, and the men found me as I traveled the roads at night. They attempted to rob me but I had nothing. They were impressed with my knowledge of the roads and made their offer. It was money I needed desperately. My family hadn't eaten more than a broth soup for several days. I was lost and angry, so I agreed." He shook his head. He looked like he was about to say more but he stopped, tightening his jaw.

"Nicholas," I said in a quiet voice. My heart thudded, but I couldn't stop my words from coming. "You are a good man. And I know you love your family very much. Sometimes our hearts do things our heads would never even think on."

His face tightened with emotion and he tipped his head away so I wouldn't see him. I was reminded once again of the boy who had lost his horse. I forced myself to look in his eyes. "We will find a way to help your mother. You need never to go back to those men." A gust of wind hit my shawl and I wrapped it tighter around me.

"One of the highwaymen was shot," he said.

My eyes widened. "How can you be certain?"

His throat bobbed with a labored swallow. "Colin. The gunshots we heard . . . it was the coachman. I saw it. He retrieved his pistol and I saw him shoot Colin. He's dead."

I remembered when Nicholas had turned the horse around. I had been unable to see the scene over his shoulders. I tried to focus on the image of the highwaymen in my mind. "And the other man?"

"He escaped—he was the man chasing us for a distance on horse-back. When I rode away with you, they must have been distracted. The coachman never could have overpowered Colin otherwise."

I could hardly grasp onto my thoughts—they were spinning too quickly in my head. "Where is he?"

Nicholas shrugged his shoulders. "Gibbs? I haven't the slightest idea."

Another shiver ran over me, making the darkness of the woods behind the property more daunting and frightening than before. I did not like the idea of one of those horrific men wandering the area. Betrayed by Nicholas. Fear clenched at my sides.

"I am glad you told me," I said in a quiet voice, trying to sound more brave than I felt. "You needn't keep secrets from me. I understand why you did the things you did. I know you regret it. The past is not one to withhold regrets from us; it has many to give. But the lessons we learn are worth it, I think."

He seemed to be considering my words deeply. Just when I thought he wouldn't respond, he said, "Thank you, Lucy." His voice was soft. His lips lifted in a smile, one so genuine and raw that I felt that warmth in my chest burn brighter and more certain. I loved Nicholas. I would never not love him. I had never stopped. Even when he had hurt me, I had still loved him.

But I kept my lips closed and tried to lock my heart up tighter. I couldn't let him know how I felt. I would not fall at his feet the way I had as a child.

Nicholas's smile lingered, but his eyes grew serious. I sensed he was returning to the place our conversation had started—when he had moved far too close to me.

"The things I said tonight . . . I meant every word." He did it again. He drew closer. The pale light from the moon caught the left side of his face.

My heart raced. Why must he stand so close? I took a small step backward so I could think clearly. It didn't work. I quickly changed the subject, hoping Nicholas's intentions would be swayed. "Do you think Mr. Parsons meant the words that he spoke as well?"

"I do not trust Mr. Parsons." Nicholas crossed his arms over his chest.

I scoffed. "I don't understand why you dislike him so much."

"I can see that you are quite fond of him. He seems to be quite fond of you. He surely takes no effort to hide the fact."

"And why should he hide his feelings? Indeed, he is a very kind, amiable man. He has given me no reason to dislike him."

Nicholas ran a hand over his hair, making it fall to the slightly unruly style I had become accustomed to. "I do not think he can be trusted."

"Why not?"

"I don't know." He shook his head as if to clear it. "But I would only ask that you be careful."

"Are you afraid he will hurt me?" It was much easier to speak the questions on my mind when I couldn't see his face clearly in the dark, when I couldn't see the golden brown of his eyes and the creases of his smile.

Nicholas looked down at the ground. "I'm afraid that he will marry you."

My ears tingled with heat and my heart skipped a beat. "What do you mean?"

Nicholas stepped closer again. I could feel the warmth of him blocking the cold air from reaching me. I wanted to step away but I wasn't strong enough. Something kept me tied to him, captivated, trapped.

"You asked me to be honest with you, Lucy, and that is my intention." His eyes locked on mine. "You spoke of regret, of the lessons it teaches us. When I think of the day you left Dover six years ago . . ." he shook his head, "The things I said to you . . . there is nothing I regret more. I have learned what a fool I am. I thought I would never see you again. I swore that one day I would go to Craster and find you. I wanted to write to you, but I didn't know how to apologize, and I was afraid. I couldn't forgive myself for hurting you, Lucy, and I still can't. Not until you can forgive me."

My legs shook and I felt the threat of emotion rising up. My eyes stung. "Nicholas—"

My head was shaking and I could hardly hear him. My feet were moving me backward, away from the sound of his voice.

He took a step closer but I moved back fast, nearly tripping over the ends of my shawl. I wanted to forgive him, but I was afraid of the things he made me feel. My heart was falling from its high shelf, barreling down to the ground where it could be trampled and tampered with. If I gave my heart to Nicholas again he might twist it and break it into even more pieces than he had the first time. My emotions choked me as I stared back at him in the dark. My chest rose and fell with quick breaths, and my legs were so stiff I feared they couldn't move even if I wanted them to. How many times had I told myself that I would never let Nicholas into my heart again? How many hours had I spent regretting every hour spent with him?

# Fifteen

Summer 1814

"We are leaving tomorrow," Mama whispered to me as she turned to leave my bedchamber. Her dark hair glowed in the orange candlelight and her mouth smiled, but her eyes were heavy. "Late afternoon. Have you enjoyed yourself here?"

I hesitated. I had never hesitated at that question before. But because I didn't want to be questioned, I nodded. I pulled my blankets up to my chin to hide my own false smile. Mama had always known the difference between a genuine and counterfeit smile.

After she gave me a kiss and left the room, I darkened the candles and rolled to my side. Nicholas had been different the last several weeks. He had hidden himself away in his house, working on the property and rarely venturing over to Rosewood as he usually did daily. I had not seen his mother or sister for quite some time—not since the previous summer when Mrs. Bancroft had nearly attacked Rachel and me. I didn't understand the condition of her mind.

Ever since Nicholas had danced with me in the morning room he had been distant, keeping away from Rosewood and away from me. I didn't understand why.

I had developed a new habit during the past several weeks. I took a walk each morning with Rachel, although she didn't know the purpose of the walk. We circled the Bancroft's home, and I often saw Nicholas outside in the garden that his mother had planted, picking weeds or *harvesting vegetables and herbs. I always brought my secret note that I had written to him on our daily walks, tucked away in my sleeve.*

*I played a game with myself. Each morning I told myself I would give Nicholas the note, but each day I was too afraid.*

*The third day, Miss Hyatt was there with him, taking her own daily walk from the other side of town. And she was there the fourth day and the fifth day too. Each time I passed with Rachel, Miss Hyatt glanced up with her full lashes and her long arm raised and she waved with a gloved hand. Nicholas glanced up too, and he smiled at me.*

*But he didn't come to see me. It had been weeks since we had spoken. I missed him. I wasn't supposed to miss him yet. Missing him was reserved for the other ten months of the year.*

*Tomorrow we would leave. I would deliver my letter and I would walk away. I wouldn't have to stay to hear what he thought of it. I wouldn't have to face him until the next summer, when I would surely be more beautiful and older than I was now.*

*My eyes were growing heavy, so I tried to close off my mind. I needed a plentiful night of rest if I intended to perform such a task in the morning. My heart raced and I heard every beat in my ear as it pressed against my pillow. My stomach fluttered violently. How could I find the courage to do it? Even if he was smitten by Miss Hyatt, I still needed him to know the things I had written.*

*I only slept for an hour or two, polishing my plan in my mind, sculpting scenarios of how my morning would transpire. I climbed out of bed at quarter to five, dressing and arranging my hair by candlelight before sitting on the edge of my bed, waiting. It was excruciating, and when the sun came out, I took the note from beneath my pillow and read it over for what must have been the hundredth time.*

*Nicholas ~*

*I know I am small and foolish and silly and many other unfortunate things. I know my hair curls much too tight, and I know I am much too short, and I know I am only fourteen years of age. But I am quite in love with you, and wish to know if you will ever feel the same. I will grow older soon. In fact, I am growing older even as I write these words, and even as you read them (but you will never actually read them because I am disposing of this note at once). Even if you never love*

*me, please stay beautiful. Stay kind and honest and good. You said that
I deserved the very best, but the only best I can think of is you.*
 ~~*With kind regards,*~~
*With all my heart,*

*Lucy*

*My hands shook as I folded the note again, tucking it into the end
of my long, pale-green sleeve. I stared into the mirror on the wall of my
room, straightening my shoulders and standing on the tips of my toes.
Before I could lose my resolve, I walked out the door and moved down the
stairs and outside, forcing my steps to be confident and not weak and slow.
And though I would miss walking with Rachel, this was a walk I needed
to take alone. Mama allowed me to take my walks as long as I stayed on
the property. Rosewood bordered the Bancrofts' gardens, so I was more
than happy to comply.*

*The sky was pale gray this morning, reminding me of the skies in
Craster. I had never seen the sky so dark here in Dover. We always left
before the weather turned colder and the sun began to hide behind clouds.*

*My stomach filled with nervousness. I wished very much that I could
hide at this moment. My chest pinched tight with anticipation. My pulse
raced. I could hardly breathe without needing to pause my walk to wipe
the perspiration from my brow.*

*It wasn't far to the point where I knew Nicholas would be, bent over
the plants. He had come to expect me to walk past, and on the days that
Miss Hyatt wasn't already there, I dared to speak to him. He was always
polite, but nothing more. He didn't laugh. His eyes shifted toward his
house and his brow was tight. I wanted to ask what the matter was, but I
didn't think he would answer. He always asked me how I was faring, and
I always replied with a simple, "I am well."*

*I could see Nicholas in his usual place as I turned the back corner of
the house. My feet felt heavy over the grass and my throat dried instantly.
How could I speak to him? In my mind I had envisioned myself simply
handing him the note, but I knew at least a greeting was in order. My
heart sunk as I came closer. I hadn't noticed Miss Hyatt standing to the
side of Nicholas. Her finger wrapped around the ribbon of her bonnet*

*and her other hand was resting on her hip. She leaned toward Nicholas and laughed.*

*I licked my lips, puffing out a breath. I turned to leave, but whirled myself back around to face them. Miss Hyatt could not intimidate me.*

*As I approached, Nicholas's eyes caught mine. I walked faster, painting a smile on my face. Miss Hyatt followed Nicholas's gaze to me. I realized I had been walking with far too much bounce in my step. I leveled my strides so my curls would stop moving. I felt every edge and crease of the parchment in my sleeve, reminding me that this time it was not allowed to stay there.*

*"Good morning," I choked as I stopped in front of Nicholas. My voice was hoarse. I tried again, clearing my throat. "Good morning!"*

*Miss Hyatt raised one thin eyebrow, and her lips pursed together in a suppressed grin. I had never stopped by to speak to them before. Miss Hyatt likely recognized me from my daily walk, but I had never spoken to her or Nicholas when they had been together.*

*Nicholas uncrossed his arms. "Good morning, Lucy,"*

*"Good morning," I said again. I bit my lip to keep myself from repeating my words like a ninny.*

*Nicholas's eyes sparked with impatience and he glanced at Miss Hyatt again. She smiled at him and whispered something I couldn't hear. My heart dropped.*

*"What brings you here?" Nicholas asked. He wasn't smiling like he usually did. He wasn't teasing me—he was asking in earnest. I opened my mouth to speak, but realized that I didn't have an answer.*

*"Oh, well, er—I wished to help you with the gardens."*

*Miss Hyatt covered her lips with her glove, but I could see the scrunching of her nose as she hid her laughter. Nicholas threw her a charming smile, the sort of smile I always craved to see when I was with him. My heart dropped a little more. He had always thrown me secret smiles.*

*Nicholas slid his gaze to me as if the action took effort. "Does your mother know you are taking your walk alone? Where is Rachel?" His voice sounded concerned, but his eyes were shining with amusement. I bit back the emotion that tore through me. This had been a mistake. Miss Hyatt giggled behind her glove. Nicholas was treating me like a dependent child.*

Fighting my tears, I turned toward the long bed of dirt at my feet and bent over, plucking the first sprouting weed I could find. Then I plucked another, and another. My eyes stung with disappointment and suppressed emotion. "I quite enjoy gardening," I stammered as I tossed aside a handful of weeds.

"Lucy," Nicholas held my arm, pulling it away from the dirt. I looked up at him, unable to hide my scowl before he saw it. His face was gentle and concerned, the way I remembered him looking at me when Miss Hyatt wasn't nearby. His body shielded me from her, so he allowed himself to brush a fleck of dirt from my cheek. He dropped his hand as if he regretted it. "You should go back to Rosewood."

"Why?" I asked.

Nicholas's eyes flicked away from my face and back to Miss Hyatt. He smiled at her again. Had he even heard me? My heart thumped with shards of loss and regret. Why had I tried to convince myself that Nicholas could ever care for me? I was a thorn beside a rose, a pesky little thing that wasn't loved and wasn't needed.

I stood up straight, brushing the dirt from my skirts. Humiliation wrung my soul dry, and I could hardly think of anything else as I stepped away from Nicholas. His stare broke away from Miss Hyatt and he looked down at the dirt where I had been standing. I quickly patted my sleeve—it was empty.

The letter must have fallen out when Nicholas pulled my arm back. Before I could react, Nicholas bent over and scooped the letter from the dirt.

"Nicholas!" I rushed forward and reached for my note in panic. "That is mine."

He danced the note out of my reach; his lips twisted in a grin. Sheer horror rushed through my veins as I jumped, trying to reach the note. My face burned at the thought of him unfolding it. "Nicholas, please return it to me." I tried to catch my breath but my heart was pounding too quickly.

"To whom is it written? Shall we find out?" He wiggled his eyebrows and tugged at the corner of the parchment. Miss Hyatt stepped close to his side, straining her neck to see the note for herself. I stopped my jumping and hung my hands at my side. "Nicholas." I tried to sound firm but my voice was shaking. I wanted to run away. "Please don't read it."

He didn't listen. He was only aware of Miss Hyatt giggling over his shoulder, tossing her soft curls away from her flawless complexion. I was certain my face had never been so rosy. My stomach lurched with dread and panic. Slowly his fingers pulled open the first fold of my note, then the next. His eyes landed on the page and his smile slackened.

"For you, Nicholas?" Miss Hyatt exclaimed. She looked down at me with a mocking grin. Nicholas's eyes were still glued to my note—to my words—my very heart was on that parchment. I had never felt more vulnerable. That was when the tears came. They sprung into my eyes without permission, and I finally found the strength to move my legs.

I turned and ran, not pausing to look back to see if Nicholas noticed, or to see if he had finished reading. I was certain I had never ran more quickly in my life. My feet hit the grass hard and I slapped the tears off my cheeks as I reached the back door of the house. I couldn't go inside, not like this. I paced in front of the door, trying to calm my breathing. It wasn't supposed to have happened like that. I never would have given it to him; I knew I would have been too afraid. It was just the thought of being brave that had excited me. I was never actually brave. He had been using me to entertain Miss Hyatt. Their smiles had been mocking and cruel—both of them.

My heart leapt in my chest. No. Across the lawn, rounding the nearest corner of Rosewood was Nicholas.

Why hadn't Mama and Papa decided to leave this morning instead of this afternoon? I didn't have a place to hide. Nicholas had already seen me standing by the back door. If I ran inside, then surely he would follow me, and I would cause even more of a scene. I needed to face him. My legs shook violently and my heart threatened to burst as he approached faster and faster. He knew everything. Everything. It was as if I stood in the middle of the sea, balanced on a tiny rock, defenseless on all sides. One movement and I would be lost in the waves.

My tears were falling faster now, even as I begged them to stop. Nicholas stopped a few strides away from me, my parchment still in his hand. He didn't speak for several seconds, so I spoke first.

*"I didn't mean for you to read that. I wanted to dispose of it. I asked you not to read it."* My voice was shaky and quiet. I wiped the moisture off my cheeks and released a quaking breath.

Nicholas's eyes were darker today, a deeper brown to match his hair and the darkness of the morning sky. He breathed out and stepped closer. For a moment I saw a softness in his eyes that I recognized. He lifted his hand toward my face but quickly dropped it again. He shook his head as if he were disgusted by the thought of touching me, and took a step back. *"Take it."*

He extended the parchment in my direction. *"Take it and we may pretend you did indeed dispose of it."*

He wasn't looking at me. His hand was stretched out holding my note, and for a moment I wondered if he would drop it at my feet. I shook all the way to my core with regret. My heart wrenched. *"I don't want to pretend that."*

Nicholas glanced at me wearily. *"Why not?"*

*"Because it was true,"* I whispered, *"All of it was true. But it does not matter if you don't . . ."* I swallowed. *"If you don't care for me at all."*

His brows drew together and his jaw tightened. He looked down at his boots that were smeared in dirt. *"You're a foolish girl, Lucy,"* he said under his breath. *"You are still practically a child! How could I care for you in the way you imply?"* His voice was harsh. *"The sooner you understand that, the better. I should hate for you to have your hopes up the next time you come here."*

His words hit me like a physical blow, striking me squarely in the chest.

Nicholas refused to look at me. I was glad, because I didn't want him to see me cry.

Turning back toward the door, I pushed it open and closed it slowly behind me. I couldn't feel myself walking. Before I realized what had happened, I was in my bedchamber with the door locked behind me. Anguish stirred feelings of inadequacy and grief in my heart until I couldn't bear it. I never wanted to come here again. I never wanted to see Nicholas again. I buried my face in my pillow and sobbed until my eyes were dry. There were a million different ways he could have said the things he said.

*In the many hours that followed, I played the same words across my mind like musical notes.* I will never forgive him. I will never forgive him. I will never forgive him.

# SIXTEEN

*T*he air was colder when I was pulled out of my memory. Tears streaked down my cheeks; I hadn't noticed them falling. I had to leave. Now. But then Nicholas bent his head over mine, lifting his hand to my face. It was warm where his fingers traced the side of my cheek. I wanted to tell myself this was only an elaborate game, a trap, but the look in Nicholas's eyes was too raw and too real.

But as I looked up at him I could only see the outline of a pale gray morning sky instead of the darkness of evening. I could only see a narrower, younger face and fierce, uncharacteristic eyes.

"Why did you do it?" I asked. "Why did you say those things?" My voice hardly escaped my throat. He was my dearest friend, and he had ruined it all in few short sentences.

Nicholas's hand cupped my cheek, and I squeezed my eyes shut against the apology in his eyes, the desperation for me to understand. "Because I didn't want you to love me."

"I know that," I choked.

Nicholas shook his head. "No. You misunderstand. There was a world you hadn't seen. I always pictured you charming away a duke and living in a home like Rosewood—you loved it so much. I knew if you loved me it would be far too easy to love you, and that wouldn't be fair. You deserved so much more than me. You still do."

My head was shaking. I couldn't believe the things I was hearing. I couldn't speak. Nicholas stared down at me, and I thought my heart would burst. He was so close. This needed to stop. How vastly inappropriate the entire situation was. My head fought to clear itself, but Nicholas had a way of banishing any rational thought from my mind.

"I need to leave," I said abruptly. I sniffed, looking down and stepping back. Nicholas's hand fell from my cheek. I tried to appear firm and strong, but inside I was weaker than I had ever been. "Perhaps we may speak tomorrow, in the light of day, and under much more proper circumstances after we have both had a plentiful rest."

Farther away, Nicholas's face was lost in shadow, but I saw his head nod. "Allow me to walk you back."

"We may be seen," I said.

"We won't be seen."

Quiet and slow, he stepped toward me and extended his arm. I swallowed, wrapping my hand around his elbow. My fingers were stiff and cold, but I forced them not to shake, which I was quite proud of. Nicholas's arm pressed against mine, and I felt every movement, memorized every step of his boots, as we walked the short distance through the dark to the back door of the house. Just being near Nicholas had my heart racing. The silence between us was tangible, and the tension was excruciating. My insides jumped and spun, catching fire and making my breath catch. After we had been walking for several seconds, I dared to glance up at him.

His eyes met mine and hovered there in the dark.

I looked away.

Finally we stopped near the set of bushes that marked the back entrance. I took a step away from him. It was brighter here, closer to the house. The candlelight from within stretched out the windows and down to where we stood. Nicholas's features were dim, but I could see them.

"Good night," I said in a quiet voice.

He watched me, eyes fixed on mine. He was silent.

"Good night," I repeated, taking a step toward the door.

His expression reflected a battle of some sort, torn over a certain decision.

Before I could question what that look meant, he filled the small space between us with two steps. "Nicholas—" I started, heart pounding. He held my upper arms, keeping me still, stopping my words. And then he bent his head down to mine and kissed me.

My lips parted in a gasp, and he kissed me again, deeply, slowly. My heart ached. I couldn't think—I could only feel as his fingers threaded in my hair and his lips moved over mine. He held my face between his hands, holding me as if I were fragile but kissing me as if I were not. His lips moved to the corner of my mouth, to my cheek, and I whispered for him to stop.

He moved back fast, dropping his hands from my face and hair. His breath came as quickly as mine did, visible in the cold air. I stared at him, my eyes wide. His cheeks were flushed.

"Why did you do that?" My voice was a weak whisper.

He hesitated before giving a half smile, barely visible in the dimness. "You've been stealing my breath for as long as I can remember, Lucy. It was far past time I stole yours."

I wanted to kiss him again, to let him steal my breath as much as he wanted. The flush had begun to fade from his cheeks and his smile was growing. Had I really just been kissed by that smile? A great knot of regret and dread tried to form in my stomach, but the fluttering joy and amazement untethered it. Without saying another word, Nicholas walked away from me.

He simply walked away.

I watched his back until I couldn't see him anymore. Then I leaned against the side of the building, willing my heart to slow and my legs to quit their shaking. I pressed my hand to my chest and waited for my emotions to realign. I brought my fingers to my lips in shock. It didn't feel real. Surely nothing so perfect could be real.

I didn't know what to believe—what was true and what was false about this evening, but I knew one thing for certain. That kiss had most definitely been breathtaking.

I had begun to doubt the wisdom of sneaking over to the Bancrofts' home and discovering the mysteries inside. In fact, I fully intended to hide in my room for the rest of my life rather than risk seeing Nicholas again. My cheeks burned with every thought of the previous night. And there had been many.

Kitty knew something was different. At breakfast she had stared at me with an inquisitive eyebrow, and I had avoided her gaze. I was busy watching out the window, hoping and also dreading that Nicholas would walk past and see me. I didn't know what to think. I only knew I needed to distance myself from him in order to gather my thoughts.

After sitting in my room for several hours, I decided to make a trip to the village. My solitude was driving me mad, and I missed perusing the millinery and admiring all the bright colors. Mr. Connor had always entertained me for hours within his shop, and I missed those days desperately. It felt like I had been away from Craster for months rather than weeks. The more I thought about it, the more things I found to love about the place I had taken for granted. It was my home. Dover was only my escape. It would likely be several days before I received word from my family. I missed them.

Without waiting for a companion, I took the walk to the village alone. It was only a short distance from Rosewood, and the crisp air was precisely what I needed to clear my mind. I played Nicholas's words over and over in my head, trying to make sense of them. He had told me that he regretted his harshness toward me. Then he had said that he had only spoken those things because he didn't want me to love him. He thought I deserved more. My heart picked up speed as I recalled everything with clarity. What had that kiss meant to him? Was he saying goodbye? Was he confessing his love? Was he taunting me? I squeezed my eyes shut to stop my thoughts. I needed to speak to him but I was afraid. There was too much between us now. Too many raw and real things. He had begged for my forgiveness.

I started at the millinery, pausing to admire the beautiful hats and ribbons that I had always loved. The shelves here were even taller, packed tightly with different fashions and colors.

After spending several minutes surveying the shelves in the millinery, I exited the door. I was met with a breeze that smelled of scones, and I was reminded of the times Kitty and I would come here with Aunt Edith for scones in the bakery. They had a delightful assortment of miniature pies as well. My favorite had been the blackberry. My mouth watered at the scents that carried to my nose on the wind. Although I didn't have money, I was quite certain that smells were free of charge. Stepping closer to the door of the bakery across the street, I held my bonnet to my head with one hand to keep it from tumbling in the breeze. I inhaled deeply.

"May we please have a pie today? Please?" A tiny voice sounded from beside me. I looked down to where a young boy with blond curls tugged on my skirts. His companion was a slightly taller boy with dark hair and freckles.

"Charles!" the second boy warned, staring up at me with wide eyes.

The blond boy looked at me in alarm, pulling his hand back. His round cheeks turned a bit rosier. "I'm sorry . . . lady. I thought you were my sister." He grinned, giggling to himself. The taller boy rolled his eyes before erupting in giggles as well.

I smiled down at them. "Not to worry. I would very much like to be your sister. I don't have any brothers of my own." I winked.

They exchanged a look, grinning without reservation.

"What are your names? Perhaps I may help you find your real sister."

The blond boy looked up at me, stretching on the tips of his toes. His eyes were blue and sparking with mischief. "My name is Charles. And that is my brother, Peter."

Peter grinned. He had two rather large front teeth that had likely just grown in. "We always run to the bakery when we come to the village. Annette knows we will be here."

"Is Annette your sister?" I asked.

They nodded in unison. My smile grew as I looked down at them. I had always wanted brothers. This Annette was a fortunate girl.

"There she is!" Charles pointed a finger behind me. I whirled around, offering a wave to the woman that approached us. She appeared to be close in age to me, with light brown hair and a pale blue dress. She carried another tiny boy on her hip, this one likely only just learning to walk. As she rushed toward us, the toddler squealed and tugged on her hair. She smiled, huffing out an exasperated breath. "Boys, please do not run off again!" She shook her head as they giggled, stepping around me and taking their places by her side.

"They are very charming boys," I said through a laugh. "I was mistaken for you just moments ago."

She laughed, covering her mouth with her free hand. "I hope they did not cause you trouble."

I shook my head. "Not at all." My eyes swept over her again. She was dressed simply but elegantly. Her face was marked with freckles and her green eyes sparked with life and joy. Her arm holding the young child was strung with bags. "You seem to have your hands quite full," I said. "I am happy to help you carry your purchases to your destination. I have nothing else to occupy my time, and your brothers are very agreeable."

She looked as if she wanted to refuse me, but seemed to change her mind, her face melting in gratitude. "Oh, I cannot thank you enough. What is your name?" She shifted her arm and I took the bags and hung them over my own arm.

"Lucy Abbot. I understand your name is Annette?" I grinned as Charles stared up at me. His tiny hand wrapped tentatively around mine. Peter giggled beside him.

"Yes, Annette Kellaway." She brushed the hair from her eyes and laughed. "And this is my son, Philip."

We started walking in the opposite direction, away from Rosewood. "May I ask where you live?" I asked.

"Willowbourne. It isn't far from here." Her voice was casual, but my eyes widened in surprise. This was the mistress of Willowbourne? It was the largest estate in Dover, perhaps even the entire county of Kent. It was beautiful. Yet here she was with her arms full, living the role of middle class mother.

"You cannot be serious! Willowbourne?"

She gave a shy smile. "My husband inherited the estate from an uncle. Where do you live? I don't believe I have seen you in town before."

"I am visiting my uncle and cousin at Rosewood." My smile felt heavy as I left out the *aunt* part.

"Rosewood is a beautiful place. I have only seen it once from the outside." She wiped little Philip's chin and turned her smile to me. I couldn't help but smile back. Charles had begun walking faster, pulling me along beside him. "How long will you be in Dover?"

I puzzled over what I should say. The journey back to Craster sounded terrible after the trouble I had undertaken to arrive here. But I missed my family so much my heart ached. I couldn't bear the thought of living under such a bitter, gray sky and wet winds. The air here was dry and crisp—rejuvenating. And the sky was blue.

"I am still deciding," I said in a soft voice. "Do your brothers occupy your home as well?"

She nodded. "Yes. My mother and father passed away when Charles was just an infant. I have cared for them ever since. We lived with my aunt in Maidstone before I met Owen—er—my husband, Dr. Kellaway. We have been married two years." She eyed her brothers. "The boys are happier now, and much more well behaved. I have never been more happy." Her smile grew with content, her green eyes shining with joy.

I couldn't help but smile. "What a wonderful improvement your life has been given. I am certain you deserve every happiness." My shoulders dropped a little as I thought about that very word. *Happiness.*

Annette tilted her head, studying my face. "What is troubling you? I may be speaking too freely, but I want to help you in any way I can. You have been very kind to me."

We made a left turn and my eyes widened at the bright golden stone of Willowbourne in the distance. It had dozens of windows, immaculate grounds, and a pond in the center of the front lawn, reflecting with brilliance under the sun. The trees surrounding the property were turning color—soft orange and vibrant yellow. I nearly forgot what Annette had asked me.

"There are many things troubling me," I said, smiling to lighten my words. "But I do not know how you can help me." I shrugged.

"You may start by speaking to me. Perhaps together we can create a solution." Charles released my hand and tapped Peter on the shoulder. Together they ran ahead, laughing as they raced to the property of Willowbourne.

She narrowed her eyes at me. "May I venture a guess? It involves a man, does it not?"

I threw her a look of surprise. "How did you know?"

"I can see it in your face." She snorted back another laugh. "Please enlighten me."

For an odd reason, I felt that I could trust her. I was not one to take down barriers with near strangers, but Annette and I felt like kindred spirits already. So I told her about Nicholas (omitting the details of the previous night), and about the secrets of Rosewood. She listened until we reached the doors of Willowbourne, and we waited on the steps as I told her the last part that had been weighing on my mind.

Annette hadn't spoken a word for several minutes—she had simply listened. Finally she said, "I know it is difficult to forget the past, but believe me when I say that there is nothing more freeing. I would not have married Owen had I not given up the things that no longer mattered, ideas that I was too stubborn to release. I cannot imagine the regret I would feel."

There it was again. *Regret.* "I want to show him that I still care for him, but I'm too afraid. And he is still hiding something from me. I cannot continue being lied to. He has vowed to not follow the path of his previous choices, but his mother's health is steadily declining. He cannot afford to help her, and nor can I. Never have I felt more helpless." I took a deep breath.

Annette's eyes grew wider. "My husband is a physician! He wished to continue his occupation as a doctor, and so he has." Her face lit up when she spoke of him, and her lips twisted in a smile. "He will attend to your Nicholas's mother. I assure you, it will be of no charge to his family."

I stared at her, emotion clawing at my throat. My eyes stung. "That is too much."

Annette smiled, shaking her head. "He will make his first visit on Thursday."

In two days. There were no words I could say to thank her for such a generous gift. I was buoyed up with hope so strong it made breathing difficult. I threw my arms around her, nearly knocking poor Philip out of her arms with the bags I held. "Sorry! So sorry." I wiped my nose and laughed, and Annette joined me.

We stepped inside the estate and I was even more amazed by the interior. Spacious and elegant, the walls were draped with elaborate curtains and flawless paintings. From around the corner, I heard footfalls echoing fast against the marble floors. A man stepped into sight, his smile wide and inviting. He had deep blond hair and striking blue eyes, and there was a twinge of mischief in his smile to match the boys. He stepped toward Annette and scooped Philip from her arms, making him giggle. Bending down, he kissed Annette, making her blush and glance at me apologetically. "Owen!" She gasped, swatting him on the arm. He chuckled.

Annette introduced me to her husband, and he assured me that he would be happy to assist Nicholas's mother. My heart swelled with gratitude. "Please do not tell Nicholas that I was at all involved in your generosity."

Dr. Kellaway tilted his head with a frown. "Why not?"

"Just please . . . do not mention my name. I would prefer that he consider it a miracle. Men like Nicholas are in need of a miracle."

He grinned. "Very well."

After visiting with them for several minutes, I offered my thanks as profusely as I could manage and excused myself. As I walked down the front path, I glanced back. Peter and Charles waved at me from the largest window before dipping their heads and hiding from my view. Before I reached the end of the property, I caught sight of both boys running toward me on the lawn. They each held a bright yellow flower in their hands.

"Owen said—Owen said that ladies like flowers. And gentlemen give them flowers." Charles beamed up at me and extended his gift. Peter did the same.

I pressed my hand to my heart in delight. "Indeed, I adore flowers, thank you!"

They laughed, both sets of their cheeks blooming in pink. Then they turned and ran the other way, whispering indiscriminate words to one another as they went.

When Rosewood came into view again after nearly an hour of walking, I hesitated. The Bancrofts' home was there too, tempting me with its secrets. The line of trees, the picket fence—it tugged me closer with curiosity.

Pulling my cloak over my head, I ducked behind the nearest tree and stared up at the tall windows of the house. I had been unable to forget the pot that had nearly landed on my head from above. The picture was vivid in my mind, and it choked me with fear. I wanted to turn back toward Rosewood, but my feet carried me closer to the house without my permission.

I didn't know whether or not Nicholas was home. I chewed my lip as I drew closer to the house. There were several things I could do. If I knocked on the door, then perhaps Mrs. Bancroft or Julia would answer before Nicholas could stop them. Perhaps then I could question them and discover the information I sought.

Deciding that this was my best option, I gathered my courage and walked up the steps. The door was large and intimidating. I swallowed hard and wrung my hands together. With a final deep breath, I struck my knuckles against the door three times. Leaning closer to the door, I strained my ears to hear any sounds from within the house. I froze. A shuffling was coming closer. My heart pounded in my ears. My feet threatened to run me away before I could see what was on the other side of the door.

Before I could move, the door eased open a crack. I looked straight ahead, holding my breath. There was nothing, just an empty house. No face. No arm holding open the door. But then my gaze traveled downward. I gasped. A small boy, likely no older than five, stood scowling up at me. His hair was a fierce red, his eyes wide and blue.

I only saw him for a moment before a slender forearm crossed his chest and hooked under his arms, pulling him backward into the dim house. I stumbled forward, pushing the door open wider.

I brought my hand to my mouth in alarm. Mrs. Bancroft was holding the boy against her to keep him from running out the doorway of the wide sitting room straight ahead of me. *Mrs. Bancroft.*

I had forgotten how beautiful she was, made to be a haunting beauty by the effects of her illness. Her hair was black and her eyes were an intense blue, glazed and sharp at the same time. Her hair was plaited neatly but the sleeves of her dress were torn. The child was calm in her arms. Comfortable. I couldn't imagine how.

Fear gripped me with icy fingers as she stared at me. I had seen the same look in her eyes before. She had nearly attacked Rachel and me.

Suddenly her gaze softened, fixed on something in my hand. *Oh, yes.* The flowers the boys had given me. I caught my breath and took a tentative step forward. "Mrs. Bancroft. My name is Lucy Abbot. You may not remember me, but we have met before, long ago." I smiled. Her eyes were still fixed on the flowers in my hand. "Would you like one?" My voice shook.

She didn't move closer, but her head nodded subtly. Taking it as an invitation, I proceeded into the house, crossing the entryway. She pulled the boy behind her as I approached, hiding him behind her full skirts. Her slim hand reached for the flowers, quaking as if the movement were strenuous. Her fingernails were cut short. I breathed a sigh of relief. At least she could not scratch me.

"What are you doing here?" A faint voice made Mrs. Bancroft draw her hand back.

My head jerked toward the sound. "Julia?" Nicholas's sister stood several feet behind me. She had likely just entered through the open door. Although it had been years since I had seen her, I recognized her immediately. She looked much like her mother, but with straight blonde hair instead of black. She was much taller, older now, and carried herself with confidence that the nine-year-old version of herself never had. When she saw me, her face lit up with recognition but quickly transformed to fear.

"You must go." Her eyes flashed to her mother and the tiny freckled hand that gripped her skirts from behind.

"Why?"

Julia grasped my arm firmly and wrenched me away from the doorway. "You cannot be here." She pulled me out the front door of the house. "I am sorry." Her eyes were weary and her shoulders were burdened as she retreated back inside the house and closed the door behind her.

I stared ahead in shock, unable to believe what I had just seen. My arm stung from where Julia had gripped it. My mind raced with so many questions I could hardly grasp onto just one. Who was that boy? And why had Nicholas failed to mention him? I remembered when the pot had fallen from the window, nearly hitting me and Nicholas where we sat below. *He doesn't know how to behave.* Nicholas had said those words and then corrected the *he.* But I had heard it. I had thought the hand I had seen from the window appeared to belong to a child.

There was no hiding from Nicholas now. I needed to find out the truth, no matter how terrifying it would be to see him again.

# SEVENTEEN

itty met me at the door when I arrived back at Rosewood. "Where have you been?" she shrieked. "We have been so very worried." She pulled my cloak off my shoulders and examined me with one raised brow.

I gave her a weak smile. "I'm sorry. I forgot the time." How long had I been gone? It hadn't seemed to be more than an hour or two. The walk back from Willowbourne had been lengthy, but I hadn't noticed—there was much to occupy my thoughts. And my visit to the Bancrofts had been very brief.

"And where were you yesterday evening?" she questioned. Her eyes were accusing and hard.

I stiffened. "When?"

"After dinner. You abandoned poor Mr. Parsons, do you remember?"

"I didn't feel well." I clasped my hands together and raised both my brows to emphasize my words.

"You were with Nicholas yesterday evening. Do not deny it."

My jaw dropped. How did she know?

"I am concerned for you, Lucy. Have you thought of your reputation? There are neighbors nearby . . . they might see you if you continue sneaking away with Nicholas." Her voice fell to a whisper. "My aunt saw you from the window."

My cheeks warmed and my heart thudded. "What did she see?" I whispered.

"Much." Kitty frowned. "I am sorry, but I was forced to tell her the truth about Nicholas's marriage. She was furious at the thought of him taking advantage of you, him being a married man with no intentions or capability to marry you. After she learned the truth, she was more easily appeased. But what she saw is nothing that she could not easily speak to Nicholas about. My aunt was once caught in a similar situation, yet more improper, years ago, with a man she loved. But he refused to marry her. Her reputation was hurt for quite some time. She has no tolerance for such conduct."

Blood rushed past my ears and flooded my face with heat. My heart pounded with dread. "She cannot force him into marrying me, Kitty. No." I shook my head fast.

Kitty placed her hand on my shoulder. "I begged her to keep silent on the matter. She agreed, but if she sees anything of the sort again, I fear she will not be so compliant. Do not let him tamper with your heart again, Lucy. I know how he has hurt you before."

I nodded, biting back sudden tears. Was that all he was doing? Tampering with my heart so he could break it again? I didn't want to believe it was true, but somehow it was easier than hoping that it wasn't true.

Kitty pulled me into her arms, patting my back like a mother or elder sister. "I know it is difficult. But he is a bad man, Lucy. If he is truly a thief and a scoundrel as you say, and by what my aunt witnessed, then you will be better without him."

I pulled back too fast, taking a step away from her. "He is none of those things, I assure you. Not any longer."

"How can you be certain?"

"I trust him." My voice was firm and resolute.

Kitty breathed out, shallow and slow. Something on the staircase caught my attention. I looked up. Mrs. Tattershall stood over the banister, watching me with a look of disdain. I felt miniscule beneath her narrowed eyes. I quickly backed away from Kitty and excused myself.

Kitty reached out her hand to grasp my wrist. "Where are you going now?"

"To the gardens," I lied.

She nodded, glancing at me with suspicion before letting go of my arm. I avoided the firm gaze of Mrs. Tattershall as I retreated down the maze of hallways and outside once again. My legs shook and my mind spun. How had Mrs. Tattershall seen us? I couldn't imagine the horror of Nicholas receiving a visit from Mrs. Tattershall and then finding me and offering his hopes of marrying me. How could I believe them to be genuine if they were induced by Mrs. Tattershall? The thought sent a pit of despair to rest in my stomach. I put my face in my hands and tried to breathe before colliding into something solid.

I screeched, pulling my hands away from my face to catch myself. I tripped backward on my dress before a hand caught my elbow. "Nicholas!" My face burned and my eyes flicked to the upper windows where Mrs. Tattershall had just been. I jerked my arm away and jumped back a step. He looked at me in bewilderment and amusement.

"What are you doing?" I looked around frantically.

"I might ask you that question. You are the one that just collided with me." His brown eyes brimmed with laughter.

"Follow me, but keep yourself at a distance." I spoke to him without looking at his face. I marched toward the gardens on the west side of the property. At least now my words to Kitty would be honest.

He laughed, low and charming, and my arms burst with gooseflesh. My palms were wet with perspiration. I didn't want to acknowledge what had passed between us the previous day. I wiped my forehead and huffed a breath. Nicholas followed behind me, chuckling to himself. I ignored him.

When I reached the gardens I didn't pause to admire the flowers and neatly trimmed bushes. Instead I sat on a solitary stone bench, crossed my hands in my lap, and waited for Nicholas to arrive. He peeked his head around a tall bush with raised brows. I scolded myself for finding the look so endearing and handsome.

"What is this charade?" Nicholas asked through a laugh.

As much as I begged them not to, my cheeks warmed. "I mustn't be seen with you."

He crossed his arms over his broad chest. His shoulders strained against the fabric of his jacket. I looked away fast.

"If you mustn't be seen with me, why did you lead me into the gardens? You might have abandoned me after you walked blindly into my chest." There was a teasing glint in his eyes.

"I am sorry. But I needed to speak with you."

His smile softened and he moved toward my bench to sit down. He leaned forward on his elbows, watching his boots before looking back to my face. There was a smile in his eyes—it always seemed to be there when he looked at me. The smile grew as he studied my face. I couldn't help my curiosity. "What?"

Nicholas looked down, laughing. "I'm thinking."

"What, pray tell, are you thinking about?"

He dropped his head with a laugh. "If you think you are entitled to my thoughts, think again."

"Well, I will tell you what I am thinking." I glanced in all directions. "We cannot continue these . . . secret meetings."

"This is not a secret meeting."

"I'm afraid it is. A coincidental one, but still a secret meeting all the same."

Nicholas's grin stretched wider, and I could see the weight in his eyes lessening. I wondered how heavily the situation of his family troubled his mind at night. I wondered if he ever slept. He stole my hand from my lap, studying my fingers casually. Then his eyes met mine again. "Do you still wish to know what I am thinking?"

I searched his eyes. There were too many mysteries there—too many scattered pieces of my heart shining back at me. He would tear them up and toss them away where I would never find them. I wanted to snatch my heart away from him but I didn't know how. All I knew was that it was far too dangerous where it was now.

"No," I answered in a quick voice.

He raised one brow and that crease appeared above it, just as it always had. "I would imagine that most women enjoy hearing how beautiful they are." His smile grew shy and uncertain.

I felt my cheeks redden. Ever since he kissed me, my control over my emotions was unsteady and unreliable. My eyes flicked to the windows again, but I couldn't see inside. There was no way to know who was watching.

I moved my eyes away, avoiding his gaze, but could feel it burning on the side of my face. "It is simply not proper that we be alone together without a chaperone. I have been raised to be strict with the rules of society. The . . ." I searched my mind for the right word, ". . . events of yesterday should not have happened." My voice was hushed, as if we could be overheard at any moment.

Nicholas shifted on the bench. I could tell he was closer, but I refused to look. Unable to accept that fact, Nicholas touched my cheek, turning my face toward his. My face tingled under his touch and I squeezed my eyes shut. "Lucy, look at me. Please."

My heart jumped with panic as I opened my eyes. He was so close. I could see the streaks of gold in his eyes, every lash and every crease at the corners. I could feel his grip on my heart like a palpable thing, unyielding and constant. "Kissing you was beyond my bounds."

I nodded in such a small movement I doubted he saw it.

He gazed at me with firmness to emphasize his words. "But I do not regret it. What must I do to prove to you that I am worthy of your trust?"

"Tell me who dropped the pot from the window," I whispered.

His brow furrowed and he fell silent.

I pulled myself away from him, gaining strength from an unknown source. "You see, you will not say it!" I shook my head and stood in one swift motion. "You should not say you feel the things you feel for me and yet deny me of the truth. You should not say you deserve trust yet keep secrets. You should not have kissed me," I choked.

My eyes stung but I held back my tears. I would not tell him about Mrs. Tattershall and the things she had seen. I would not tell him how afraid I was of him—how afraid I was that he would change his mind and crumple my heart like he had the first time. I took a deep breath. "My feelings have changed since I was a child. I do not love you like I once did." The lie ached in my throat, robbing me of air.

Nicholas looked like he had been physically struck, vulnerable and broken. He stood, but I was already moving away. I had forgotten the things I came here to say to him. I needed to leave before we were seen by the Rossingtons again and things became worse than they already were.

When I burst through the door of the house, I spied Mrs. Tattershall and Mr. Rossington at the end of the hall that led to the drawing room, leaning on the windowpane, speaking in hushed tones. My stomach dropped with dread. It was the window overlooking the gardens. They had seen Nicholas and me in the gardens.

In one swift motion, I turned around and rushed up the stairs to my bedchamber. I shut the door behind me and squeezed my eyes closed. Why had I been so foolish? I should have run away the moment I saw Nicholas today.

If Mrs. Tattershall approached Nicholas about the two encounters she had witnessed, then he would surely propose or never speak to me again. She had seen us alone in the dark the night before. But he was not titled or wealthy, so why should she push him to marry me? It was not in my best interest.

But I also had an inkling that she did not particularly like me, so perhaps she would try to force the engagement anyway. Nicholas had told me how he felt, but no matter how much he spoke of his own feelings for me, I simply couldn't believe him. His words to me in his garden years ago were instilled on my heart, and I couldn't erase them. How could he be happy with me? Surely his judgment was weak. If he was going to propose to me, then I didn't want it to be influenced by anyone. I wanted him to truly mean it. How could I know it was genuine if Mrs. Tattershall spoke with him first? I did not want Mrs. Tattershall telling him to marry me if he did not truly desire it himself. One day he would regret choosing me and I would be hurt all over again.

I leaned heavily against the wall. How could I prevent it? To start I would need to avoid Nicholas as to not give Mrs. Tattershall any further reason to speak with him. A pinching started in my chest but I stopped it. There was no need to despair over Nicholas. I had other prospects, including Mr. Parsons. The thought sickened me.

But I had many other things to occupy my thoughts, like the mystery of the dispute between the Bancrofts and Rossingtons. Indeed, I would hardly miss Nicholas at all.

My body told me I was exhausted, but my mind would not relax no matter how hard I tried. To distract myself, I wrote a letter to my family.

*Dearest Mama and Papa,*

*Adequate time has not yet passed for me to receive word from you, and although I am not quite certain I deserve it, I must tell you that I love you and miss you. Rosewood is not the same place I remember. While it is fascinating and beautiful, it is also a place of secrets. Much has changed. I have enjoyed seeing Kitty again. Nicholas Bancroft is here as well, and*

My quill stopped moving. After several minutes, I crumpled my note in my palm and threw it away. My parents would accuse me of being a fool for chasing after Nicholas again. They knew how hurt I had been. I could not tell them of my renewed attachment to him. Nor could I tell Kitty, Mrs. Tattershall, or anyone for that matter.

It seemed I had a secret of my own.

I was beginning to realize that I was often wrong. Very wrong. It had been two days since I had last seen Nicholas, and I missed him much more than I ever had. More than any summer I had departed from Rosewood. Even after months of being away I never missed him *this* much. Sitting on my bed, I leaned toward the window and watched the Bancrofts' house. My vantage point faced the front path perfectly.

I had been performing quite well in my efforts to avoid Nicholas, but it was making me anxious. Without him, there was no one to speak to that didn't make me want to run across the country to my home in Craster.

Kitty was suspicion personified in every glance she cast my way. We talked and laughed over old memories, but it had been so long since we had been together that we had grown apart. We disagreed on much now that we were older and had experienced our own separate lives. It broke my heart a little. William was sweet, always lending an ear to my prattle when I was lonely. He didn't speak much, but he listened.

I hadn't been able to stop thinking about the little red-haired boy I had seen at the Bancroft's home. I didn't share the details with anyone. The only person I knew that could explain was Nicholas, and I couldn't allow myself to see him.

Mr. Rossington was disturbingly unreserved in his attentions toward me. He rarely spoke to me, but rather fixed me with prolonged stares and wide, unsettling smiles. Mrs. Tattershall frowned at me all hours of the day, whispering things to her brother when I turned my back.

But I knew they were speaking of what they had seen out the window.

My nerves were constantly in motion, waiting for the moment Mrs. Tattershall would turn to me and announce that she had taken measures to preserve my reputation, but not by keeping quiet about what she had seen, no—she carried every trait of an incurable gossip. She would preserve my reputation by telling Nicholas to marry me instead.

My longing for Nicholas was growing every hour that I was apart from him. I missed him. I hated myself for it, but I couldn't lie to myself. But then I remembered that he hadn't come to visit me either. If he did care for me as he said, would he not try to find me? It was my fault. I was too harsh the last time I had seen him. I had accused him of lying and keeping secrets, but *I* had lied about my feelings for him. All this time I had been holding his words to me six years ago against him . . . but hadn't I just done the same thing to him? Spoken the same words? I was a hypocrite. A cruel hypocrite.

Leaning my forehead against the cold window, I breathed, watching my breath create a film of fog on the glass. My skull throbbed with a headache.

When my eyes opened, I sat up straight. Out the window I could see someone approaching the Bancrofts' door. I squinted. Dr. Kellaway walked with long strides, carrying a leather case. I scrambled to my feet, leaning both hands on the window to get a closer look. It was certainly him.

My eyes widened as Dr. Kellaway moved up the path and knocked on the door. I held my breath. How would Mrs. Bancroft react if she opened the door to another stranger? To my relief, the door swung open and Nicholas stepped outside. My heart raced as I watched their muted conversation. I was too far to read their lips, but I saw Nicholas step back and run a hand over his hair. Dr. Kellaway smiled, and Nicholas gripped his arm and slapped him on the shoulder in gratitude. He dropped his head and smiled in disbelief.

Suddenly, Nicholas's gaze moved toward the window I was peering out of. I screeched and ducked my head, spying with just my eyes above the windowsill.

Nicholas was shaking his head in disbelief, rubbing the side of his face. His expression was distorted with emotion as he invited Dr. Kellaway inside and closed the door.

A knock at the door to my room made me jump. I cleared my throat and stood, turning away from the window. "Yes?"

Kitty's head appeared behind the door. "Mr. Parsons is here." Her smile grew to a wicked grin.

"Kitty!" She was already retreating out the door. I rushed forward and threw it open. She grinned at me from the hallway. I scowled. "Why is he here?"

"To see you, of course." She winked before bursting into giggles, stifling it behind her hand. "He wishes to see you in the drawing room immediately. He seemed quite determined."

I felt the color drain from my face. "For what purpose is he here?" I repeated.

Kitty swatted her hand through the air. "Oh, calm yourself. There is a handsome, highly eligible man in the drawing room that wishes to see you."

"And why does that give me reason to be calm? It is quite the contrary. I don't wish to see him! Tell him I'm unwell."

She rolled her eyes and straightened the lace at the cuffs of her sleeves. "You must come down, Lucy." There was no room for argument in the look she cast my way.

I breathed an exasperated sigh. "Very well."

Kitty clapped her hands and reached for my wrist. I might have turned around if not for Kitty's unrelenting grasp. With her free hand she smoothed my curls and tugged the fabric of my dress down, forcing the neckline to scoop lower.

"Kitty!" I jerked it up again, throwing her a look of dismay.

"We must entice him to marry you in every capacity."

I stopped on the stairs. "Marry me?" I whispered angrily.

She leaned closer, pulling me after her down the staircase. "You cannot continue to pine after Nicholas Bancroft. It is time you claim what is directly before you. Mr. Parsons is smitten by you. Do you realize what this means?"

I shook my head, hoping to drown out her words. "I don't want to marry Mr. Parsons."

"Lucy, my aunt has not spoken to Nicholas. You need not rely on securing a marriage with him."

"I am not relying on him!" My voice was too defensive.

Kitty planted her hand on her hip, cocking her eyebrow. "You have wanted to marry him since you were twelve years old."

I couldn't lie to her. She knew me too well. There wasn't a time I could remember that I didn't dream of marrying Nicholas. Until now. How could I marry him now? I told him I didn't love him. My head spun with a rush of pain and regret, tingling out to the tips of my fingers.

*My last pearl rolled across my hand, settling in the crease between my fingers and palm. I had already used the other four. The wishes I had already made collected in my mind: That Nicholas will never forget me. That I could see him again, but only so he could apologize. Then I had wished that he would never fall in love with anyone else. That he would dance with me when I was all grown up.*

*I thought I would have forgotten Nicholas by now, but it had been a year and I still thought of him every night as I fell asleep. I replayed his last words to me in my head, over and over. I traced the moments he spent with me in my memory, searching for the most wonderful things about him to remind myself that he was good. That loving him was not foolish. There were far more things about Nicholas to love than there were to hate.*

*We were not going to Rosewood this summer. Mama had told me that this morning. I had suspected as much, but I had been obedient and good, sensible and patient all year. No matter how good a daughter I was, my parents' minds could not be altered. Aunt Edith had died in the winter, and Mama did not wish to go back.*

*I stared at the fireplace and let my last pearl roll over my hand again. I was much too old to believe in such ridiculous things as a wishbox and magical pearls, but here I stood.*

*How had I wasted so many dreams on Nicholas? Even acknowledging that I was a fool didn't stop me from being foolish. I was foolish and fully aware of the fact. Closing my eyes, I made another wish—that one day I could marry Nicholas. I whispered it as I threw the pearl into the flames.*

I balanced on the staircase and looked down at the door to the drawing room. Kitty was speaking.

"What?" I blinked.

"I will wait here." She smiled but it only unsettled me further.

Commanding my legs to stop shaking, I descended the stairs and paused at the drawing room door. I planned to fully explain my intentions to Mr. Parsons. I did not have any interest in courting him at all. Kitty nodded with encouragement as I stepped inside the room.

Mr. Parsons clamped his book shut in his hand and stood, straightening his shoulders and fixing me with a look of admiration. I stared at him. There was something false about the expression on his face—the admiration seemed forced compared to the way Nicholas had sometimes looked at me. Before I could puzzle over his expression further, Mr. Parsons moved across the room until he stood directly in front of me. He held a bundle of roses in one hand, the crimson red and tightly wound buds far from blooming. I didn't take another step. I didn't make a sound.

"Miss Abbot, what a pleasure it is to see you." He took my hand and kissed the top of it, prolonged and firm. I tried not to visibly cringe at the wet mark he left on my hand as he pulled away. When he straightened his posture again, he turned my hand over and placed the roses there, smiling down at me, just a twinge of his lips and a tip of his head.

"Oh—er—thank you, Mr. Parsons. The roses are lovely." When he looked heavenward with another smile, I wiped the top of my hand off on my skirts.

"You need not thank me. A gentleman cannot help but give roses to the woman that so easily steals his heart." His blue eyes tilted down to look at my face, and his stare was so intent and penetrating that I cleared my throat as loud as I could manage.

"I have no intention of stealing your heart."

His lips pressed together and half his mouth quirked in a grin, making his cheek crease handsomely. "Oh, but I have every intention of stealing yours."

Despite my every effort not to, I felt the unwelcome flooding of heat to my face. "Mr. Parsons—"

"Would you like to join me at a party Saturday evening?" he interrupted. "It is at a residence of a family friend just a few miles up the road at Stanton manor. I believe they have also extended their invitations to the Rossingtons and asked that I extend an invitation to the Bancrofts as well. Particularly Mr. Nicholas Bancroft."

I frowned. Nicholas?

Mr. Parsons must have noticed my confusion, so he added, "They knew Nicholas as a child and insisted that he be in attendance. Please do insist that he accompanies you there." He gave a charming smile.

I nodded to appease him, although I had no intention of seeking Nicholas out to invite him to a party influenced by Mr. Parsons. I had no intention of seeking out Nicholas at all.

"I will see both of you there, then?" His voice was quick and his eyes pulled at my gaze, begging for an affirmation that I couldn't give.

"I will do everything in my capacity to ensure our attendance." I tried to sound polite and convincing, but I could still hear the confusion in my own voice. If Mr. Parsons did indeed have every intention of stealing my heart, why would he be so adamant that Nicholas attend this party with me? Surely he viewed Nicholas as a potential competitor. My brow tightened.

Mr. Parsons touched one of my curls. "I will look forward to our reunion."

I couldn't speak. All I did was nod as he bid his farewell and exited the room. I heard him ushered out by the butler and heard the door close with a firm thud. What a strange encounter. I scowled at the pianoforte for several minutes as I tried to make sense of that man. Kitty eased the door open, breaking my trance.

"Give me every detail," she squealed.

As expected, when I finished relaying the exchange, she slumped in disappointment. "Is that all?"

I hadn't included the bit about Nicholas being strongly encouraged to attend the party, but it was a minor detail. So I nodded. "That is all."

# EIGHTEEN

The interior of Rosewood usually began to bore me a little before noon. So today, I secured my bonnet to my head and slipped outside, enjoying the warm rays of the sun as they spilt through the clouds, trying to forget about my strange encounter with Mr. Parsons that morning. I loved days like this, when the wind was cold but the sun was stronger, cutting through with a happy warmth that reached my soul.

There were many areas of the property that I hadn't explored yet upon my return here. It had only been a few days and I had visited the stables, gardens, and north lawn, but I had yet to venture into the woods behind the lawn—the area I had spent most of my time playing in as a child.

Careful to escape unseen, I approached the trees and entered between the two largest ones. I smiled to myself. This was the place I had always entered, and I was surprised it still stood. Kitty and I pretended that it was a mystical doorway that led to another land. The woods behind Rosewood might as well have been another land. They were drastically different from the neat orderliness that marked the lawns and gardens. They were wild and free.

As I stepped farther into the trees, the sun was shaded from me, and I watched in awe as the dried leaves fluttered with the breeze and tiny pockets of light filtered through the surviving leaves on the trees, creating tiny dots of light on the dirt ground. The image filled me with nostalgia for the many hours I had spent here.

I remembered the exact location of the pond—the one I knew so well for its abundance of toads. I couldn't stop my squeal of excitement when I saw it, in the same place as always, tucked behind a clearing of trees. The water was murky and thick with debris. My mind created an image of a gigantic toad living beneath the water, waiting for its next meal. My arms shivered with cold as I circled the small pond, grinning at the memories that surfaced in my mind.

"What are you smiling about?" A voice from behind made me jump. The perimeter of the pond was slick with mud, and my boot was too close to the edge. My arms flailed at my sides and I fell backward into the pond with a screech. My head submerged for a brief moment before I shot up out of the water, spewing and slapping at the dead leaves that clung to my hair. I was unintentionally floating deeper into the pond. When I gathered my wits, I tried to scramble toward the edge of the water, but my boot was encased in the mud at the floor of the pond. The water reached my waist, but I was drenched from head to toe. I tried to take another step, but my feet were stuck in the mud.

To my dismay, the voice belonged to Nicholas. He stood at the edge of the pond, crouched down with his hands reaching toward me. "I'll pull you out!" His voice brimmed with laughter.

I tried to take another step, staring down into the water. I couldn't see anything.

Oh . . .

I squinted into the murk.

"Nicholas! Pull me out! Pull me out!" I thrashed and splashed in the water, and Nicholas burst into laughter. A large, bumpy toad was swimming straight toward me, with just its eyes poking above the surface.

Nicholas stepped into the water and waded toward me, the water only reaching the middle of his thighs. He wrapped his arm around my waist and leaned toward the edge of the pond, hoisting me out of the mud. He held me against him above the water, one arm tucked under my knees. I could feel his laugh rumbling against me. My eyes squeezed shut with embarrassment before I burst into laughter of my own. I threw my head back, my laughter obnoxious and loud. Nicholas's eyes widened and he laughed so hard that he struggled to breathe. He couldn't walk, so we stood in place in the pond.

When my laughter subsided, I dropped my head against his shoulder without thinking of the dangers of doing so. His arms were strong, and he held me without any apparent effort. Water dripped down my hairline and onto his shirt but he didn't seem to mind at all. I was frozen there, and I could almost hear the steady beat of his heart through his shirt. I laughed softly again to dispel the silence, tipping my smile up to him.

He was looking down at me, his eyes filled with tears from his laughter. His smile was so endearing I had a fleeting thought of kissing him again. It seemed Nicholas had the same thought, for his eyes grew more intent, searching my face and pausing at my lips.

"You may set me down now, Nicholas," I said, laughing again at how I must have appeared flailing backward into the water.

He smiled, but then his jaw tightened before he trudged out of the pond. He set me down on my feet and laughed again. "You have a something in your hair." His hand reached down to my head and pulled a twig out of my soaked curls. He held it in front of my face. I swatted his hand away and gave him a half-hearted glare.

I remembered my visit from Mr. Parsons that morning. "Would you like to attend a party with me Saturday evening? It will be quite the smash I hear." I gave my most cajoling smile.

"Another dinner party?" His voice was pained.

"Nicholas, please, I beg you. You have two days to prepare, and it will be much more tolerable with you there. And only slightly less comfortable." I grinned.

He raised a skeptical brow. I had intentionally omitted the detail that Mr. Parsons had extended the invitation. Surely if Nicholas knew that detail he would not attend.

"Very well. I *am* very charming at parties."

"Not as charming as I am, I'd wager."

He chuckled before shaking his head in disagreement.

"I believe there will also be dancing," I said in a cheerful voice. "You know how I enjoy dancing." I immediately regretted bringing up the night years ago that I had drafted my note to him, when he had danced with me in the morning room when I had been all alone. My heart stung with melancholy.

His eyes met mine, a smile shining through them. "I will only attend if you will save your first dance for me there. You must also save a waltz."

I looked down at my muddy feet, feeling strangely shy. It was easy to be shy when he was looking at me in that way. "Very well, but I cannot promise I will not stomp on your toes."

"But will you stand on my feet?"

I laughed, hiding my face behind my hands. When my laughter subsided, I dropped my arms to my sides. "Did you follow me here?" I asked, raising one eyebrow.

He looked down at his own mud-covered boots. "I needed to tell you something." He lifted his gaze to mine, making my heart jump in my chest. "A man, Dr. Kellaway, has insisted upon making visits to my mother." The corners of his eyes were tight with emotion and gratitude. "He is providing his services without charge."

My eyes widened and I gasped in false surprise. I cringed. When I was attempting to put on an act, I was never very subtle. "You cannot be serious. That is wonderful, Nicholas!"

His smile was genuine and grateful as he nodded. "I asked him how he found us, but he would not say." Nicholas raised a skeptical brow. "Were you involved?"

I eyed him from under my wet, grimy eyelashes. "No, not at all. It sounds quite like a miracle to me. How is your mother faring?" I pretended I hadn't already seen her and the mysterious little boy beside her.

He studied me with suspicion for one more moment before releasing a heavy sigh. "She is comfortable. Not as anxious as she once was. I have seen progress during the warmer months."

I itched to ask him who the little boy was, but I didn't want to argue with Nicholas today. I wanted my time spent with him to feel the way it once had—light and safe and comfortable. "I would very much like to see her."

"Perhaps she will consider receiving visitors soon. She seemed to take well to Dr. Kellaway." His voice sounded hopeful. "But I still lack the money to repay the specialist in London. I don't know how I will come by it. And there is also the innkeeper I must pay for looking after my horse." He rubbed his forehead.

My heart ached for him. "In Craster there is plenty of work for everyone that seeks it. You need not have attended university. My dear friend Charlotte's husband knows many places you could begin to earn wages. Of course, then your family would be here alone . . ." I bit my lip.

Nicholas seemed to be thinking deeply about my words. His eyes locked on mine. "I have thought of that before." His voice was soft.

"What do you mean?"

He gave an audible breath. "The day I met you at the inn . . . I was traveling to Craster."

"Craster?" I choked. "Why?" I wrapped my arms around myself to keep warm as a shiver spread over my entire body.

Nicholas's brows drew together with concern. "We need to get you to a warm place." He offered me his jacket, just as he had the day I fell in the trough in the stables. I wrapped it around my shoulders before changing my mind and handing it back to him. He gave me a confused look.

"I should go alone."

His chest rose and fell with a deep breath. I couldn't look at his eyes any longer. They had already weakened me far more than they ever should have.

"Was this another secret meeting?" He was smiling again—I could hear it in his voice.

"An unintentional one, yes."

"They are becoming a very common occurrence."

I accidentally looked at him. "We must put an end to it before we are discovered." He didn't know that we already had been discovered. My heart beat with dread.

He looked like he was about to say something more, but the words stopped before they escaped, lingering between us like a broken promise.

"I must go. Thank you for saving me from the toad." I forced a smile so he would know that I didn't hate him. Just that I was afraid of him breaking my heart.

His smile was faint compared to the usual smiles he gave me.

With a final glance over my shoulder, I traipsed back to the edge of the woods, cringing at the water that dripped down my legs and puddled in my boots. I squeezed the water from my hair, shaking it onto the grass below as I stepped back onto the lawn. I snorted back another bout of laughter as I imagined Nicholas's face as I fell into the pond. He was my dearest friend. The thought filled me with sorrow. If only I knew if he was genuine, that his feelings for me really had changed. I told myself that I trusted him but maybe I still didn't. Not completely. If I did trust him, then I would let him have my heart; I wouldn't be running away. I wouldn't be so afraid. And now there was an entirely different matter that I hadn't considered before. Nicholas needed money. He could win any lady of fortune with his charm, I was sure of it. I did not possess the wealth he needed for his family. If he married me, it would be selfish of both of us. And if there was anything I knew about Nicholas, it was that he was quite the opposite.

Lost in my thoughts, I opened the door to the house. For the second time today, I jumped, pressing my hand to my chest in surprise. Mrs. Tattershall stood just to the right of the doorway with her arms crossed and her eyes narrowed.

"Good morning," I squeaked. My stomach tightened with panic as I tried to slide past her.

"Where have you been?" Her voice stopped me in my escape attempt. Every muscle in my body stiffened as I met her accusing eyes. I maintained my stance for a short few seconds before melting into a confession.

"I know I should not have been in the woods alone, but I missed the old pond, and then I fell into it, which was not pleasant, and—"

"But you were not alone in the woods."

My heart pounded in my ears. "Indeed, I was."

"Do not lie to me, child." Every feature of her face was sharp. Her cheekbones could shatter glass. "I saw the Bancroft boy follow you." Her stare was unwavering.

I shook my head. "You are mistaken." I couldn't believe that Mrs. Tattershall had seen us again. It was the third time now. I had been so careful. If she had not seen the kiss she might have been more forgiving this time.

Mrs. Tattershall intertwined her fingers, glancing down at them casually. "Perhaps I might take my questions to him."

"No! I mean, no. You must not do that, please."

She leaned her head closer to mine, emphasizing her words through partially clenched teeth. "You are a guest in this house, Lucy Abbot. My brother's hospitality will only stretch so far, and I can assure you that it does not give place for wanton women begging for scandal. One scandal from my brother is quite enough for this house to endure." When she finished speaking she clamped her mouth shut, standing up straight and smoothing her hair. She cleared her throat.

*Scandal?* My thoughts whirled. "I assure you that I will not associate with Nicholas in such circumstances again . . . but I beg you, do not try to compel him to marry me. If he intends to marry me he will propose. He is an honorable man."

Mrs. Tattershall scoffed. "You do not possess the wealth he needs. He is desperate for money; the family always has been. He would never choose to marry a woman without a dowry to speak of. I do not respect a man that toys with hearts he has no intention of keeping." She huffed a breath. "I would very much like to see him suffer at the prospect of marrying you."

Her words struck my chest with the strength of a physical blow. It was true what she said. Nicholas could easily steal the heart of a wealthy heiress. Why had he not done that already? It would have been so easy, swift, and lawful. Instead he had opted to help a group of highwaymen. It didn't make sense. Surely the thought of marrying an heiress had crossed his mind so why had he not done it? If he ever set foot in a London ballroom he would be flocked within seconds.

No matter that he wasn't titled. He was handsome, and men as handsome as Nicholas were not a common occurrence.

"Please do not say a word to him. Please." I begged with my eyes as much as my words.

Mrs. Tattershall hesitated, but shrugged one shoulder. "I cannot give you my promise."

My eyes stung with tears as she turned her back on me and walked back to the sitting room. I shivered again and crossed my arms, standing alone in the vast hallway. With defeat in my steps, I moved down the hall toward the staircase. All I could do was behave as a proper lady, and hope that she took pity on me. Tearing my gaze away, I made my way up the stairs, eager to change my wet clothing and distance myself from Mrs. Tattershall. I put my face in my hands and tried not to think about any of my problems.

Perhaps if I stayed up here the rest of the day, they would disappear.

The day before the party at Stanton manor, I avoided Mr. Rossington and Mrs. Tattershall as much as possible. Mrs. Tattershall's warning still hung in my thoughts, filling me with anxiety and restlessness. At breakfast, she had asked me a question that I didn't hear, and I had failed to give an answer because I was so distracted. After that she had left the house.

Since then, I had been certain she was venturing to the Bancrofts' home to send Nicholas over to me with a proposal. And so I stayed in my bedchamber late into the afternoon.

I wanted to go home. I needed to escape with my heart while I had the chance. Nicholas did not need me here as a distraction, but he needed to find a wealthy heiress to provide for his family's intense needs and his debts, just as Mrs. Tattershall had told me.

Reminiscent of the previous day, a firm knock sounded at my door. I sat upright from where I had been laying on my bed. I fixed my curls and said, "Come in." My voice came out raspy.

It was Kitty at the door again. Her eyes were wide enough that I could see white surrounding each iris. Her hands twitched at her skirts with concern. "Nicholas is here to see you."

Certainly my eyes were wider than hers. "What?" Mr. Parsons yesterday and now Nicholas? "Why is he here?"

She swallowed, shaking her head. "I do not know, but my father will not be particularly delighted at the fact." She hesitated. "Surely you must know why Nicholas is here."

"I don't." My heart hammered against my ribs. I was not prepared to see Nicholas. I had just spent hours preparing myself to avoid seeing him until the party tomorrow evening. A sick feeling of dread dropped in my stomach. Had Mrs. Tattershall spoken to him? Had they come to an agreement?

I stood on shaking legs, moving toward the door. Kitty put her hand out to stop me. "I can tell him you are ill if you wish."

I hesitated. "No. I will go."

Kitty stepped out of my way, pressing herself against the door frame. When I reached the stairs I glanced back at her. She was watching me with a look of worry. I gave her a reassuring smile that I didn't feel, and walked down the staircase. I gripped the banister with both hands and held my breath until I reached the drawing room. The footman welcomed me inside and closed the door behind me. I waited several seconds before turning around.

"Good afternoon, Nicholas," I said, trying to sound more calm than I felt. I moved away from the door. "I thought we agreed to put an end to secret meetings of any sort."

Nicholas stood in front of a red settee, smiling. It was a different smile—a nervous one. The space between us was excruciating and silent, and I heard Nicholas's shaky inhale before he spoke. His dark hair was neat and his eyes were soft.

"This is not secret, so it does not apply to our agreement." He walked toward me before saying, "You are a liar."

I gasped in bewilderment. "I am not."

He was still moving toward me, so I took a step backward, crashing into a round table, capsizing a stack of books. I straightened them, face burning. When I turned around again, Nicholas was directly in front of me, close enough to touch. I had no place to go except straight into the wall behind me, so I stopped moving. I could smell clean soap and leather and fresh parchment on him. I stared straight ahead at the top button of his waistcoat where I didn't have to see his eyes.

"Dr. Kellaway and his wife are recent acquaintances of yours, are they not? You sent them to help my mother."

I choked on a breath and my gaze flew up to his. "How did you know that? I told them not to mention . . ."

He pressed closer to me until I was against the wall, stopping my words. He searched my eyes, as if looking for permission to kiss me again. I was weak all over. My heart pounded. I couldn't manage to bring a refusal to my eyes. So he bent his head down, brushing his lips first over my cheek. I couldn't breathe. Without consulting me, my hand reached up, sliding over his chest and to his neck, pulling him down closer to me. He drew a breath and moved his kiss to my lips, slow and gentle, achingly tender. I touched his cheek, his hair, and Nicholas pressed me closer to the wall. He whispered my name against my lips.

Then he whispered something else.

I pushed hard against his chest, making him stumble back a step. My heart thudded. "What did you say?" I choked.

"I love you." Only now could I see that his eyes were wet with tears, vulnerable with emotion. "I said I love you." His voice was hoarse. "I always have, Lucy. Even if I did not realize it before."

"What do you mean?" I couldn't believe his words. My heart ached with longing and hope, but I pushed it away.

He raked a hand over his hair before filling the step between us again, touching my cheek. "It means that I wish to marry you. If you will have me."

I was shaking, fighting the lump that rose quickly in my throat, tightening it with tears. I closed my eyes, warding off the desperation to say yes. "Mrs. Tattershall sent you." With my words came my tears, flowing out onto Nicholas's fingers on my cheek. "She saw us t-together multiple times, and sh-she told me she would pressure you into m-marrying me. But it isn't fair."

"She did not." He bent down to look closer in my eyes. "She did not send me. She has not spoken to me at all."

I shook my head. "I wish it were true."

"It is true!" His golden brown eyes locked on mine. "I would not lie to you, Lucy. And even if Mrs. Tattershall had spoken to me, it wouldn't change that I love you and wish to marry you. Since the day I called you Mrs. Bancroft I had longed for a chance to call you that and have it be real." His voice cracked. "Please trust me."

I couldn't speak or breathe. "You would not lie to me? Keeping silent can also be a lie, Nicholas. Why should I believe that you love me if you will not tell me everything? Why should I trust you if you do not trust me with your secrets?" I drew a breath but it came out as a shudder. "You do not wish to marry me. It would be foolish. Your family needs the money a wealthy heiress could provide you in a marriage." I was proud of how strong my voice sounded, how unwavering. "You must think of your mother and Julia."

His brow tightened with emotion and he reached for me, but I slid away from the warmth of him, crossing the room where I could see him more fully. He didn't approach this time. I wiped the remaining moisture from my cheeks and crossed my arms. Silence hung in the air between us for a long moment.

And then Nicholas's expression hardened, masking the hurt and rejection that had burned there on his face before. His voice was quick. "The day I met you at the inn I was traveling to Craster. I was on what I knew to be my last assignment from the highwaymen, and I planned to leave the next night without their knowledge. I was lost—angry—and the only person I thought could help me was you. And I knew that Craster would provide me with an opportunity to work." He watched the ground as he spoke, but then he met my eyes.

"But above all, I needed to find you. I needed to apologize and I needed to see how you had grown—if you were still short and little, and how beautiful you had become in my absence. After that I knew I would somehow have the strength to return here to my family and face my burdens again."

My shoulders shook with quiet sobs and I covered my mouth with one hand. He took one step closer to me, but changed his mind, standing several feet away. His face was serious, determined, and full of hurt. "That is my first secret. The other secret is not entirely mine. As you know, my mother has been ill for several years. What is not commonly known is how the illness of her mind intensified when my father died, showing itself through her grief and sorrow, eating away her emotions until she couldn't feel anymore. In her unfit state, Mr. Rossington, the boor that he is, took advantage of her."

Nicholas's jaw tightened and he crossed his arms. I could see him shaking. "She had always respected Mr. Rossington, and after my father died, his interactions with her became more frequent, more secret, and as her mind deteriorated she convinced herself that he was a good man." He shook his head in anger. "The one honorable thing he ever did was marry her. The prospect of an illegitimate child drove him to the decision."

My heart thudded, my stomach lurching in disgust and dread over what I was hearing. My mind raced after each of Nicholas's words. "He married your mother?"

Nicholas nodded. "After your aunt's death, he married my mother. But when her madness became too much for him to bear, he annulled the marriage, leaving my mother even more of a social outcast, and leaving Simon as illegitimate as he would have been had he been born outside of marriage. Or never born at all."

I couldn't believe what I was hearing. "Simon?"

"Simon, the son of Mr. Rossington and my mother, is the boy who tossed the pot from the window. He is nearly six years old." Nicholas's voice grew solemn, quiet.

The red-haired boy I had seen . . . it was Mrs. Bancroft's son. Mr. Rossington's son. I covered my mouth in shock, shaking my head as if it could dispel the truth of what Nicholas was telling me.

"To his inner circle of acquaintances, Mr. Rossington still claims he is married and that is wife is simply ill and unable to join them, keeping himself free of ridicule. He brought her to social events for the first several months of their marriage, but soon her behavior became too much to bear, and he was pitied and humiliated for it. So he annulled the marriage and shunned my mother and his own son to a house directly beside his. Leaving them to my care—a twenty-year-old, basely educated boy." Nicholas clenched his jaw and met my eyes. They were wet again, broken and heavy.

"He ruined them. Illegitimate, Simon cannot inherit or show himself in society by the name he was given. Simon Rossington. He is ruined and he is only five years old."

I was grounded where I stood, my head swimming with disbelief and revulsion. I had never been more appalled, more shocked than I was by what Nicholas had just revealed to me. Anger roiled within me. Mr. Rossington's wicked ways must have been discovered by Aunt Edith and my own parents that summer we left Rosewood.

My stomach was uneasy, hollow, thoroughly disturbed, and seething with anger. Aunt Edith had died shortly after. How her heart must have been broken. My own heart burned with sorrow and pain for Nicholas, Mrs. Bancroft, and Aunt Edith. For little Simon. I understood why Mama and Papa had refused to return here.

They knew Mr. Rossington for the monstrosity he was.

I remembered Nicholas standing across the room. I had been silent for so long, absorbing the words I wished weren't true. "Nicholas . . ." I shook my head. "How horrible. I . . ." My words refused to come the way I wanted them to. "I am very sorry." My voice burned on the way out.

His eyes were deep set and full of hurt, staring into mine from across the room.

I didn't know what else to say.

"Now you know my secrets, Lucy. Are you satisfied? Was that precisely what you wished to hear?" His voice was tight and hoarse.

A fresh wave of emotion came over me, but Nicholas didn't wipe my tears this time. Instead he took his hat from atop the pianoforte and left the room without glancing back. The door shut and the tenseness in my body released, and I slumped to the sofa in sobs. I don't know how long I stayed there, but when the door cracked open, I looked up, hastily swiping at my cheeks.

The face of Mr. Rossington poked through the doorframe. I narrowed my eyes at him, squinting through my tears. I moved to my feet and crossed the room toward him.

"Miss Abbot, what is the matter?" His voice grated.

I tugged the door from his grip and stormed past him. It took all my concentration not to slap him across his face.

Back in the safety of my room, I collapsed on my bed, burying my face in my pillow as I cried. It was unfair and cruel what Mr. Rossington had done. Nicholas had told me the truth; he had poured his heart out in front of me and held nothing in reserve. He had not given me a chance to accept him after he told me the truth. Would my answer have been different? Simply because he told me the truth didn't change the fact that he needed the money that I could not offer him. He had claimed it did not matter. It was my way of protecting my heart, but what was I protecting it from? Did I still not trust Nicholas, even after all he had revealed to me? I searched my soul, but had no answer. Surely he thought me to be a coward and a fool, asking for too many answers of him. It was dreadful, the things he had told me. Of course he had worried over telling me.

I drew a long, shaking breath and propped myself up on my elbow, trying to calm my tears. Nicholas would not attend the party tomorrow after what had just passed between us. I didn't expect him to.

I was a pathetic, stupid girl. A foolish girl, just as he had said years ago. He was right. He had always been right.

# NINETEEN

*I* stood in front of the tall looking glass in my room the next afternoon, studying the deep red gown that had been made for me by the Rossingtons with the money that should have been given to the Bancrofts. I looked at the dress in disgust in an attempt to stop admiring it. But the color was striking, with long, fitted sleeves and beads placed intricately at the neckline. The satin skirts hung elegantly around my legs. It was the perfect length.

My maid, Helen, assisted me in styling my hair, pulling it up into a loose coil at the crown of my head, decorating my curls with tiny silver pins shaped like roses. My cheeks were flushed with nervousness already, so she had no need to pinch them. My large brown eyes stared back at me in my reflection, sparking with confidence. I couldn't decide if I wanted Nicholas to be at the party or not. It would only be awkward and painful if he was. But if he wasn't there, I would spend the evening wishing he was there to dance the waltz with me.

When I walked outside that evening to enter the carriage, my heart leapt.

Sitting inside was Nicholas.

His eyes met mine in the dim light, flashing with admiration. But there was also the reflection of broken things in his face, and it stabbed me with remorse. He looked too handsome with his hair combed and his jaw freshly shaven. Taking a deep breath of fortitude,

I smiled at him, trying to assure him somehow that I was sorry. He stared at me in silence. He didn't offer a smile in return, but turned his head toward the window.

The ride to Stanton manor was every bit as uncomfortable as I imagined it would be. Nicholas sat straight across from me, Mr. Parsons directly beside me, and thankfully Kitty and her husband took our carriage instead of riding with her father and the Tattershalls. I had noted the tension between Nicholas and Mr. Rossington, so it was not surprising that they had taken separate carriages. But the tension between Mr. Parsons and Nicholas was heavy as well.

Mr. Parsons didn't seem to mind at all. In fact he seemed quite pleased that Nicholas had arrived in the first place. But I could see the annoyed looks Nicholas threw Mr. Parsons through the dimness of the carriage each time Mr. Parsons leaned his head close to mine and whispered, which he had done many times already.

I met Nicholas's gaze several times throughout the drive, and our knees brushed every time we hit a bump on the road. Nicholas's gaze burned through my face as we drove; I could feel it without needing to look back or make eye contact. For most of the ride, I focused my attention out the window beside me, wishing I could jump out of it. I wished I could tease and laugh with Nicholas, apologize for not understanding why he wanted to keep his secrets, but nothing would be same after I rejected his proposal. Never had I wished to erase a moment in time more than I did now. But it was impossible.

Just when I had determined to ignore him, I glanced up involuntarily and he met my eyes with a smile in the dark.

Why?

I flitted my gaze away as quickly as I could, staring at my hands in my lap. My heart beat fast and my palms were slick with sweat. It was suddenly far too hot in that carriage. Perhaps he didn't hate me now. Perhaps he had seen the apology in my smile when I entered the carriage. We had always been able to communicate well without words.

I blew a puff of air at my forehead to clear the fallen curls from my eyes. Mr. Parsons leaned over and asked if I was well. Nicholas frowned at him.

At last we arrived at Stanton manor, and I scrambled out of the carriage before Nicholas or Mr. Parsons could offer to help me down. I almost sighed as the cool night air breezed past my skin. Nicholas approached from behind and wrapped my hand around the bend of his arm, just as he had so many times. I caught my breath, pressing my lips together and glancing up at him.

"I told you to be careful about throwing that look to every man that glances your way," he said in a quiet voice.

"I do *not* throw this look to every man that glances my way."

"Just the ones you wish to torture?" His head was leaned down far too close to my ear, and his breath tickled my hair against my cheek.

"I have never tried to torture you." My voice was weak.

"Then why do you push me away?"

My heart leapt and I watched the ground as we walked. I didn't know how to answer. I cleared my throat, attempting a smooth change of subject. "Are you looking forward to seeing Lord and Lady Stanton again?"

He was silent, frustrated by my avoidance of his question no doubt. "Again? I have never made their acquaintance."

I scowled at the ground. How strange. Mr. Parsons had told me that Nicholas had once been acquainted with them, and that was why they insisted upon his attendance tonight. "Mr. Parsons believed you to be well acquainted with the family. He insisted that you come tonight."

Nicholas's brow furrowed. "Mr. Parsons insisted that I come?"

I bit my lip. I hadn't meant to tell him that part. Luckily we reached the house and were joined by the rest of the party as they arrived. We followed behind Kitty as we entered Stanton Manor. I understood why Mr. Parsons had been so enamored by the prospect of attending this party. The house was simple yet elegant, brightly lit by the sconces on the walls. It wasn't as large or grand as Rosewood or Willowbourne, but there were many fine decorations and ornaments that sparkled in the candlelight. I felt slightly overdressed in my red gown, as most of the ladies that entered the house were dressed in pale colors and simple sleeves. It was a larger group than I had anticipated, and I noticed the eyes of several gentlemen flit in my direction as we gathered in the expansive drawing room. I had often drawn many gazes for my eccentric choices of headwear and jewelry, but never dressed as simply as I was now. I could feel Nicholas standing nearby, and I gained the courage to look at him. Nicholas didn't speak, but just offered me another of his devastating smiles, fluttering my heart and warming me to my toes. A dramatic gasp came from behind the pianoforte where we stood.

"Nicholas Bancroft?" a sly voice asked before Nicholas could speak to me. I turned toward the sound. For a moment I didn't recognize her, but then my heart dropped.

"Miss Hyatt." Nicholas gave a polite smile, his expression lifting in mild surprise.

A pretty young woman standing beside her piped in, "Not Miss Hyatt any longer."

"Ah, are you married now?" Nicholas asked. I studied his face, my pulse pounding as I watched the interaction from beside him. He didn't appear to be genuinely curious, but asking to be polite. But I didn't like the smile she gave him, fluttering her lashes the way she was. I didn't like it one bit. She looked the same as I remembered her, with honey blonde hair and thick eyelashes and bright hazel eyes. Although she was older now, her face still carried the youthfulness and flirtatiousness of a girl at her first London season.

"It is Mrs. Elkins now, but I am recently widowed." She cast her eyes down before glancing back up at Nicholas.

"I offer my condolences," he said. "Have you fallen on difficult times?"

The woman beside her leaned forward, as if by a previously planned strategy, and remarked, "She is lonely, that is all. But her thirty thousand pounds are supporting her quite well financially." Her voice trailed off at the end and she eyed *Mrs. Elkins* with a miniscule grin.

"I am happy that you will be comfortable in that aspect, then."

My eyes were glued to Nicholas, trying to analyze every expression that crossed his face. But his features were smooth and unreadable. He didn't blink. Did he realize what Miss Hyatt was scheming? The way she looked at him made me ill—the obvious longing and flirting. Here was a beautiful, wealthy woman that would marry Nicholas without a second thought. As much as I had supported the idea the day before, it now sat dull and painful in my chest, twisting against my heart, threatening destruction. But I thought of Nicholas's family. Of the debts that weighed on him and the small child that needed to be fed.

Miss Hyatt seemed to realize I was standing there. My petite size could not hide me forever. I swallowed as she appraised me with a discreet eye, her face hovering with recognition. She jerked her attention back to Nicholas. "Who might this be?" Her hand swept in my direction.

He glanced down at me. I was sickened with dread. In my mind I could still see the expression he had worn six years ago when I had approached him and Miss Hyatt at the garden. He had glanced down with casualness and annoyance then, treating me like a pest.

My heart hammered with vulnerability and I could hardly manage to look at him. I was afraid of what I would see. I felt like I was sinking into the floor; I desperately wished *I could* sink into the floor.

Nicholas shifted closer, and I felt myself stop sinking. My nerves settled and I dared to look at his face. "This is Miss Lucy Abbot, my dearest and most unexpected friend." Every doubt and fear dispelled under his gaze and I gave him a shy smile.

Mrs. Elkins cleared her throat, tearing my gaze away from Nicholas. "I thought I had seen you once before." She rubbed her chin with one delicate finger. "Miss Abbot, have you and Nicholas been long acquainted?"

"Yes . . . since we were children." My voice shook and I hated myself for it. Jealousy and inferiority boiled within me until I could hardly breathe. Mrs. Elkins was obviously interested in marrying Nicholas. She was wealthy and beautiful.

A heavy aching started in my chest. It was the perfect opportunity for Nicholas to repay his debts and help his family. He would be a fool not to take it. And I suddenly felt like a fool for endorsing it. I was destroying my own heart in the process.

"Please excuse me," I said in a quick voice before I could be questioned further. I didn't want her to remember that I was the little girl that had given Nicholas a love note.

"Lucy," Nicholas said as I stepped away. His voice faded away before I could hear the rest.

Kitty was on the other end of the room, and thankfully as I reached her, our hosts guided us to the dining room. I was escorted by a young man named Mr. Drew, with thick black hair and a severe brow. In the dining room, I noticed Mr. Parsons sitting between two young women. His eyes never ventured my way. It confused me—he had appeared so attached to me. Why was he now acting as if he didn't even know I was in the room? Occasionally I saw his eyes shift to Nicholas, narrowed, discreetly watching.

I ate just a little of my meal, not feeling well enough to enjoy the delicious-looking courses that came to the long, full table. I didn't engage in any conversation either. I drank my entire goblet, but with each sip seemed to feel more and more ill. I was nauseated, and more than once I felt my food come halfway up my throat. I refused to vomit in the middle of the dining room. Mr. Drew leaned toward me.

"Are you well, Miss Abbot? You are quite pale."

I shook my head, afraid if I spoke that I would faint or vomit.

"Perhaps a bit of fresh air would be beneficial? I would be happy to escort you."

I nodded, grateful for Mr. Drew's attentiveness. He mumbled his excuses to our host before standing. The group was large enough that they didn't notice Mr. Drew help me stand from my chair and escort me from the room. Nicholas did notice, though. I saw his eyes follow me with concern. He moved, as if he intended to stand, but Mr. Parsons asked him a question before he could leave. The entirety of the table focused their attention on Nicholas and his eyes flicked to me one more time before he sat back in defeat.

Kitty nudged her husband before leaning to whisper to our hostess as well.

The hallway was well lit outside of the dining room, and Mr. Drew led me outside. He was a very small, stout man, likely only a few years older than me. I thanked him, but my voice was muffled to my own ears. Kitty and Mr. Turner appeared beside me just as I vomited on the neat grass. She must have worried over me being alone out of doors with a strange man.

"Oh, Lucy," Kitty said in a nurturing voice. I shook as I stood up and faced her. "You look quite ill. Shall we send you back to Rosewood?"

Mr. Drew eyed her with annoyance, as if her presence here was not welcome. I thanked her with my eyes for coming out here. "I will be just fine, but the outside air is quite refreshing. Will you stay with me a little longer?"

"We shall stay out here as long as you need, Miss Abbot. Take as long as your recovery requires." Mr. Drew cut in. His voice was friendly and loud.

Kitty motioned for me to take her arm to steady myself. I could not leave without dancing with Nicholas. I needed him to know that I was not pushing him away. That I trusted him. But Miss Hyatt was here . . . would he not dance with her instead? As much as I told myself to support the idea of Nicholas marrying her for his family's advantage, I couldn't bear the thought of him dancing with someone else but me.

I stayed outside for several minutes, and I could see the ladies already in the drawing room through the nearest window. Taking one last breath of fresh air, I put on a smile. "Shall we return to the party?"

Mr. Drew eyed the window with speculation, searching for someone through the glass. Kitty clasped her hand around my arm and nodded. "If you are feeling well enough."

"I am." My voice was distant. I was focused on Mr. Drew and his intent study of the window.

"Do not walk too quickly," he stammered. "It will unsettle your stomach."

Something was very strange with the way Mr. Drew was behaving. I glanced back at him with a false smile. "I feel quite recovered, Mr. Drew."

Mr. Turner opened the door and Kitty led me through it. Mr. Drew kept close behind us as we walked through the hall. As we passed the dining room, the men were exiting, jeering heartily as they made their way to the drawing room. The candlelight glowed off each of their faces as they passed me, but Nicholas was not among them. I frowned, tipping my head to catch a glimpse inside the dining room. The door was ajar, but the group of men hid most of the room from my sight. But then I saw the end of the table. Nicholas and Mr. Parsons were the only two that remained sitting. As Nicholas stood, Mr. Drew stepped in front of me. "Are you certain you're well, Miss Abbot?"

"Yes!" I said in an exasperated voice. Kitty shot me a look of dismay. "I mean—yes, thank you for asking." I strained my neck to see Mr. Parsons cross the table to Nicholas. He leaned his head down and whispered something. Nicholas's eyes widened just as the door closed them from my sight.

"Come now, let us claim the comfortable seats in the drawing room before they are all occupied." Mr. Drew smiled and hooked my arm around his. Mr. Turner and Kitty joined arms as well as we entered the room. What had I just witnessed? Why were Nicholas and Mr. Parsons interacting? As far as I could tell, they despised one another.

The other ladies in the room took turns at the pianoforte, but I sat in silence in the corner settee beside Kitty, trying to figure out what was happening with Nicholas and Mr. Parsons. When the men joined us in the drawing room, I noticed that Nicholas and Mr. Parsons were absent. Where had they gone? What had Mr. Parsons whispered to Nicholas in the dining room? My thoughts whirled. Nicholas had suggested that he did not trust Mr. Parsons. Had he been correct not to trust him? My stomach stirred with unease, suspicion toward Mr. Parsons flooding me. Did he intend to harm Nicholas?

Several minutes later, Mr. Parsons entered the room alone. My heart sunk. He smiled at me for the first time all evening, but I didn't smile back. Crossing the room to me, he walked with purpose, his neat, handsome appearance enough to catch the eye of several women of the room. I noticed a small group of women whispering as they watched him, as if they had never seen him before. I found that strange. An eligible, wealthy bachelor such as what Mr. Parsons claimed to be would not go unnoticed in a town like Dover. He would be the prize to be won among so many unmarried ladies.

As Mr. Parsons approached, I stood, stopping him from moving past me.

"Where is Mr. Bancroft? Have you seen him recently?" I tried to keep my voice free of the suspicion I felt.

"He was not enjoying the party, I'm afraid. He took the carriage back to his home. Not to worry, by the time we finish here the carriage will be back to return you to Rosewood." Mr. Parsons turned to leave, but I caught a handful of his sleeve. He glanced down at me with annoyance. I was shocked by his behavior . . . it was as if he had never admired me—never even tolerated me for one moment. But his eyes also slid over me with caddish focus. I let go of his sleeve fast.

"Nicholas would not have left without informing me," I said in a loud voice, recalling his eyes back to my face.

"That is simply what he told me. I am sorry I do not have further information." Mr. Parsons brushed his sleeve off and stepped away, rejoining the women he had sat with in the dining room.

Nothing made sense. My mind spun in circles as I sat down beside Kitty once again. She had been watching the exchange with half her attention, carrying a conversation with the woman beside her at the same time. A minute later, she leaned close to my ear.

"What did you do to divert Mr. Parsons' attentions? You nearly had him!" she half-whispered.

"I did nothing. I asked him where Nicholas was and he told me Nicholas traveled home." The words didn't sound true.

Kitty rolled her eyes. "I do not understand why Nicholas attended at all. Quickly now, you must make amends with Mr. Parsons before it is too late."

I couldn't believe her lack of worry for Nicholas. Something was wrong. Why would he leave without warning?

What must have been no more than thirty minutes later, we were ushered into the ballroom on the other side of the manor. The assembly seemed smaller now within the larger room, and Nicholas was still nowhere to be found. The widowed Miss Hyatt studied the room as well, likely searching for the same person I was.

The music began, but I did not feel like dancing. I was beginning to feel ill again. I did not trust one word that had been spoken by Mr. Parsons. Lady Stanton, our hostess, interrupted shortly after the first dance, cutting off the ensemble. Her hair was tightly curled and pale, frizzing out on the sides. She was dressed in an elegant blue gown with gold trim, but it was her eyes that caught my attention, wide with consternation.

She took a deep breath and her husband moved beside her, his face twisted in panic as well. The room fell silent as Lady Stanton spoke. "Several of our antiques have disappeared, as well as many valuable relics from our travels in the continent. I do not mean to alarm or accuse, but please, if you know of their location do come forward at once."

A hush fell over the crowd before they erupted with whispers. My heart pounded with a question that I didn't want to acknowledge. No. I tried to shush my thoughts, but Mr. Rossington's voice cut through them before I could.

"Mr. Nicholas Bancroft was in attendance, but I have not seen him for the last hour." He seemed far too happy with the prospect of accusing Nicholas. I wished his embarrassingly tight breeches would split right down the middle in front of every woman in the room.

"It is true," Kitty said.

I gasped, jerking my head toward her. Every head in the room turned toward her too.

"That does not prove his guilt," Lady Stanton said, her voice shaking.

"He was acting rather suspiciously, I confess, and he exited the dining room alone." Mr. Parsons stepped forward, his voice sharp and nauseating. I refused to believe that Nicholas was involved in this. My spine chilled with uncertainty, but I shook it away. My eyes stung with tears as I begged myself to trust him, to believe in his promised innocence. If he had done this, then I could never trust him again. He was a good person; I knew he was. How could I doubt him? Every person in this room doubted him; he needed someone to believe in him. I knew he was innocent. The knowledge spread through my veins and strengthened me, and my suspicions returned to another source. Mr. Parsons.

Kitty slid her eyes to me before speaking again. "It is rumored . . . that he has conspired with highwaymen in the recent months, and I fear he may have reverted to old habits, my lady." She threw me an apology with her eyes.

The crowd buzzed with Kitty's words, and I refused to hear it any longer. I stared at Kitty, unable to believe that she had just revealed the words I had spoken to her in confidence. My muscles stiffened in defense and courage.

"He is not that man!" I shouted over the rumble of voices. "He is good and innocent and kind, I assure you. I have known him all of my life. Take your accusations elsewhere."

My words seemed to go unheard, for the party was still abuzz with whispers and plans to apprehend Nicholas. The party was soon cut short, and an assortment of wheels was sent after the carriage that had taken Nicholas home. After several minutes, the remaining party dispersed with their fresh gossip. When we were outside, I gripped Kitty's shoulder from behind and turned her fiercely toward me.

"What have you done?" My voice was shrill and tears streaked from my eyes.

Her face fell. "Lucy, I could not keep quiet in a situation like this, surely you understand! If Nicholas is truly as innocent as you claim, then he will not be held accountable. But if he is indeed guilty, then the demands of justice will be served, as they should."

My heart was in my throat. I shook with anger and fear. "He will be brought to trial, Kitty! He could be executed!" I pressed my hand to my forehead and bit my lip to keep from crying harder.

Kitty scoffed in disbelief. "He is a thief!"

I could hardly see her through my tears. I narrowed my eyes and backed away from her. "He is not."

She was silent as she pulled me toward the coach. I reluctantly climbed inside on my shaking legs. The moment I sat down, a small phaeton entered the drive ahead of us. Two men descended from their seats and approached Lord and Lady Stanton. I leapt down from the coach, nearly tripping on my skirts. I hurried over to where a cluster of the remaining guests stood, straining to hear the conversation.

"We tried to apprehend the carriage ten miles down the road, but Bancroft appeared to be in a hurry, not stopping until arrival at his home. He appeared confused, and claimed to have no knowledge of the thievery, but we found this in the carriage, my lord." The man lifted a small antique to the moonlight. It didn't appear to have much value. "The constable has made plans to speak with him this evening."

My heart sunk. What was Nicholas doing with that item? In my peripheral vision, I saw Mr. Parsons mounting a horse. He was tucked around the side of the manor, where he couldn't be seen by the majority of the party. Without thinking, I marched over to him, anger pounding through my steps. Mr. Parsons was involved in this; I knew it with a certainty that chilled my bones. Nicholas had always been brave. It was time I did the same for him.

"Where are you going?" I snapped as I reached the side of the horse.

Mr. Parsons appraised me from above, his gaze pompous and casual. "No place of consequence."

I hardened my gaze. "Why have you ignored me this evening?" I couldn't let him know my suspicions or he would likely ride away.

His expression faltered for a brief moment. "You bore me, Miss Abbot. You do not return my attentions."

My stomach lurched with disgust. How had I ever considered this man handsome or agreeable? I studied his face, trying to decipher his motivations. I breathed deeply, formulating a plan in my mind. It was horrifying, but I had an odd suspicion about the overly filled sack that hung from Mr. Parsons's saddle on the other side of the horse, hidden from view.

"I do."

His eyebrows lifted. "You have said nothing of the sort."

"I am saying it now. Please, Mr. Parsons," I tipped my head flirtatiously and leaned closer, lowering my voice. As I moved closer, I caught sight of something in the sack on the other side of the horse, shining gold under the moonlight. It appeared very much like an item I had seen upon my arrival at the house tonight. He was the thief. He had framed Nicholas. But why?

I tried not to cringe at the wry smile that twisted his mouth. My words stumbled out. I needed more time to formulate a plan. "I would very much like to speak to you about my feelings. Allow me to accompany you to this place."

The people on the property had begun to disperse, and my carriage was waiting on the other side of the house. My heart pounded. I was placing myself in horrible danger. He seemed to consider it, sweeping his gaze over me distractedly. "Your words mean nothing."

I swallowed. Fear crept over my shoulders but I forced myself to remain strong and calm. "Then I will show you how I feel. I am quite smitten by you," I whispered.

He cracked his neck, clenching his jaw as he fought over his decision. I waited. It would be simple. I would mount the front of his horse and we would ride away in the dark. I would beg him to steer the horse. We would drive in front of the remaining party and I would throw the sack to the ground where it would open and reveal the items Mr. Parsons had stolen.

He had been quiet for too long. He was close to giving in.

I reached up and touched his arm, tracing my finger down to his hand. I shivered in revulsion at the caddish expression on his face as he looked down at me. He dismounted his horse and I took an involuntary step backward. We stood where no one could see us, and I experienced a surge of regret and fear. He pulled me toward him and I pretended it didn't disgust me. My heart raced, and I was tempted to kick him and run away. This had not been my wisest plan. He slid his hand around my waist and gathered me closer, running his other hand along my cheek and neck.

"Mr. Parsons!" I said in a panicked voice. I dislodged myself from his arms and tried my hardest to hide my fear. "Not here. We might be seen." I transformed my voice to a demure one, walking around him toward the horse. It shifted restlessly, but I stroked its muzzle softly, in part to calm the horse but mostly to calm myself. "My father taught me to ride when I was very young. Might I take the reins? You can direct me to your destination."

I stared straight ahead, heart pounding in anticipation. I heard him step closer behind me, and I reeled in disgust as I felt his breath on the back of my neck. He breathed in my hair, gripping me at the waist. I was about to jerk myself away when he lifted me effortlessly onto the saddle.

"You are surprising this evening, Miss Abbot. Perhaps I was wrong in considering you a bore." He mounted behind me.

I struggled to breathe with the fear that choked me. I had one chance to do this. The voices from the other side of the manor echoed in the dark and I gripped the reins with both hands. I sat sideways on the saddle, giving me a clear view of Mr. Parsons where he sat, far too near, behind me. "Where shall I direct us?" My voice shook. I hoped he couldn't hear it.

"South." He gestured in the opposite direction of where I intended to go. "I need to meet an acquaintance, but we may spend an hour or two at my home first." His voice was low and much too close to my ear. "It isn't far." I felt his touch on my shoulder, sliding down my waist again. I shifted forward on the horse and let the reins loose. I wanted to throw Mr. Parsons off the horse at this very moment. He would lead a woman away and willingly ruin her reputation without a second thought? Nicholas had been correct in his warning me to be careful. Mr. Parsons was a dangerous man. A wicked, wicked man. I was confident that he had framed Nicholas for the robbery. Somehow.

I could hear my heartbeat in my ears as the horse stepped forward. Before I could lose my nerve, I steered violently in the opposite direction, making Mr. Parsons lose his balance as the horse turned swiftly. I slapped the reins and we lurched forward in a trot, then a run. The speed of his horse shocked me, and within seconds we were in sight of the party once again.

Mr. Parsons yelled something behind me, but I couldn't hear. He grabbed my arm and wrenched it backward. I cried out, and Lord Stanton's eyes shot up in our direction.

I cried out for help as Mr. Parsons wrenched my other arm.

The crowd stared in bewilderment for a moment before several men moved toward our oncoming horse. I had managed to maintain my grip on the reins, so I pulled them tight, bringing us to an abrupt halt. The horse whinnied in annoyance. An elderly man reached for me and helped me slide down. I could hardly stand on my shaking legs. Mr. Parsons caught his breath, pushing his hair off his forehead, glaring down at me before sitting up straight. "This woman is . . . mad! She mounted my horse and carried us off like—"

"Look inside his bag, sir," I interrupted. "I assure you will find the items you are seeking." I was out of breath, and my words were garbled. Lord Stanton seemed to understand, stepping toward the horse. I watched Mr. Parsons. His eyes flicked to mine as his hands slipped discreetly over the reins.

"No!" I screamed as he set the horse in motion, rearing back and then flying over the grass with ghostly speed. Lord Stanton fell to the ground, rolling away from the hooves that threatened to crush him. Lady Stanton rushed to his side.

"Who the devil is that man?" she shrieked.

"Your thief," I said, slumping my shoulders in exhaustion and defeat. I made a sound of frustration as I watched Mr. Parsons's retreating form, but remembered that I should also be relieved. Nicholas was safe. Mr. Parsons had just proven his own guilt. But there was still the item that had been found in Nicholas's carriage . . .

"Are you well, miss?" I was not well. Mr. Parsons had escaped. I still didn't know why Nicholas had rushed home. But I knew one thing for certain: Nicholas was not involved. I trusted him. I loved him. My heart confirmed the truth of my words, but it also reminded me of my inability to give Nicholas what he needed. He needed to marry a woman like Miss Hyatt, or rather, *Mrs. Elkins*. My brain hurt from thinking too much.

After explaining all I knew and suspected of Mr. Parsons—including that he had framed Nicholas with the other item found in his carriage—I proceeded back to Rosewood.

The carriage was taut with silence, and I didn't try to break it. Kitty avoided my eyes and I avoided hers. Mr. Rossington stared out the windows, and Mrs. Tattershall looked at me occasionally, as if she were attempting to solve a puzzle. I didn't want to be angry with Kitty, but she had thrown Nicholas under accusation, even though she knew I trusted him to be an honorable man. I closed my eyes and tried to shut off my thoughts.

But when we arrived at Rosewood, I couldn't stop worrying over Nicholas. I almost sneaked out to see him, but no doubt Mrs. Tattershall would be keeping a close watch on my bedroom door for the rest of the night. She made certain that I arrived in my room, leading me by the elbow the entire way. When we stopped at my door, she pushed it open and watched me walk inside. Just before she closed it behind me, she cleared her throat. "You are a brave one, Miss Abbot. I am sorry if I have . . . thought little of you. I do hope Mr. Bancroft is well."

She didn't give me an opportunity to respond. The door closed and I was left alone with my thoughts.

# TWENTY

It amazed me that I had managed to fall asleep at all. I awoke before the sun and decided to venture outside by the gardens. I picked several flowers and walked to the other side of Rosewood—the side bordering the Bancrofts' home—and waited with my bouquet until a more appropriate hour for a visit. Mrs. Tattershall could not accuse me of anything but delivering flowers to an ill, lonely woman. If I happened to see Nicholas, then so be it. I needed to know what had happened last night and warn him of Mr. Parsons. I had been assured that there would be a search for Mr. Parsons, but I worried that he wouldn't be found.

The early morning air was crisp and cool, biting through my shawl and scratching at my arms. A lone bird sang a song of joy, of daybreak and sunlight, a song I didn't remember. Nicholas would not like me knocking on his door uninvited, but the last time I had done it he hadn't been home. Perhaps now that I knew the truth he wouldn't mind me stopping by unannounced.

With a deep breath, I approached the door. Before I could reach it, however, I heard a sound from the other side of the house. It sounded like laughter, but I couldn't be sure. With slow steps, I followed the sound to the back of the house where Nicholas and I had sat the day the pot had fallen from the window. I stopped.

The little red-haired boy—Simon, Nicholas had called him—sat on the grass with his legs crossed, pulling handfuls of grass out of the ground and tossing it into the air. I took a step closer to greet him, but his eyes flew up to mine first. He threw a handful of grass angrily in my direction before jumping to his feet and running toward the garden. I stood in surprise, brushing the grass from my skirts before following the boy silently, trying not to appear threatening. I saw Mrs. Bancroft's sheet of black hair in the corner of my eye. Before I could move away, she was in front of me, her hands gripping my shoulders. My bundle of flowers fell to the ground. I smiled, willing myself to not be afraid. Her breath was short and quick as she studied me. I could clearly see every faint wrinkle of her face, every line of color in her eyes. She mumbled something I couldn't hear. I waited. I was proud of how calm I felt, and when her grip finally loosened on my shoulders, I scooped my flowers up from the grass and held them out to her.

"Good morning, Mrs. Bancroft. It is Lucy. I remembered how much you love flowers." My voice was too loud and friendly. I softened it slightly. "They would look quite pretty in your hair, I daresay. Would you like to see?" I selected the smallest flower, a delicate yellow, and threaded it behind her ear.

"Beautiful," she whispered, raising one slender hand to touch the flower.

I smiled and nodded. "Take all of them," I placed my bouquet in her other hand. She stared down at them, raising them to her nose and inhaling their scent. Simon ran across the grass toward the back door. Julia stood under the frame, eyeing me with displeasure as the boy reached her and clutched onto her hand.

"Good morning," I called out to Julia. Mrs. Bancroft covered her ears, and I watched her as she moved to the stone bench beneath the window. Her eyes focused on something I couldn't see, and her lips moved without sound. All the while, her fingers caressed the petals of the flowers in her lap.

Bending down, Julia scooped up the boy's hand in her own. She stepped out the doorway and met me on the grass. "Are you in search of Nicholas?"

I nodded.

"I have not seen him since very late last evening. He rushed back here and raced off soon after, and I haven't the slightest idea where he has gone." Her voice was weak, trying to sound strong. I tried to ignore the fear and worry that erupted inside of me, feigning calm for her sake.

"I am certain he is all right," I said, but I wasn't sure I believed it. My chest tightened with unease. Where would Nicholas have gone? What had Mr. Parsons done to him?

Her brows turned downward. "I saw a man here last night. He wore a mask. He followed Nicholas into the woods."

I inhaled sharply, pressing my hand to my chest. My heart pounded with dread. "How was this man dressed?"

"In fine clothing . . . he wore a coat with several brass buttons. He was very tall and rather thin . . ."

The only image I could conjure from her description was the man from the night my coach was robbed. The highwayman that had dragged me from my seat. Nicholas had told me that one of the men was shot. Could this man Julia spoke of be the man that survived the attack? Could he be seeking revenge for Nicholas's betrayal? My breath came fast and my thoughts refused to calm themselves. But how had Mr. Parsons been involved? I squeezed my eyes shut and opened them with another gasp. I had met Mr. Parsons in the village the day after the attack. Perhaps this highwayman had found himself a new accomplice that night.

"What is it?" Julia reached for my arm.

"The man you saw—he is dangerous. Perhaps you might leave your house, go to the village. I don't think it is safe to remain here if that man might return."

Julia looked on the brink of dissolving into emotion. Her chin wobbled but she tightened her jaw to stop it. Her eyes were hard one moment, staring into mine, but then she seemed to melt, putting her hand to her forehead and slumping her shoulders. When she looked up again, her eyes were vulnerable and trusting. "Will you look after Simon?" she blurted, shifting her grip on the young boy's hand. "I cannot look after both him and my mother outside of these grounds."

"Of course." I swallowed my fear and put on a smile. Reaching forward, I touched Simon's small shoulder. His nose scrunched at me and he squirmed his shoulder away.

"Would you like to spend the day with me, Simon? My name is Lucy. We may play games and explore, and I am certain we will become friends." He refused to meet my eyes as Julia let go of his hand. An idea struck me and I gasped. "May I take him to visit an acquaintance of mine at Willowbourne? I know for certain she will welcome him. She has two young brothers that I am sure Simon will benefit from interacting with."

Julia nodded, her eyes glazed with fear. "Please return him here by the afternoon." Her face was firm again, hiding all emotion. "Thank you, Lucy. I do hope Nicholas returns soon."

I pressed my lips together as my stomach twisted. "As do I."

Simon was a strange child. He was shy and sweet at one moment, and wild and angry the next. As we walked to Willowbourne, I tried to quiet my mind of its worries, but it was impossible. Simon refused to hold onto my hand, and many times throughout our walk I was forced to chase him before he could be lost.

I caught my breath and planted my hands on my hips. Simon had finally stopped running, standing beside a birch tree on the opposite side of the village. We had almost arrived at Willowbourne, and I had dealt with quite enough of Simon's mischief. I puffed a curl out of my eyes. "Simon, you must never run away from me again, do you understand?"

Simon giggled, backing away from me. I rolled my eyes. Why could I not be intimidating? I was never taken seriously. A small, curly haired, large-eyed woman that appeared to be much younger than she truly was did not make for a convincing threat. If I looked more like Julia, then perhaps I could be taken seriously. She was tall with firm features and straight, long hair. Simon continued walking away, and I begged him not to run again.

"If you become lost I will be very angry with you," I said in a scolding voice.

This caught Simon's attention, and he walked over slowly and took my hand. He looked up at me, his freckles darker under the sun. His crystal blue eyes widened. "Mama is lost."

I frowned. "What do you mean?"

"Julia and Nicholas said—they said she is just lost. Her mind is lost and she can't remember some things sometimes. She's lost." His voice was clear and quiet. He shrugged and kicked the grass as we walked. My heart ached. I was so distracted that I didn't notice Simon tear his hand away from mine and take off running again.

"Simon!" I yelled, scooping up my skirts and chasing after him. "Simon, come back!"

His giggles echoed through the air. I may have had short legs, but Simon's legs were shorter, thank heavens. I caught up to him just as Willowbourne came into view. He stopped, gazing up at the estate in awe. Sneaking up behind him, I lifted him into my arms, heaving with his weight as I carried him over the grass. He squirmed, but I tightened my arms around him.

At last we reached the front doors and were greeted by Annette. Her hair was hanging loose around her face today, and her freckles illuminated her cheeks when she smiled. Her husband welcomed us as we entered the house. They ushered us to the drawing room, where Simon and I sat across from Annette and Dr. Kellaway. I introduced them to Simon, calling him the Bancrofts' cousin, although I knew it wasn't true.

"He has quite the spirit," I said. "I chased him the majority of the way here." I wiped a trickle of sweat from under my lower lip.

Annette exchanged a look with her husband, and they both burst into laughter. Dr. Kellaway eyed Annette before turning to me. "We are quite experienced with the mischievous workings of young boys. Perhaps Simon will benefit from a day spent with our boys."

I sat forward on my chair. "Yes, that is precisely what I was think-ing upon bringing him here."

Annette grinned. "Peter and Charles will love to make a new friend. Their cousins have been away for several weeks now, and they have been bereft of socialization. I am certain they will love Simon."

Dr. Kellaway stood to leave the room to retrieve the boys. He kissed Annette in farewell, as he had to go visit a patient. I patted Simon's shoulder. He glanced around, his brow furrowed with nervousness. His hands fidgeted in his lap.

"What is wrong?" I asked. Annette crossed the room to join us.

"A friend?" His voice was just a squeak.

"Yes . . . Peter and Charles will be your friends. They are little, just like you."

Simon's eyes widened.

"You have nothing to fear, Simon. A friend is a very good thing. I am your friend, am I not?"

His eyes met mine and he gave a slow nod.

"You see? Not to worry."

The door eased open and Peter and Charles stepped in, chattering in quick voices over who should be Simon's favorite. They stopped, grinning when they saw me sitting beside Simon. The hurried over, pausing when they saw the critical stare Simon was giving both of them. After making their introductions, Charles pulled on one of Simon's arms, and Peter pulled on the other, dragging him to his feet. Simon giggled, grinning up at them as if they were the Prince Regent himself.

"May we play outside?" Charles asked Annette.

She nodded, ruffling his hair as the three of them left the room, Simon trailing tentatively behind them. Annette and I followed them to the back property. I wanted to admire the bright colors of the many trees and gardens, but my worry and fear over Nicholas consumed me. We sat on a wooden bench that overlooked the boys as they played.

"So." She raised one arching eyebrow. "Have you confessed your love to that Nicholas?"

My cheeks flushed. My voice was stammering and not nearly as smooth as I intended. "No. I have much to tell you."

When I finished telling her of the events of the previous night and the day he had proposed to me, and how Nicholas had not been seen all day, I felt the familiar choking of emotion in my throat. I gave a shaky breath. "But I do trust him. I think I always have; I have just been afraid. I know he is honorable. He has forsaken his past wrongdoings. But he is gone, and a dangerous man was seen pursuing him." I pressed my face into my hands. "He could still have been involved in the robbery with this man, given the circumstances, but I do not believe it. If he is not involved in the robbery, then where is he? The only other option I can contemplate is that he is in danger."

Annette chewed her lip, thinking. She fell back against the cushions, at a loss. "It is very strange . . . would he not inform you of his departure had it been planned? He trusts you with all of the workings of his past and the many secrets he has."

"But I told him not to visit me alone ever again. He could not have informed me. I didn't return until dark, and he could very well have been gone by then."

"If he cares for you as much as he has proclaimed, then surely he would not abandon you without word."

"Julia said he rushed off somewhere. He was not abducted or hurt . . . It seemed to be a choice. But he was indeed followed. Perhaps he does not care for me at all."

"I know he does. How could he not? He proposed to you. And I have never met a more adorable and lovely person than you, Lucy." Annette smiled with reassurance. "There must be some other reason."

I strained my mind to remember every detail of the night. Mr. Drew had tried to delay me from entering the house. Mr. Parsons had spoken to Nicholas—an encounter Mr. Drew had also tried to prevent me from seeing. Surely Mr. Drew was not innocent either. I closed my eyes, scrunching my face in focus. They had been hiding me from Nicholas. What had Mr. Parsons said to him in the dining room? Did it involve me?

Annette's grip tightened on my arm and I jumped.

"Did Nicholas know where you were during dinner?"

I shook my head.

"Did he see you at all after you left the dining room?"

I suddenly knew what she was hinting at. My heart thudded and I sat up straight. "No!"

"No!" she repeated, clapping her hands together. "Mr. Parsons needed to draw Nicholas away from Stanton Manor somehow in order to carry out his plan. Mr. Drew was involved, taking you outside so you would not be seen. Nicholas believed you to be in danger! That is why he left in such a rush."

"He was looking for me." I gasped.

She sat back in triumph. I couldn't think or breathe. Where was Nicholas? And where had Mr. Parsons told him I was? I shot off of the bench, pressing my hand to my chest. "How will I find him?" If this other highwayman had pursued him, how could he be safe? Dread poured over me in a fresh wave.

"I haven't the slightest idea."

My face was sullen and stiff. Panic laced through all my limbs, making me feel frozen where I stood. The cool air outside created chills on my arms, but I didn't feel them.

"Sit down, Lucy. Relax. You will find him."

"Or he will find me." I sat down in a daze, watching as Nicholas's half-brother raced on the grass, giggling and chattering with Peter and Charles. It was still incomprehensible to me that this was the son of Mr. Rossington, and yet he provided him with no education, no clothing from his pocket, and forced his family to keep him hidden. He annulled the marriage with Mrs. Bancroft, leaving her to ruin and his son illegitimate. I wanted justice for Aunt Edith, for Mrs. Bancroft, for Simon . . . but I didn't know how.

Annette was staring at me as I chewed my nails, still in my daze. I blinked.

"Leave Simon with me," she said. "I will look after him while you return to Rosewood. Perhaps Nicholas is already there, and it will put your mind at ease. Philip is with his nursemaid, down for a nap. I am quite capable of caring for three little boys."

I hesitated, tempted by her offer. Julia had trusted Simon to me; I couldn't leave him. But my mind was already elsewhere, stricken with worry. I had nearly forgotten to look after Simon already. "Very well . . . but I will return within an hour or two."

I stood to leave, and Annette insisted that I take their carriage. I was relieved that I would arrive back at Rosewood sooner. I thanked her thoroughly before setting off toward where I hoped Nicholas would be.

# TWENTY-ONE

When the carriage pulled into the drive at Rosewood, I jumped out without waiting for assistance, hurrying across the property to the Bancrofts'. The autumn air was harsh today, chilling my cheeks and the tip of my nose as I approached the front door. I couldn't see any signs of Nicholas's return. I stopped, catching my breath before striking my knuckles against the door. And then I remembered that Julia had taken her mother to the village.

I sat down on the steps in defeat, at a loss over what to do. Nicholas was likely in danger, possibly searching for *me*, and I was here, completely helpless. Never had I felt more powerless. The road that approached the property from the east was clear, without many trees to conceal it from view. After watching it for several minutes, I looked down at my hands, wringing them until they were white and warm despite the cold.

After staring at my hands for what felt like hours, I glanced up at the road again. I leapt to my feet in shock. A man was trudging in my direction, passing a bend of trees, but he was too far away to recognize. I wrapped my arms around myself to keep warm as my heart thudded with hope. As he came closer, I gasped. It was Nicholas. I could see his soft brown hair and his height and broad shoulders. I stumbled down from the steps, fighting the urge to run to him.

As I moved toward him, I waved my arms, jumping up and down like a madwoman. Perhaps I was one.

I knew he must have seen me, for he stopped in his tracks before lengthening his strides toward me. I noticed the way he walked was a little strange, as if he were in pain. But my smile stretched over my entire face with relief that he was here—that he was alive—and I couldn't help but run. When I had almost reached him I stopped, and my eyes filled with unexpected tears. I scowled at him.

"Nicholas! I was so worried."

At close range, I could see the raw relief in his eyes, the emotion as he filled the remaining steps, wrapping his arms around me. He held me close, and I could feel him shaking. His face was buried in my shoulder. Then he gripped my upper arms and held me back from him so he could study my face. My heart melted at the look in his eyes. He stared down at me as if I were the most precious thing in the world to him; tears wet his eyes and spilled down his face, and his lips pressed together, creasing his cheeks.

The only other time I had seen him cry had been with the death of his old horse. He reached down and touched my face, my hair, as if I weren't real. And he wrapped me up in his arms again. I had never felt more loved. My heart pounded with the revelation I had been too stubborn to acknowledge. Nicholas did love me. I trusted him. I had no doubt anymore. Every inch of me cried out in regret over what I had done, how I had rejected him. I wanted to stay here in his arms forever.

"They told me you were dead," he said into my shoulder, his voice tight.

I tipped my head up to look at him, my eyes wide with shock. "What? Who?"

"I need to move you to a safer place."

"Nicholas, what is happening?"

He placed his hand on my back and guided me toward his house, but I turned around to face him again. Fear pounded through me. I had never seen Nicholas so uncollected.

He rubbed his hand over his hair. "At the party, Parsons told me you were being held captive here, under the control of Gibbs. I hadn't seen you for a long time, and you could easily have been abducted by Mr. Drew."

"Gibbs?" The name sounded familiar.

"The highwayman that I used to work under—the one that escaped that night we met."

The man that Julia had seen.

He continued guiding me toward the house, glancing behind him every few seconds. "So I came to find you, but you were not here, and I was accused of robbing Lord and Lady Stanton. I searched for you all night, and this morning I was apprehended by Gibbs and Parsons." His voice was hard. "Parsons is the new man they acquired in my place. He was sent to befriend us, to gain our trust in order to frame me. They told me they had already . . . killed you." He could hardly speak the words, and his voice shook. "I attempted to fight against them, as they intended to murder me as well, but I knew I wasn't a match for two men. I was shot in the leg and I barely escaped with my life."

I gasped, glancing at the limp in his walk, stopping him with my hand on his arm. "You must see Dr. Kellaway. Are you in pain?"

He shook his head fast. "We cannot worry over that yet. They are coming back."

My chest flooded with fear. "What are we to do?"

"We need more men." He rubbed his head and glanced back at the road again. I noticed the bruises on his cheeks and a cut on his forehead. Anger boiled inside of me. I wanted to fight Mr. Parsons myself for what he had done.

"Mr. Turner! I will alert him. And Mr. Rossington."

Nicholas's chest rose and fell with quick breath, but he was silent.

I pulled on his arm, recalling his eyes. "We must ask Mr. Rossington. He has weapons. I will send Kitty to find the constable and any others that may be inclined to help us."

Nicholas nodded. "But we must hurry. We don't have a lot of time. I must retrieve my family." He turned toward his house, but I shook my head.

"They took a trip to the village. I thought it would be a safer place for them. Julia saw Gibbs pass the house last night." I paused. "And Simon is at Willowbourne with his new friends."

Nicholas gave me a look of confusion, but didn't ask me to explain. "I heard Gibbs and Parsons. They plan to steal from Rosewood should they have a chance. When Parsons first discovered we intended to travel there, robbing Rosewood was their goal. But when you did not return Mr. Parsons's attentions, he was unable to spend as much time in the home as he intended."

My pulse flooded my ears. I had never been more afraid. We hurried to the back door of Rosewood as quickly as we could with Nicholas's wounded leg. I burst through the door with Nicholas beside me, slamming the door against the adjacent wall with a crash. Mrs. Tattershall rushed around the corner, hand pressed to her chest. "Good heavens." She gave us a look of deep disapproval.

I stepped forward. "There are two wicked men on their way to Rosewood, including Mr. Parsons. They intend to harm and steal. We need the assistance of Mr. Rossington and Mr. Turner with their weapons at once. Send Kitty or yourself to find the constable and any others willing to defer these men." My voice was edged with panic and fear. I could hardly breathe. I didn't want Nicholas to fight them. He was injured! They could so easily kill him. The thought choked me.

Mrs. Tattershall's eyes flew open and she nodded, disappearing around the corner of the hallway. The audacity of these men frightened me. To pursue Nicholas in broad daylight likely meant they were confident in their ability to remain unscathed. I swallowed, holding Nicholas's arm tighter. I didn't care what he thought of it. I needed him. He had always kept me safe, and I was determined to keep him safe tonight.

Mr. Rossington rounded the corner, scowling as his eyes fell on Nicholas. "What is the commotion about? Have you trailed your criminal acquaintances to Rosewood?" His face was pompous and cruel.

I had endured quite enough from this dreadful creature. "Are you a man?"

Mr. Rossington tore his glare from Nicholas and moved his gaze to my face. "Pardon me? Yes, of course," he sputtered.

"Then you will step outside with your weapons and defend your property and your family. These men intend to steal from Rosewood."

His face reddened and he muttered something under his breath before retreating into the hallway. My shoulders relaxed and the fire in my expression faded. I wasn't certain, but I thought I felt Nicholas pull me closer.

Several agonizing minutes later, Mr. Rossington emerged from the hall, tossing a pistol to Nicholas. Mr. Turner followed behind him. Both men had swords on their belts and pistols in their hands. Mr. Rossington offered his extra sword to Nicholas without a word and pushed the door open behind us.

"Where are these men?" Mr. Rossington barked.

"They were not far behind me," Nicholas said. I walked beside him, but he stopped me. "You must accompany Mrs. Tattershall away from the property. It is not safe."

My heart pounded and I shook my head.

"Please, Lucy. It will be all right. Trust me." His eyes bore into mine for several seconds before he ran after Mr. Rossington and Mr. Turner. I didn't move. I couldn't breathe.

There on the road, two dark horses galloped toward where Nicholas and the other men stood, directly beside the Bancrofts' home. I trusted that Kitty and Mrs. Tattershall were gathering more men to help fight, but I couldn't bring myself to move from where I stood. Mr. Parsons dismounted, drawing his sword. The man Nicholas had called Gibbs did the same. I recognized him from that night. He was the tall, thin man that had pulled me down from the coach. My lungs froze.

Gibbs moved toward Nicholas first, and I muffled a scream behind my hand. Nicholas deflected his blow, pressing back with impressive skill. Mr. Parsons approached Nicholas from behind, his sword drawn as well, but Mr. Turner jumped between them, engaging Mr. Parsons in a duel.

Mr. Rossington staggered back, away from the dueling men, raising his pistol and pointing it at Mr. Gibbs. I tensed, shaking my head.

He could easily hit Nicholas. I covered my mouth, afraid to watch, yet unable to look away. I glanced around in desperation for a way to assist, but I thought of nothing. I was helpless yet again.

Something caught my attention from the opposite side of the Bancrofts' property. I gasped. Julia and Mrs. Bancroft walked arm in arm toward their house from the opposite direction, unaware of the fight occurring just around the corner. Julia's head turned toward the sound of the commotion. The scene before me played out in slow motion, unimaginable. Julia and Mrs. Bancroft were coming closer to the fight, curious to see what was causing the commotion. I gasped, my muscles tensed, and before I could stop myself I was running across the property toward them. But I was too far to warn them to stay away.

As they stepped around the house, in clear view of the confrontation, Mr. Rossington, the only man not engaged in the fight, saw them.

I was still running, getting closer. I tried to conceal myself along the border of trees between the houses as I moved. Mr. Rossington stopped. I followed his gaze as he stared at Mrs. Bancroft as if he had not seen her in years, and perhaps he hadn't. His head was turned toward them, his pistol still withdrawn and pointed at Gibbs, and for a moment I saw his face. Pity, shock, and a bit of regret.

And then I heard the shot.

I jumped, covering my mouth with another scream. My eyes darted to Mr. Rossington's pistol, but I found that it had fallen from his hand. And then I saw Gibbs, lowering the aim of his pistol from Mr. Rossington's chest. Mr. Rossington fell to the ground, and the fight continued between Mr. Parsons and Nicholas.

Mr. Rossington's aim had been on Gibbs, but he had been distracted for long enough for Gibbs to shoot him instead.

Mr. Rossington lay on the ground, motionless. Julia pulled her mother back toward the house, flying up the steps and through the door. My head alternated between clarity and smog, seeing the wound in Mr. Rossington's chest and the blood that soaked his jacket one moment, and blocking it from my mind the next. My stomach lurched, and I ran closer to him. Metal scraped against metal beside me, bringing me back to my senses. I needed to help Mr. Rossington. No matter how horrible he was, he didn't deserve to die like this.

"Lucy!" It was Nicholas's voice. "No!" I stumbled away from the two pairs of men as they fought. I could not distract Nicholas like Mr. Rossington had been distracted by Mrs. Bancroft. His eyes were trained on me, and Gibbs took the opportunity to strike Nicholas's sword from his hand.

Nicholas backed away, nearly tripping on his wounded leg. Gibbs swung his sword, moving tauntingly toward Nicholas. I searched in desperation for an idea, a way to help him. Then I saw Mr. Rossington's pistol hewn across the grass beside him. Scrambling forward, I jerked it from the ground and positioned my finger on the trigger. I had never even held one before, but I had a basic idea of how they functioned. It was walnut with intricate silver wiring. My eyes focused on the trigger.

Nicholas backed farther away from Gibbs, barely missing a strike from his sword. I had little time to act. Raising the pistol, I aimed it toward Gibbs. I didn't trust my aim. My heart thudded and my palms slickened with sweat, making it difficult to grip the weapon. Mr. Parsons was facing me now in his fight with Mr. Turner. His eyes widened and he opened his mouth to warn Gibbs. When Gibbs swung his sword again and Nicholas jumped to the side, I screamed and squeezed the trigger.

My ears rang and I wasn't sure where the bullet had landed. I held my breath, lowering my shaking arm. Gibbs screamed a number of curses and fell to the ground, clutching his knee and writhing in pain. Nicholas reclaimed his sword and held it to Gibbs's throat, making him freeze.

Another gunshot rang through the air, and I turned around in alarm. Three men I did not know were approaching on horseback, one with a pistol pointed toward the sky. For a moment I worried that they had come to assist the wicked men, but then I saw Kitty and Mrs. Tattershall huddled close to the doors of Rosewood in the distance. Could they see Mr. Rossington? I glanced at him again, lying there in his own blood. He was dead.

I tore my eyes away. Mr. Parsons had begun to realize he was outnumbered. When the men on horseback dismounted and stormed toward him, he dropped his weapon and put his hands in the air, pleading his innocence. It didn't work.

After Gibbs was tied and led away along with Mr. Parsons, Nicholas crossed the grass to me. His face was caked in dirt and sweat, and his arm was sliced deeply with another cut. The sight of him then brought all the terror inside of me to the surface. I buried my face in his chest and cried, and he held me, shaking with relief and fear. It was over.

But Mr. Rossington was dead. I ached with grief for Kitty. How would she bear the news? Only twenty years of age and an orphan. I could hear her behind me, but I didn't look. I was too afraid, too weak. She sobbed, and her husband's voice comforted her. I couldn't believe what had just happened, and all so fast. Guilt choked me as I thought of the words I had spoken to Mr. Rossington. I had been the reason he came to fight at all. Nicholas whispered words of comfort to me but I couldn't hear. I was too tired and too focused on the sound of Kitty and Mrs. Tattershall as they cried behind me.

Never had I imagined that a trip to Rosewood would bring about such circumstances. I had expected a relaxing, freeing escape, but I had been granted this instead. I still didn't believe any of it was true. I didn't believe that Mr. Rossington was dead or that Nicholas was holding me in his arms. But I did believe in Nicholas.

# TWENTY-TWO

*T*he funeral of Mr. Rossington was a small service with very few in attendance. The town was fresh with gossip over how he had died, spinning the tale however each preferred to tell it. After the night of his murder, Gibbs and Parsons were taken to trial and found guilty. I didn't sleep for days, living the horrific events over and over again. Gibbs and Parsons had tried to accuse Nicholas of his involvement with their crimes in trial, but Kitty and Mr. Turner had vouched for him, among many others. I had seen little of Kitty in her mourning, and hadn't been given a moment to thank her for defending Nicholas.

Rosewood was a solemn place, always wrought with tears and black dresses. After discovering Mr. Rossington's wicked ways, I had felt nothing but disgust for him. But he was still Kitty's father. And it hurt me to see her and Mrs. Tattershall so solemn. I had never been very close to my uncle, so the grief that I felt for Mr. Rossington's death was only determined by the shock and the depth of sorrow that surrounded me. It made Rosewood a dreadful place, and it took great effort not to allow the memory of his violent death to resurface every moment I was alone. And there were many.

Dr. Kellaway treated Nicholas's wounds that night, or so I had heard. A fortnight had passed since my uncle's death and I had only seen Nicholas twice. When I did, he was distant, reserved, and far too polite. I had broken his heart that day he had proposed to me, just as he had once broken mine. I hated myself for it, and my own heart felt as if it were shattering more each day. We hadn't spoken of that day he had proposed. I hadn't yet apologized. Nicholas had been keeping to himself, surely waiting for me to make the decision that grated on me.

Today, Kitty and Mr. Turner were returning home, leaving me at Rosewood with only William and Mrs. Tattershall as my company. And soon they would leave as well, for a distant cousin of Mr. Rossington would claim the property of Rosewood as heir. With Mr. Rossington's death, no will had been discovered. Therefore, the laws of primogeniture would give his property to his nearest male relative, which happened to be a cousin living in Leeds.

I would be leaving Rosewood soon too.

I stood outside the carriage that would take Kitty and her husband away. The air was cold today and the trees shed their leaves all around me, swirling in the wind, making the black of our dresses haunting instead of beautiful. I embraced Kitty, smiling as she stepped away from me. I offered her my most sincere gratitude for defending Nicholas and ensuring that he was no longer accused. For a while I had held a grudge against her for the night she had accused Nicholas at the party. But she was like a sister to me, and I couldn't let anything ruin that. And she needed to be loved during such a difficult time.

"I will visit again before you leave," she promised. Her eyes blinked back tears.

"Of course. I will miss you."

She gripped my hands before stepping into the carriage. "I have seen the pain in your eyes, Lucy, and I do not like it."

I frowned.

"I know that I haven't always approved of Nicholas, but I can see now that he is a good man. Do not let anything stop you from claiming your happiness. You came all this way to find it."

The crisp wind whipped my curls into my face but I pushed them away. I had once been so certain that Rosewood was the epitome of happiness, the one thing that would pull me from my feelings of being trapped and bored, lonely and cold. But the things that made me happy were not tied to this place. It was my family, my friends, and most of all . . .

"Nicholas," Kitty said, leaning close to my face. "Do not convince yourself that you cannot be with him. He loves you, I can see it. You love him, for I have always known that. Tell him."

My cheeks warmed and my heart pounded. I missed him. I had been restless, anxious, waiting for him to come to me again, so I could admit that I was wrong. But he had not come, and that convinced me that he had changed his own mind. He had always been the brave one. Perhaps Kitty was right. Perhaps it was my turn, once again, to be brave.

"I thought you did not approve of Nicholas for me." My voice was breathless.

She smiled. "I only worried that he did not deserve you. But it is obvious now that the two of you are perfect for one another. After all he did to ensure your safety, I can see that I have misjudged him. I declare I have never seen a more perfect match."

I laughed, biting my lip. "Farewell, Kitty. I will see you soon."

She climbed into her carriage and clung to her husband's arm. How fortunate it was that she was well-married and had a home to live in since she was not willed any property from her father.

I hadn't had an opportunity to speak to her about what Nicholas had revealed to me about Simon and Mrs. Bancroft. Did she know that she had a half-brother living directly beside her? Or did she scorn him because he was considered by law to be illegitimate, an outcast by society? It was not fair what Mr. Rossington had done to his only son and his second wife. He had banished them from social existence. I tried to shush my angry thoughts, but simply because he was dead did not mean I had to dispel all my feelings of anger toward him. Simon would suffer because of him. So would Mrs. Bancroft and Nicholas and Julia. They were poor and exiled from society. But perhaps now that Kitty's father was gone, she might be bold enough to reacquaint herself with Simon. When she came to visit again, I would need to arrange it.

*If I am still here.* I missed my family more each day. They had written me a letter, and I had received it one week ago. They missed me, and forgave me for leaving. Mama said she loved me and wished me to have a wonderful time here. I wished I could see their faces and tell them how foolish I was. I had been foolish many times over the last month.

But there was one person here that I needed to speak to face-to-face and confess my foolishness to. Perspiration gathered in my palms with the very thought of approaching Nicholas. My feelings were raw, and so were his. He still needed the wealth for his family that I could not offer. How could I be so selfish as to deprive him of that opportunity? And Julia was nearly of marriageable age . . . I didn't want the pressure to fall on her to make a wealthy match.

I sat in my room as I had done for countless hours over the past fortnight. I chewed my nails, begging myself to have the courage to find Nicholas. I could not live without him. I could hardly breathe. I felt as if a piece of myself had been missing these last two weeks, and I knew it was my distance from him that was causing it.

Why was I so afraid? How could his feelings have been changed over two weeks? *Two weeks.* My feelings had not been changed in six years. My heart hammered and I was filled with courage. I was not averse to work. Surely I could learn to make hats and other fashionable items, and even assist the seamstress in the village to help gather the funds for Nicholas's family. Perhaps we could even move to Craster together. My mother was the most hospitable, kind woman that I had ever known. She would take all of the Bancrofts into our home.

My soul sprung with hope, making me jump to my feet. I pushed my hair from my eyes and tried to breathe normally. I needed to be brave. I was going to find Nicholas, and I was going to tell him I was sorry. I would tell him all my secrets, just as he had told me his. I loved him, and I always had.

I was quite certain I had never been more afraid or more vulnerable. I walked across the grass toward the Bancrofts' home. Leaves crunched under my feet, leaving little flecks on the tips of my boots. I could hear my heart in my ears. *What was I doing?* I felt as if I were floating, unable to control my own movements as I knocked on the front door. After waiting two seconds, I regained control of my mind and my legs, turning around, intending to run back to Rosewood and never show my face to Nicholas again. But then the door clicked open, and I whirled back around to see who would be standing there.

My heart beat so hard it hurt. I wrapped my cloak around me and tried to look calm, as if I weren't about to burst into thousands of pieces.

Julia peeked out from behind the door, smiling when she saw me. "Lucy, come in."

My throat was too dry to speak. So I nodded and stepped through the doorway. Simon stepped up behind her, offering a shy grin.

"Where is Nicholas?" My voice was quick, and not at all the courageous tone that I had practiced.

Julia reached behind me to close the door. I hadn't realized I left it open.

"He is in the library."

It had been a long time since I had ventured past the entryway of the house, so Julia led me to the library door. My mind flooded with memories of playing cards with Nicholas in the library, reading books and listening to him tell me stories.

My hand froze on the handle and Julia gave me an encouraging smile. "He is not the same without you," she whispered. "He does not smile and laugh . . . He needs you." And with that she walked away, leaving me there at the door.

I let Julia's words blossom inside me, filling me with strength. With one final breath of fortitude, I pushed the door open. It slammed against the wall and I cringed. Nicholas stood at a bookshelf, and when he heard my entrance he looked up from his book and glanced over his shoulder. I imagined how I must have appeared, standing in the center of a large, open doorway, cringing at the commotion I had just created. *Well done, Lucy.*

Nicholas stood up. "Lucy." He stared at me, waiting for an explanation for my presence there, a greeting, anything. He looked so handsome with the look of surprise on his face. My heart pounded, but I felt my courage returning, drop by drop.

I walked forward until I stood in front of him. He watched every step, a sort of restraint in his expression, defenses built up around his smile. "I'm sorry for coming to your home uninvited, but . . ." I couldn't find the words. Nicholas's eyes searched mine. I stopped, measuring the distance in our heights with my gaze. I could not kiss him if his posture remained firm and straight as it was. I needed to kiss him so he knew my words were earnest. He had kissed me, but I had never kissed him.

I turned toward the bookshelf, removing several thick books. Nicholas's expression remained guarded as he frowned in confusion. When I was satisfied with my selections, I hefted the books into my arms and moved back to where he stood. I set the books on the ground at his feet, positioning them in a stack.

"What are you doing?" Nicholas finally asked, a hint of amusement in his voice. But he was still quiet, careful.

I grinned at him, unable to hide my smile any longer. When my stack was complete, I placed my hands on Nicholas's shoulders and stepped on top of the stack of books. My eyes were level with his. He smiled now. I met his gaze again. Before I could lose my nerve, I moved my hands from his shoulders to his face, one hand on each side. His cheeks were slightly rough where he had neglected to shave. His eyes stared back into mine, reserved at first, but then brimming with laughter.

Taking a deep breath, I counted to three in my mind. And then I kissed him, quick and firm. I pulled back, keeping his face between my hands. His eyes were wide with shock. My cheeks were certainly bright pink, but I didn't care.

"Nicholas. I am sorry. You are correct: I am a liar. When I said my feelings had changed since I was a child, I was lying. When I rejected your proposal I didn't know the difficulties you had endured—the reasons behind your secrets. But now I know you weren't lying to me. I—I understand why it was not easy to share such things." My voice was quick and choked with emotion. "I love you. I have for longer than I can remember. I know it is not fair of me to ask you this, but I must. I ask that you forgive me—that you give me another chance to be your wife because that is all I have ever wanted. I was a fool for hurting you—a—a buffle-headed niddicock."

I was practically squeezing his face between my hands to empha-size my words. "But I also understand if you would rather marry Mrs. Elkins, because she is wealthy and quite attached to you and—" I shrieked, feeling my stack of books sliding away underneath me. I faltered, but Nicholas caught me, wrapping his arms around my waist and lifting me off that stack of books before I could fall. I laughed uncontrollably, and he laughed too, holding me against him. Then he kissed me, holding me above the floor and spinning me in a circle. He set me on the floor, keeping me close enough to kiss me a little longer. When he pulled back, he brushed my hair from my eyes, kissing the tip of my nose. We laughed, breathless.

It was his turn to hold my face in his hands, emphasizing his words. "I am only certain that I will not marry Mrs. Elkins if you are certain that you will not marry Mr. Parsons," he said in a teasing voice.

I gasped. "Do not ever say that again!"

He laughed.

"I am serious, Nicholas. I cannot provide you with the money your family needs. How long will it be before you can no longer afford this house?" Panic spread in my lungs, making it difficult to breathe. Why had I done this? Nicholas needed much more than I could give him. Emotion choked me all over again.

He sighed in exasperation, bending down to kiss my forehead, pressing his thumb to my quivering chin. "We are both intelligent people; surely we can make a plan. I will find work. All will be well. If I cannot marry you, then I will not marry at all. There will never be a woman that makes me laugh as often as you do, or one that is so thoroughly unexpected, breathtaking, and . . . beautiful." He wiped a stray tear from my eye and I burst into laughter, sniffing, making an ugly sound. He laughed, gathering me into his arms.

"Are you saying yes?" he asked. His eyes stared into mine, fragile and vulnerable, reflecting my heart back to me, whole and safe. I was breathless, so I nodded. He spun me around again, making me shriek and laugh. He set me down on the floor and took my hand in his, pressing his lips to the top of it.

"May I have this dance, Miss Lucy Abbot?"

Tears were still pouring from my eyes—tears of joy and unexplainable peace. It was not at all how I had always imagined our dance, but I gave my most flourishing curtsy anyway, stepping toward him. He slid his hand around my waist, pressing me close to him. Our hands fit perfectly together just as I had always imagined it. The last time we had danced I had been fourteen, unsure and afraid. Now I was brave and certain. I laughed through my tears, stepping my small feet on top of his boots.

"That is not the proper way to dance." His brown eyes stared down at mine, his lashes crinkled at the corners with a smile. I grinned, sniffing through my laughter, creating a snorting noise that made Nicholas laugh harder.

Although we had no music, we danced an imperfect and rather broken waltz. But it was perfect to me. My heart soared. Although our future was uncertain, and our plans for a secure living shaky, I believed in Nicholas. I believed in the beauty of this moment, of this dance I had been waiting for my entire life. So I calmed my fears, clung to hope, and tilted my head up to look at my dream.

# TWENTY-THREE

Nicholas and I sat in his drawing room with Julia and Mrs. Bancroft, attempting to play a game of whist. Julia assisted her mother, trying to remind her of the rules. Simon had been at Willowbourne with Peter and Charles all morning, and Nicholas and I had just returned from bringing him home. Annette was overjoyed to hear of our engagement, and little Charles was a bit jealous to hear of it.

It had been three days since our engagement, and I had written my father, hoping for his approval of the marriage. He had always thought Nicholas to be a respectable young man, so I had no worry, especially since my father had no knowledge of Nicholas's past practices. I was also eager to tell my family that we wished to move to Craster where we would get married and where Nicholas would find work with my friend Charlotte's husband, James. I would assist in the millinery with Mr. Connor. I was confident he would give me work to do. Nicholas and I had discussed the matter for the last several days. I dreaded the gray skies and cold but knew they would be better with Nicholas there too.

Mr. Rossington's cousin would be moving to Rosewood within the week, so Nicholas and me and his family would be leaving for Craster soon as well. Through the generosity of Dr. Kellaway, we had been lent one of his private coaches that would convey us there.

I heard a banging sound at the door and jumped out of my chair. I exchanged a look with Nicholas. No one ever came knocking here.

Nicholas slid around the card table, and I followed him to the front entry. He swung the door open to reveal Kitty standing on the steps. I gasped in surprise, throwing my arms around her. "Kitty! What brings you here?"

When I stepped back, I noticed the wideness of her eyes and the quickness of her breath. She appeared to have run here with something urgent. She held a stack of papers in her hand. "John insisted that we do some research upon our return home. We spoke to a series of legal men and have discovered something remarkable." She shook her head, swallowing hard. Nicholas motioned for her to enter. He exchanged a worried look with me before pulling me close to him. Kitty opened her mouth to speak, but paused when she saw Nicholas's arm around me. "You two have resolved everything, then?" She squealed. "Are you engaged yet?"

"Kitty!" I laughed, but nodded.

She clapped her hands together, crumpling the papers she held. After offering her congratulations, she seemed to remember her purpose in coming here.

"Oh, yes." She cleared her throat. She breathed in, long and slow. "They discovered that my father . . . well, he was not entirely honest."

"Not entirely?"

She swallowed and looked at Nicholas. "Although he owned a large amount of land, he was not among the gentry, therefore he could not annul a marriage legally and remain unscathed by society. So he didn't."

My jaw dropped. I tried to make sense of her words. Nicholas stepped forward, crossing his arms. "What do you mean?" His voice was careful.

"The day he died just weeks ago, he was still married to your mother. His circle of acquaintances was small and very local. They did not even know of his second marriage. To those of us that knew him well, he claimed an annulment. He knew that should it be discovered by society that he had annulled his marriage that he would be scorned. I did not know all these years that the annulment was falsified."

My heart raced and my eyes shot to Nicholas. His jaw was tight, his expression flooding with disbelief.

"The marriage has stood all along, which means . . ."

"Simon is heir," Nicholas said.

I covered my mouth, flicking my gaze between Nicholas and Kitty. *Simon was heir to Rosewood.* The marriage was never annulled, all this time. I couldn't believe what I was hearing.

"Simon," Kitty breathed. "Another secret my father has kept. I did not know I had a brother. He was born after my father sent your mother back to this house."

Nicholas stepped toward Kitty, taking the papers from her hands, studying them. After several minutes of waiting, he stepped back, rubbing the side of his face. He exhaled fast, a sound between a sigh and a laugh. My eyes were wide, waiting for him to confirm it. He nodded slowly, turning to face me. "Simon is heir to Rosewood."

"The staff is prepared for Simon and his mother and any others that wish to move there." Kitty's voice was soft as she turned to Nicholas again. "He will need a suitable guardian." She smiled, and her eyes blinked back tears. "I should very much like to become acquainted with my brother."

I nodded and hugged her, still reeling with astonishment. "Simon is here in the drawing room if you wish to see him now."

Her eyes widened. "Yes, I would."

I squeezed her arm before she stepped around me and rounded the corner that led to the drawing room. I brought my hands to my head, circling to face Nicholas. He shook his head in bewilderment and wrapped his arms around me. How had our fortune turned so quickly? I couldn't comprehend it. We laughed in disbelief.

"Perhaps my family will travel here for our wedding instead?" I questioned as Nicholas set me on the floor again. With Simon heir to Rosewood, and with Nicholas as his guardian, we could live there together until Simon grew old enough to manage the home on his own.

Nicholas kissed the top of my head. "I am certain they will."

"I always dreamed that I would be married here."

Nicholas took my hands in his, giving me a smile that fluttered my heart and stole my breath. "Did you always dream that you would marry me?"

I laughed, nodding my head in embarrassment. "Do you remember the box of dirty pearls you gave to me? You told me they were magical wishes and dreams."

His lips twisted in a grin. "Did you believe me?"

"Of course! And I used them all on you. Surely that is the only reason you love me at all."

He threw his head back with a laugh. "Are you comparing my heart to a box of dirty pearls?"

I nodded, shrieking as he pulled me closer and kissed me again.

When I finally pulled myself from his arms, we walked to the drawing room hand-in-hand, where the tiny, red-haired heir to Rosewood sat, meeting his sister for the first time. Everything broken was aligned, every injustice was resolved. Happiness soared in every inch of me, every beat of my heart. It was difficult to believe that just weeks ago, I had been sitting in our drawing room in Craster, dreaming of things I never thought I'd have. But here it was in front of me. Fate had sent me to Rosewood that day.

Nicholas smiled down at me as we observed Kitty and Simon, and I smiled back.

# EPILOGUE

$\mathcal{M}$ama smiled at me in the mirror as I tried on my wedding gown for the third time that day. I spun, admiring the many frills of lace and strands of pearl that covered it.

"I love it, Mama!" My smile reached my ears as I threw my arms around her.

Rachel stood in the corner of the room, eyeing me with a suppressed grin. "The gown I wore at my wedding was much simpler, and I preferred it that way. But I daresay this one suits you quite nicely." She crossed the room to me and patted the oversized sleeve, erupting into laughter the same moment I did.

It had taken several weeks to dispel the forlorn feeling in the air at Rosewood, but with the prospect of my wedding and with my family coming to visit, Rosewood was becoming the place I had always remembered it to be.

The Bancrofts had adjusted well to their new home. I had seen Julia smile for the first time in years, and Mrs. Bancroft appeared at peace, calm and relaxed. It warmed my heart to see her in the early hours of the morning, stroking Simon's hair and smiling as she watched him read simple stories to her in the library. Kitty came to visit often, and Simon looked forward to each visit. The two of them had grown close in the last several weeks, and Simon quite enjoyed that he had another sister. Nicholas and I had taken to tutoring him in our free hours, and I had coached Julia in fashion. She did not seem to apply my advice to her own wardrobe. As I stared in the mirror at my extravagant wedding gown, I couldn't imagine why.

Nicholas did not know it, but I had prepared an early wedding gift for him. Our wedding was tomorrow, but I planned to surprise him with my gift today. So after changing from my gown into a ordinary morning dress, I thanked my family for their assistance and skipped out the door with my cloak. The weather had turned slightly cold, but it was warm compared to the autumn chill in Craster. I hurried across the grass, enjoying the brisk winds that blew leaves all around me. I had instructed Nicholas to meet me by the stables at precisely twelve, and as I approached I found him there, smiling in greeting.

"You're late," he called as I crossed the grass toward him.

I stopped in front of him, planting my hands on my hips with a grin. "I am not! It is precisely twelve. You were simply anxious for the surprise."

He wore a simple waistcoat and jacket today, in a pale blue. His eyes sparked with amusement and he took a step closer. "I was anxious to see you."

"I can assure you, the surprise will be much more exciting."

He laughed, lifting his hand to my hair to pull a leaf from my curls. How did that get there? He ducked his head to kiss my cheek. "I don't believe that."

I pressed my lips together to stop my squeal of excitement. Then I took his hand. "First you must close your eyes."

He obeyed, dropping his head with a chuckle. Nicholas went riding most mornings on the many fine horses at Rosewood. I accompanied him on his rides some mornings, but on the days I did not, we met at the stables afterward. Today was much like any other day, but he did not know that my surprise was now waiting inside.

After affirming that his eyes were closed, I pulled him by the hand through the doors. I glanced over my shoulder every few steps to ensure that he was not looking. His smile was wide as he followed behind me. When we reached the stall I was searching for, I turned my face up to him. "You may open your eyes now."

I watched carefully as his lashes twitched and his eyes opened to the sight before him. His eyes immediately widened. "Jack!" He stepped toward his sleek black horse, stroking its muzzle and head, laughing in disbelief. He turned back to me, his expression bright with surprise. "Lucy, how did you ever retrieve him?"

"In my letter to my family I asked that they make a stop at the inn where we left your horse to return him here to you. We have been hiding him for two days." I stifled a laugh before reaching forward and patting Jack's head.

Nicholas shook his head, his smile stretching wide. "I should have known you would be so thoughtful." He tipped his head down and my cheeks warmed under his praise. "I do not know how to thank you."

"You may begin by marrying me tomorrow." I shrugged.

He chuckled, bending down and kissing me with so much fervor that my heart skipped. He pulled back, tracing a line on my cheek with his thumb.

"And you may kiss me like that every day of my life," I said through a laugh. Nicholas pulled me close once again before opening the stall and saddling his newfound horse. Outside, he helped me mount before he mounted in front of me on the saddle. The last time we had ridden this horse together, I had been convinced Nicholas was a thieving scoundrel, much less the good, kind man that I loved. Now, instead of trying to push him from the horse, I wrapped my arms around him, safe, secure, and free.

Without warning, we raced across the grass. I screeched before melting into laughter. I felt the rumble of Nicholas's laughter against me as we rode across the grass toward Rosewood.

# ACKNOWLEDGMENTS

This story wasn't easy to write, but there were several amazing people that made it easier. Big thanks to my family, as always, for your love and support. I needed your encouragement. Big thanks to my roommates, for your support as well, especially Eliza, my own personal reminder every day to "finish my words!" Believe it or not, my procrastination would have been even worse without you keeping me on track. Thanks to Mom, Joanna, Johanna, Sally, Heather, and Anna for helping me brainstorm titles. Anna, my buddy, thank you for letting me talk through the plot with you when it could hardly be considered a plot, and for your helpful feedback.

Thanks to the Cedar Fort team, especially Jessica Romrell for helping me through that first very, very rough draft and seeing the potential in it. Thank you to Shawnda Craig for putting up with my many requests and creating such a beautiful cover. Big thanks to the rest of the Cedar Fort team for always believing in me and putting in so much hard work to make my stories come to life.

And above all I express my thanks to my Heavenly Father for giving me the imagination, strength, and perseverance to write this story when I felt like giving up. Only through Him can we can achieve great things.

# About the Author

*A*shtyn Newbold was introduced to the Regency period early on, and the writing soon followed. Fascinated by the society, scenery, and chivalry, she wrote her first novel, *Mischief and Manors*, receiving a publishing offer before high school graduation. Ashtyn is currently attending college with plans to obtain a degree that will help her improve in writing and creativity. In her spare time she enjoys baking, singing, spoiling her dog, spending time with friends and family, and dreaming of the day she'll travel to England.

Scan to visit

www.ashtynnewbold.com